JORJA DUPONT OLIVA

Chasing Butterflies

In The
Magical Garden

Chasing Butterflies in the Magical Garden by Jorja DuPont Oliva
Copyright © 2013 by Jorja DuPont Oliva
Copy Edit by Nancy Quatrano

Cover design and layout by MRK Publishing
Interior layout and pagination by Michael Ray King
Chasing Butterflies in the Magical Garden by Jorja DuPont Oliva
220p. ill. cm.

ISBN 978-1-935795-23-0 (hardcover) 978-1-935795-24-7

Library of Congress Control Number: 2013954773

MRK Publishing
PO Box 353431
Palm Coast, FL 32135-3431

Table of Contents

REVIEWS

"Emotional roller coaster that touches every emotion and sensation-smell, touch, taste, sight- an indulging voyage of amusement."-Rhonda Bracewell

"An amazing story, believable, heartwrenchin' and fun"-Michael Ray King

This story, and the fresh, unpretentious voice, is reminiscent of Lisa Verge Higgins' THE PROPER CARE AND MAINTENANCE OF FRIENDSHIP in mission. Oliva tells it with such innocence that we're on this journey of friendship's magic, once again. Been a long time since I've been innocent, but this was a fast and fun read that is touching and powerful at the same time. New Adult readers should enjoy this young women's fiction and look forward to the next! – Nancy Quatrano, Editor/Author

DEDICATION

To everyone I have shared memories with. There has never been a regret, only a fabulous life to look back on. To friendships and lost loved ones...living on. To God for showing me the way.

"I never exactly made a book. It's rather like taking dictation. I was given things to say."--C.S. Lewis

"Any writer worth his salt writes to please himself...It's a self-exploratory operation that is endless. An exorcism of not necessarily his demon, but of his divine discontent."--Harper Lee

"Your intuition knows what to write, so get out of the way."--Ray Bradbury

PROLOGUE

In the clearing, creatures of the air and earth were gathered.

"The humans don't always understand that change is constant and good. How will they ever fly if they do not embrace the changes that enable them to do so?" **asked the Butterfly.**

"And if they can believe that every living thing is sacred, then a lesson can be found in all things and experiences," **added the Armadillo.**

"Life is about Honor, Love, and Respect to self and all others. That we are connected with all the things around us. That we are an integral part of everything that as a whole makes up the universe," **said the dog.** *"All would be happier if we behaved with honor and forgiveness."*

The cats swished their tails. The calico spoke first. *"They must learn honesty in all things."* **The black cat snickered.** *"They need to take the time to understand the dreams. The meanings. Not all is what they think it is."*

The dragonfly fluttered her wings. *"How true, Black Cat. Change is constant but not always seen."*

"Humans struggle with understanding, but many learn to do so. They eventually embrace both the dark and the light of life," **said the Eagle.**

"Easy for you to say," **said the Bull.** *"From where you soar, you can see how dark and light work together. You are the Great Spirit. You know that both are needed. Humans don't like the dark."*

And in the circle of creatures, the long rays of the setting sun lit the clearing in orange and gold light, punctuating the conversation. Light would soon be dark. The fragrance of an afternoon rain shower lingered in the air.

The Hummingbird settled his tiny body on the back of the Bull. *"But the ones who don't shy away, the ones who keep looking forward learn that they cannot understand light without dark. They cannot embrace joy without knowing heartache."*

And as the light in the clearing completed its metamorphosis into darkness, the scene began to fade.

There were big changes coming her way...

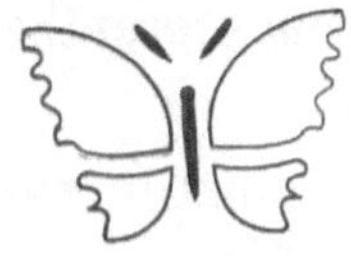

CHAPTER ONE

Rear View Mirror

I can of mine own self do nothing... *(John 5:30)*

At twenty-one years of age, Lizzy's most significant dream was dead. Well, not physically dead, he stood in the driveway of their rented house watching her prepare to drive away. The ring that had been on her finger, now tucked away in her pocket, was about the only thing she was sure of at the moment. There'd be no white picket fence in her immediate future–at least not one around her happily-ever-after with Lee.

Her Father, quiet and strong as always, walked from the U-haul to the driver's side window of her mother's car. "Everything is loaded up, Lizzy Girl. Are you okay to drive?"

She looked in the rear view mirror one more time, sighed and nodded. "I'm okay, Daddy. Let's just go. I really want to go home." As he walked back to the U-haul with all her belongings in it, she sniffed. *Is this the right thing to do? Please God... don't let them see how I am dying inside!*

Her momma patted her leg. "First loves are the hardest to get over, honey."

Lizzy forced a weak smile and turn to her mother. "Momma...Do you think it will ever stop hurting?"

Her mother just stared straight ahead almost as though she hadn't heard Lizzy.

"It won't stop. It will just get easier," she rasped after a long moment.

Momma's had her heart broken, too. Somehow, that secret they just shared made Lizzy feel a tiny bit stronger.

"You can and will love again," her mother said. "Sometimes even stronger and more beautiful than the first. The kind that lasts a lifetime."

Lizzy lifted her chin an inch, flexed her hands on the steering wheel, and nodded. "I sure hope you're right, Momma."

They drove for hours; love songs played on the radio, and the U-haul continued steadily just ahead.

Lizzy's thoughts cluttered her mind. What she knew was that all her plans for the future now veered off in a different direction, a new path, a road not yet imagined. She was scared to death.

"Momma, I can't drive. I think I'm going to puke!" She pulled the car off the interstate into a rest stop. Her momma took over the driver's seat and drove so Lizzy could pull herself together.

Lee was the only man she'd ever been with, and ever planned to *be* with. Now everything had changed. Lee and Lizzy had been inseparable since they were thirteen. In middle school and high school they were called *The Double L's*. In most conversations, people never mentioned *one L* without the other.

Lee was no angel. Through the years he'd strayed from their relationship, but Lizzy had stayed faithful through it all, never even considered dating anyone else.

"Sowing his oats," her mother would say. *"That's what boys do."*

Lizzy accepted that explanation readily and welcomed him back when the time came. She just believed that they couldn't live without each other for very long, because they were *The Double L's*.

She grew up in a family of "Christian up-bringing" and the small town outlook on marriage and family at a young age suited her just fine.

Lizzy dropped out of college when she decided to follow Lee to the foothills of the Carolina's for work. When she got settled in, she would return to school and finish that teaching degree. Of course, that never happened.

Women don't have need for careers unless it's teaching children, Lizzy would remind herself every time she considered changing her major. That was just how it was. Many miles later the U-haul ahead exited the interstate; Lizzy took a deep breath, then blew it out through her lips, long and slow.

After they passed the county line, Lizzy's chest started to burn. Everyone would know she'd come back home without the "other L." *How will I face any of these people?* Lizzy almost smiled. *Well, I can face Ripley. She'll understand. She'll even be sad for me, I'll bet. Knowing Ripley, she'll want to kill him for me.* Lizzy glanced at her mother, who was now driving then looked straight at the road ahead. An on-coming car approached and Lizzy waited.

She caught a glimpse of the driver. Ripley! Lizzy ducked down in the seat. She wasn't ready to see anyone just yet, not even Ripley. Lizzy looked at her mother wide eyed. Hoping Ripley didn't see her, she eased her way to an upright position.

"Momma? Do you think she saw me?" Lizzy asked.

"Probably didn't know it was you," her momma answered. "But, she is eventually going to find out you're home and she might be hurt if you don't reach out to her."

"I know. I just need a little time is all," Lizzy said.

The pressure in her chest subsided as they pulled into the driveway, but the knot in her throat and the sour in her stomach remained. *How am I going to do this?*

As she got out of the car, her father opened the door to the U-haul. He gave her a wink. That was his way to assure her everything was going to be all right.

He wasn't much of a talker, but just his presence was enough. Today Lizzy wasn't much for words either, but without words, her daddy always said the right thing with his expressions.

Deep down, Lizzy knew her daddy hadn't cared much for Lee, but he never said it to her and he never let it show.

She sighed and fought back tears. Lee was in North Carolina and she was back home. There'd be no reunion this time.

She still had a future–didn't she?

CHAPTER TWO

Moving In

The Phoenix - a mystical bird which consumes itself in fire and rises from its own ashes

As Lizzy entered her parent's house, she dropped her suitcase on the floor. Everywhere she looked baby toys and stuffed animals decorated the floors and furniture.

Her older sister Lynn, recently divorced, had moved in with her momma and daddy a month before Lizzy had left for the foot hills. With four kids.

Lynn, local beauty queen, recipient of athletic scholarships, and product of the small-town-young-marriage society, was pregnant before the ink on the college applications were dry. *Oh, dear God, how can I add to all of this?* Lizzy's stomach twisted. Her parents didn't need another mouth to feed.

She trucked her suitcase into the small den she'd be calling home for a while. Lynn and the kid's occupied the other bedrooms, including Lizzy's old one. She'd just dropped into the worn sofa when the phone rang.

For a split second she hoped it was Lee wanting her to come back. That's how it had always been.

Her mother called to her from the kitchen. "Lizzy honey, it's Ripley. She wasn't sure it was you in the car with me, but now she is and she wants to talk to you. Come get the phone." Lizzy got to her feet and squared her shoulders. Maybe there was no better time than now to get started on that new life. Besides, Ripley had recently moved out of her parent's home and moved in with a classmate named Dee.

As she reached the hallway, she felt lighter. Maybe she wouldn't even have to unpack.

Maybe she could stay with her school mates.

***

Lizzy slowly opened her eyes. Warm and cuddled in a soft pillow, her smile faded as she realized it had only been another dream of her and Lee. *Why do these dreams feel so real?* She looked up through blond curls that had fallen across her face and saw Dee, Ripley's roommate, staring at her, a cigarette hanging from the corner of her mouth.

Dee had cinnamon-red hair, sported thick black eyeliner and a look that could kill.

"Didja sleep good?" she barked.

"Ok, I guess," Lizzy answered slowly sitting to an upright position. "I'm sorry to still be here. Ripley was going to wake me when she left for work."

"No biggie." Dee took a drag on her cigarette. "I told her to let you sleep. You looked like you needed the rest."

"I did. I haven't gotten much sleep lately".

"You and Lee broke up." Dee stated, or asked; Lizzy wasn't quite sure which it was.

"Yeah. I guess," Lizzy responded.

"Well, you did or you didn't?" Dee asked again.

"Yes, we did," she said with a sigh. "But–"

"But what?" Dee broke in. "That guy was no good for you. He's a player and players are no good for girls like you."

"Girls like me?" Lizzy asked. "What's that supposed to mean?"

"You know ... righteous and all," Dee replied.

What the heck does that mean? Tears filled her eyes. "I'm not righteous ... I ... I just don't do things that aren't right."

"Yep. Righteous," Dee said as she exhaled the cigarette smoke and then walked out the front door.

Lizzy sat on the couch for another minute. She wasn't sure if she was supposed to be insulted or proud of herself. But she knew what the right thing was to do. She stood and headed to the front door to thank Dee for letting her stay the night.

Lizzy opened the screen door. The bright sun warmed her face. Dee stood in a beautiful garden with fairy statues and flowers that smelled so sweet that Lizzy almost forgot the reason she went out there.

As she inhaled the fragrance of gardenias and honeysuckle she remembered her mission. "Thank you, for letting me sleep on your couch, Dee."

"Welcome," Dee answered without turning around.

Once again, Lizzy wasn't sure how to take Dee's words. Was she welcome to stay or was it just a polite come back? She decided that Dee was just being polite.

Much as she hated being a burden to her parents who already had more than enough to handle with Lynn and the four kids, Lizzy didn't have a job or any way to contribute to her own household. Even if Dee invited her to move in with them, Lizzy couldn't just live there for free. She was darn lucky that her daddy's old hunting Jeep cranked or she wouldn't even have transportation.

Since Dee didn't pick up the conversation, Lizzy went back into the house and spotted the local weekly paper on the table. She needed a job, right? She'd better start looking for one.

As she thumbed through the pages, she realized that the job opening page was gone. She dropped the paper back on the table.

She felt hopeless again. She could hear her Momma saying, "A woman needs a man to take care of her." The heaviness in her chest, the knot in her throat and the churning in her stomach came back. *Is this pain ever going to stop?* After a minute or two passed, she walked to the window and watched Dee in the garden talking to herself, the fairies, or someone Lizzy couldn't see. A few minutes more passed before Dee walked back into the kitchen.

That's when Lizzy realized if anyone knew how to handle the loneliness, it was Dee. Ripley had told her that Dee had lost many people that were close to her. Her older brother died at a young age from some kind of fever, then her younger sister died in a car accident when she was in middle school, and cancer took her mother when Dee was in her senior year of high school. She never even knew her father. She'd inherited the house she lived in with Ripley. She had no real family, but she had a home.

Silence dangled in the air. "How do you deal with it, losing people you love?" Lizzy asked.

"I don't," Dee snapped. "They're still here." Her voice relaxed. She cleared her throat and started again. "Here," Dee said pointing to her heart. "Here." She pointed to her head.

CHAPTER THREE

Missing Mr. Right

The empty vessel makes the greatest sound- William Shakespeare

Lizzy swallowed hard and felt her heart skip a beat. Could a person die of embarrassment? *Why did I ask such a personal question? All I know about her are the rumors.*

Dee laughed. "You don't have to look so terrified." Then she sobered. "I know, you're remembering all that high school crap, aren't you? Well, let's get it cleared up, then." Dee raised her hands in front of her face and ticked off each item one finger at a time.

"No, I do not speak to the dead. I do not practice voodoo or witchcraft. Yes, I was more comfortable wearing black than any other color and I wore a lot of it. And after a while, I did it just to piss people off."

Lizzy felt the color drain out of her face, but that was exactly what she needed to hear. "I'm sorry, Dee. I don't know you and I was just trying to remember anything that would help me understand you, that's all. Ripley says we're not, but we're different as night and day."

Dee shrugged. "Maybe yes, maybe no. You're good people, Lizzy. Naïve maybe, but good people. And Ripley said you needed a place to stay, so stay here. It's okay."

Before Lizzy could reply, Dee pushed through the wooden screen door and rejoined her flowers in the garden.

***

Two days later, Dee walked into the kitchen with an application for the fancy yacht club in the next town over. She worked there and earned pretty decent money. She tossed it on the table in front of Lizzy.

"One of the girls quit and they're looking to fill the spot," Dee said.

Lizzy put down her book, "Wifey" by Judy Blum and looked at the application.

Is this the start of my new life? Is this where I will find the man to take care of me? What if Lee wants me back?

"Thanks, Dee. I..." Lizzy said. "Thank you very much."

"Welcome." Then she gave a nod and went out to her garden.

Thoughts bobbled around in Lizzy's head as she filled out the application. *Now I can pay my own way around here–pay Dee back for letting me sleep on her couch.*

***

The next ten days settled into a new routine for Lizzy. She learned her new job at the yacht club, helped with laundry and the garden, talked to her parents and even babysat for Lynn one afternoon when Momma had an appointment. She was even losing her dread of what was apparently to be a "Lee-less" future.

She walked through the front door of Dee's house with her first check from the yacht club. She stared down at it, smiled, and felt a sense of accomplishment. She jumped when the screen door slammed behind her. Dee came out of the kitchen with her signature peanut butter and jelly sandwich in one hand. "I see you got paid," Dee said.

"Yes, I did," Lizzy said. She passed the check to Dee with a slight bow. "Here, it's yours."

Dee shook her head. "Nah you keep it." She took a bite of her PB&J. "Besides, you need to get back on your feet before I start taking your money." Dee smiled her PB&J smile at Lizzy and walked out the screen door to her garden.

Lizzy clutched the check to her heart and smiled, twirling around in a tiny circle, her black apron swinging with her. Life was getting better, at least at the present moment.

She started thinking about how Ripley wasn't around much the last couple of weeks. She'd met a guy and she was spending a lot of time with him. Lizzy felt a twinge of envy before she pushed it aside with a genuine smile for Ripley's new found joy.

Ripley worked for her father in the family hardware store since she was legal to work and she worked hard. She could name every tool and tell you what the tool was used for before she was thirteen years old.

And, she also knew how to save money, another thing Lizzy envied her best friend for. Ripley had every dime she ever made in an account at the local bank. Well, except for the rent money she gave Dee, and the money towards the groceries or whatever that stuff it was they ate.

I've got it! Her first check would go toward groceries. Lizzy loved to cook. Lizzy's love of cooking began as a young girl when she tried recipes out on her father. She figured if he liked them, surely her future husband would as well.

She dropped into the kitchen chair, completely deflated. *Who am I kidding?* She hadn't cooked in months. Hadn't really been a need for it after the *Double L* break up. She felt the tears starting up again and she sniffed them back.

No matter how hard she tried, she still couldn't escape her thoughts of him. Some nights before she fell asleep, she would cry in her pillow so Dee or Ripley couldn't hear. Lizzy prayed for God to give her what was right for her.

Angry with herself for sinking like a rock once again, she pushed to her feet and marched to the bathroom to wash her face and change out of her uniform. She reminded herself, *God doesn't give you what you want. God gives you what you need...God only gives you what you can handle...God has a plan for each and every one of us.*

She pushed out the front door and hopped into her Jeep. She was done feeling sorry for herself. At least for the moment.

When she returned from the store, Lizzy pulled a roast, potatoes, carrots, and celery out of the grocery bag. She didn't care much for celery but it flavored the meat good. Lizzy found a roasting pan in the cabinet that looked like it had never been used.

She seasoned the roast with salt, pepper, onion powder, tiny bits of garlic and a pinch of sage, and then put it in the oven. She preferred to cook the roast real slow, so it would soak up the juices.

Lizzy realized she was *actually* enjoying herself. Cooking felt therapeutic. An escape from her pain. After an hour or so she added the vegetables and returned it to the oven.

The scent of food floated through the house and out to the garden where Dee chatted to who knew who or what. Lizzy watched Dee sniff the air and then follow her nose into the house. Lizzy pulled the roast out the oven as Dee stood behind her.

"Wow that smells great. What is it?" Dee asked.

"Supper. It's not ready yet, though. I like to cook it until the meat is real tender."

"You cook?" Dee looked amazed, as though someone their age shouldn't know how to cook.

"I do," Lizzy answered.

Dee commented with a grin, "Not only righteous but a Suzy Homemaker too."

Over the weeks, Lizzy had learned that Dee's sarcasm meant she liked her, so she took Dee's words as a compliment and smiled.

Before the roast finished cooking, she opened the oven and added a cookie sheet filled with buttermilk biscuits. Lizzy took out a stick of butter from the fridge to soften enough to spread on the hot biscuits when they were ready.

Lizzy set the table for two. Ripley and her new-found joy were heading to the movies in the next town. Their little town was lucky to have the hardware store, bank and grocery store, much less a theater.

When supper was ready they sat down and Lizzy said grace. With her mouth full of biscuit Dee said, "I can't believe how yummy this is. You really can cook."

Lizzy smiled in her heart for the first time in months. During the course of supper they talked about kids they'd gone to school with and what they were all doing now. Once supper was over they cleaned off the table and started on the dishes.

"You know, Ripley gets on to me about not cleaning my dishes after I eat," Dee said with a chuckle. Then the chuckle turned into a laugh. "I'm just pre-warning ya."

Dee dried her hands and walked out of the kitchen to have a smoke in her garden, leaving Lizzy to daydream.

She drifted back to a time when Ripley and she were in middle school. Ripley's mother had made both of them do the same dishes three times because they'd left them in the sink after they'd eaten and run off to go swimming at the lake with Lee and his friend Stan.

"Ripley is turning into her mother," Lizzy muttered out loud as she shook her head.

***

Everything seemed to be looking up for Lizzy, except her heartache. Thoughts of Lee popped into her head all the time. Where was he? What was he doing? Is he happy? Everything reminded Lizzy of him.

The first anniversary of their breakup crept up slowly on the calendar so she kept herself busy by working. She took on a second job for when she wasn't working at the yacht club.

In the meantime, Dee met a terrific guy named Raymond. He worked at the body shop across the street from the house. Dee always said he did "r-e-a-l nice body work" as they watched him from the garden.

One evening, after a long day's work, Lizzy pulled into the drive way. She chuckled to herself when she saw Dee across the street sitting on the hood of a car Raymond was working on. Dee looked at him the way Lizzy once looked at Lee. Lizzy felt that twinge of envy again.

"He must do r-e-a-l nice body work to make that girl smile like that!" Lizzy said out loud. Loneliness had haunted Lizzy the last couple of months since Ripley had moved back home to her parents.

Ripley's new-found joy had turned out to be a con and pretty much took her for every dime she had. Some of the town's people said he had a gambling problem. Some said it was drugs. Others said he was just no good.

Lizzy and Dee both wished they'd noticed more to save her the heart ache, but after Ripley had moved home again, it was time they stopped grieving over the past. *"Can't cry over spilt milk"*, Lizzy's grandma always said.

Lizzy headed into the house to get a cold drink and go back out to sit in Dee's beautiful garden. There were flowers everywhere and butterflies flew from flower to flower *"to pollinate"*, Dee would say.

Lizzy didn't know much about gardening. She knew how wonderful the garden made her feel and enjoyed its beauty. Visiting the garden became an everyday occurrence for her.

Lizzy talked to the bumble bees, the butterflies, and the flowers when she sat out on the swing. Dee had the swing built when she added the room to the back of the house that became Lizzy's room. Dee had told Lizzy that she intended the room to be for storage. She didn't want Lizzy to feel that it had been built especially for her, but Lizzy knew the truth. That's why she loved Dee so much.

And so, every evening Lizzy sat out on the swing and watched Dee and Raymond across the street as they fell more and more in love. Lizzy so much wanted that feeling again. Sometimes she prayed to God for someone to love her like that. What she really wanted was someone to love and someone who would love her back just as much.

Lizzy used her time alone to get to know herself. *What do I want out of life*? Something was missing. *Is it Mr. Right?*

CHAPTER FOUR

End of the world

It's better to have loved and lost than never have loved at all-

unknown

Lizzy was enjoying the garden, swinging on the swing one day when she noticed "the love birds" (Dee and Raymond) were fighting or at least that's what it appeared to be. Dee slapped Raymond's face and yelled at him. Then she stomped back across the street to the house.

"Is everything okay?" Lizzy asked as she got to her feet. Dee didn't answer except with the slam of the screen door.

Lizzy kept her distance. In her opinion, it was best to stay out of the middle of things like that. People did better figuring things out without an outside opinion.

That night without seeing Dee again, Lizzy said good night to "WRANGLER MAN", a poster of a cowboy that hung on her wall. It was her imaginary boyfriend. As she crawled into bed and pulled the covers up she looked over at the door way to see Dee standing there.

"Can I come in?" Dee asked.

"Sure," Lizzy answered.

"I told him I never wanted to see him again. I lied. I love him. I *do* want to see him again. Every day, for the rest of my life!" Dee said as she plopped down on the bed. She grabbed Lizzy's teddy bear and bawled all over it.

"I'm sure he knows that. Wait till tomorrow. You'll see." Lizzy sat up and hugged Dee, not wanting to let her go and wishing she could keep her safe in her arms, always. Dee had become a precious sister to her.

The next morning, Lizzy woke up and made a pot of coffee since Ripley was not there anymore to leave her some. Dee rushed into the kitchen.

"I'm going to call off from work and go talk to Raymond."

"Ok, I'll explain to Dottie. She'll understand," Lizzy answered.

The phone rang and Dee shouted, "I hope that's him." She ran to the phone and answered it. "Hello...What? Oh, no, no....noooooooo!" and her legs crumbled under her.

Lizzy ran over to Dee and helped her to her feet. "What's going on?" she whispered, terrified to think of what it could be. She got Dee to the couch and knelt in front of her.

"He's dead. He's... dead!" Dee answered, and completely dry-eyed, stared into the air.

Lizzy hung up the phone then settled on the couch beside her heartbroken friend. She wrapped her arms around her and they sat together for what seemed like hours.

"Can you tell me what happened, Dee?" Lizzy asked once Dee's sobs had subsided.

Between sobs and long minutes of silence, Dee got the important facts out.

It seemed that after their fight, Raymond was so upset he went to the store, bought a bottle of whiskey, took it home and drank the whole thing in an hour. Then he got into his car, cranked it up in the garage, and passed out.

Totally spent, Lizzy tucked her friend into bed and slept that night on the floor beside her. She was going to be there if Dee needed anything. She knew how bad it had hurt to drive away from Lee, but she suspected Dee's pain had to be much worse.

"I'll be here for you," she whispered into the darkness.

***

Some of the town's people said that Raymond's death was suicide. Others said it was just a case of real bad luck. Some even whispered that he'd been on his way to see Dee and simply passed out.

All Lizzy knew was, Dee blamed herself.

"If I hadn't stormed home like a spoiled brat, we'd have worked it out. Everything would have been all right," Dee told Lizzy more than once in a few days. "Raymond would be alive."

Lizzy understood guilt, but she had no idea how to help Dee. In the days before the funeral, she did what she could to ease Dee's pain, but nothing seemed to help. She ate very little, talked even less.

***

"Dee hasn't said much," Lizzy told Ripley as they drove to the funeral. "All I can do is let her know I'm here for her."

Dee had gotten up early and gone to the funeral home. She told Lizzy that she felt the need to stay close to Raymond as he transitioned to his next life.

Lizzy and Ripley knew Dee held deep spiritual beliefs, so it didn't seem odd that she wanted to be with him. They'd long ago accepted Dee's code of love, respect and honor for all things, although all the spiritual stuff made Lizzy feel uncomfortable because of her "Christian" up-bringing. But if Dee found comfort in all that stuff, Lizzy would do whatever it took to give her the space to practice her beliefs. Lizzy realized every one probably handled death differently. Lizzy hadn't experienced many deaths in her life. *Maybe Dee's right-on with all her beliefs, because of all the death she's had around her,* Lizzy thought.

"You know, some are saying it was suicide," Ripley said as she parked the car.

"I know, but I ... I saw it. I saw how much they loved each other. He would never do that to her. It had to be an accident," Lizzy said, pointing to her chest, with her voice cracking and eyes tearing up.

Ripley broke down in tears too and they hugged each other until someone knocked on the window. It was Dee.

"It's almost time...time for his transition," Dee said in a monotone voice.

Her expression matched her voice-cold, stony, matter-of-fact, almost as though she was paralyzed and couldn't feel anything.

The three of them entered the building where the services were being held. Lizzy and Ripley let Dee lead the way. Raymond's family sat in the front staring at her. Everyone was whispering when Dee walked in.

Lizzy and Ripley both knew what was being said. At the same time, they put their hands on Dee's shoulders to let her know they were there for her. Dee's expression remained stony as they walked to the front to say goodbye.

Dee stood in front of the casket and looked at him. She bent down, kissed his cheek and put a rose in his hands. As Lizzy watched, she heard an overwhelming ringing in her ears, almost musical, then it was gone. Dee turned to Lizzy and Ripley. "He is gone now."

The three of them walked to the back of the room and remained sitting until the service was over and everyone left. At the grave side, they stood with Dee until everyone went home. Dee kept her silence, even on the ride home.

At the house, she got out of the car and marched to her room.

The days drifted into weeks and Lizzy's number one priority was to get Dee to eat. She stayed locked in her room unless she was at work. Even there she was only a shell of a person. The garden missed her as much as Lizzy did.

Lizzy tried to cook something every day that would be aromatic, or as Dee would say, *"yummy smelling."* Lizzy tried hard to get her to snap out of it. She even made an effort to get her back out into her beautiful garden. Nothing worked.

One day when Lizzy came home from work, the front door was locked. "Dee never locks the door," Lizzy said. She tried it again— it was locked.

She fished her keys out of her pocket and opened the door. She smelled gas. Gas filled the air as she walked further into the house. She saw Dee lying on the floor holding a rose.

"Noooooooooo!" she screamed and ran to Dee's body.

Lizzy shook her. Dee didn't respond.

"Oh my God!" she screamed, "Oh please, God! You can't leave me like this, Dee. I need you!" She felt for a pulse. Dee's heart was barely beating.

"Thank God, I still have her."

Lizzy got up and ran to the phone and called 911. She dragged Dee's limp body out the door and held her tight. She was determined not to lose her.

The ambulance came and the paramedics pulled Dee from Lizzy's arms. One paramedic said, "I think this one is going to make it," to the police officer who was making his way to Lizzy.

After the officer finished his questions, Lizzy learned that Dee had put out the pilot light on the stove and turned all the burners to high. She'd closed all the windows and the doors. She laid on the floor and went to sleep.

"You got here just in time, Miss. Five more minutes and your friend would have died," the officer told her.

Lizzy was almost sick to her stomach and her knees buckled. The officer helped her to sit on the garden swing. "I was supposed to work until six, but it was slow, so they sent me home. I'm so glad they did."

The fire fighters opened all the windows and vented the natural gas out of the house. While the officers spoke with Lizzy, she watched the men move through the house that she now called home. In an hour or so, they began to close the windows.

"The house is all clear. We lit the pilot again for you. Take care of yourself, Lizzy," the Fire Captain said. He'd been in the yacht club once or twice for meetings and he was always very nice. He patted her shoulder and left her in the garden with the police officer.

"Are we done, sir? I really want to get to the hospital."

"We are. You drive safe, okay? Your friend isn't going anywhere for a few days."

As soon as he was out of sight, Lizzy raced to her father's Jeep and headed to the hospital.

She stopped at the pay phone outside the door of the hospital and called Ripley to tell her what had happened. Within minutes, Ripley joined her. They sat by Dee's bed for hours, watching their friend sleep.

The nurses explained that they'd had to sedate Dee because she was upset that she was alive when she came to. The girls stayed until visiting hours were over and the nurses assured them that Dee would not wake up during the night.

The next morning as the sun came up, and glowed through the window. Dee's eyes started to flutter. Lizzy had just arrived, holding a steaming cup of coffee in her hand. She tiptoed to Dee's bedside and gently swept Dees hair out of her eyes.

"Hi, how you feeling?" Lizzy asked. She forced a smile she didn't feel.

"I want to die," Dee said with a raspy voice.

Lizzy gasped. "Noooo... You can't leave me. I need you. Ripley needs you. Your garden needs you!" she took a breath. "I've thought of dying myself, but I couldn't do that to you! You gave me hope, Dee." Almost exhausted with reasons, she took a deep breath and released it.

"Raymond wouldn't want you to do that. He would want you to live. I know that. I don't know how I know, but I do! We love you and our lives wouldn't be the same without you! *Please Dee, don't leave me!*"

Dee turned her head, looked out the window and stared at the rose bush just outside the window. To Lizzy, those few minutes of stark silence seemed like hours. Dee turned back and looked Lizzy in the eye.

"You are right. Raymond does want me to live," Dee said in a soft whispering surrender. "And he wants you to have hope."

Lizzy wrapped her arms around Dee and sobbed.

CHAPTER FIVE

Breaking Free

***Wisdom is nothing more than healed pain*-Robert Gary**

After Dee was discharged from the hospital, she returned to her job at the yacht club.

Each day became easier, but she missed Raymond so bad, it almost killed her at times. When she was home, she spent more and more time in the garden, where she talked to her flowers and the bumble bees.

Odd thing was, the butterflies had disappeared. *There should always be butterflies around.*

Where are you, Raymond? Without their fluttering, colorful presence, I feel all alone, as though you aren't with me.

She sat on the swing and stared off into space. Raymond once told her that she represented a caterpillar, and she would cocoon to chrysalis state, and transition to a beautiful butterfly.

Where are you? She wondered again.

Lizzy found her sitting on the swing when she got in from work that afternoon.

"Hi. What-cha doin?" Lizzy asked.

"Just out here getting some fresh air and thinking," Dee said as she glanced across the street.

"I'm happy to see you out here in the sunshine, Dee," Lizzy said. "I know you're still hurting a lot, but you know that your love and Raymond's is still alive, right?" She pointed to her heart and smiled.

Dee didn't answer right away. She understood that Lizzy was a good friend and loved her like a sister. But without the butterflies, Dee wasn't so sure. "Tell me about love, Lizzy," she whispered.

"Well, I've learned that love survives even when people are gone out of our lives. We can still love them— maybe even deeper than when they were here." She glanced across the street, and then turned her gaze back to Dee. "Not every loss is death maybe, but the loss still hurts bad."

Dee knew Lizzy was thinking of Lee and she'd heard Lizzy crying herself to sleep all those nights on the couch, even though she'd never said a word to Lizzy about it.

"I remember you telling me about your mom's saying about setting something free and if it comes back, it's meant to be," said Dee. "Raymond can't come back in person, but I keep hoping I'd have a sign he was still here."

Lizzy patted her hand and sighed. "I know. But maybe he's just not ready yet. Maybe he's waiting for you to be stronger. I don't know. You understand these things better than I do."

Do I? Thought Dee. Maybe what I thought was wrong. Maybe what I made up to help me understand death as a child was wrong. She rocked the swing just a little. "Have you seen any of the butterflies lately?" she asked.

"As a matter of fact, I haven't. There were always butterflies out here." Lizzy looked up at the sky. "Maybe they left because summer is almost over and the nights are cooling off."

"I keep looking across the street to see if he's there" Dee whispered.

"They really have had a lot of business lately," Lizzy said quickly.

"Raymond sent them the business," Dee said. But she knew that Lizzy thought it was all due to the write up in the local paper about Raymond's death. Whatever the reason, the shop was so busy they opened up a mechanic shop adjacent to it.

Lizzy smiled. "Yes, he did. A gift from the heavens."

Dee was thankful that Lizzy had come into her life. She may not have shared Dee's beliefs, but she respected them. And, Lizzy made sure that she was always there for her, no matter what.

"How fast would you move out if Mr. Right showed up?" Dee asked her after a while.

Lizzy looked stunned. Then she gave a little laugh. "Well, it would take a while. First, I'd have to make sure he *was* Mr. Right. Then I'd have to make sure he was *really* Mr. Right. I sure know that it takes a long time to get to know someone. And even then, you can't be sure you really know them." She looked out over the garden. "Yup, it would be a while, Dee."

Again, they settled into silence and rocked on the garden swing. "Déjà vu!" Dee mused. "We've done this before in a past life."

"Done what?" Lizzy asked.

"You and I, sitting and talking about Raymond, but it wasn't Raymond. It was someone else that I loved very deeply." Dee shook her head, trying to shake the thought away.

Lizzy just sat quietly as though she was thinking about what Dee had said. Dee loved that about her. She never laughed at her ideas and beliefs, just sort of soaked them up and tried them on.

"Hey let's go for a ride," Dee suggested. "I've got to find a butterfly!" She smiled. "After I find a butterfly, I will take you armadillo huntin'." Lizzy just grinned at her.

It felt good to smile again.

They closed up the house, took the top off the Jeep, jumped in, and headed out.

"Look. Let's stop, and get some peanuts." Dee pointed out an old man on the side of the road selling boiled peanuts from an old steel drum that had steam escaping around the lid. They traded two dollars for the cup of steaming nuts and climbed back into the Jeep.

Dee realized how much she'd missed the wind mussing up her cinnamon-red hair. She looked over at Lizzy whose blonde curls were wrapping around her face. *This is living.*

***

People considered their small town country, but it wasn't even close. They headed west of town, to the real country: cabbage farms, dirt roads, and cowboys!

The young women sang songs, laughed, and ate their boiled peanuts, as they drove the dirt roads. They talked about the *Double L's,* and sometimes about Raymond. When Lizzy recognized the pain in Dee's green eyes, she was quick to change the subject.

When she looked over at Dee, the hurt was still there and that's when Lizzy could hear her mother's words.

"Honey, God didn't give you feelings to hide them. He gave them to you to feel." That was when Lizzy realized that Dee needed talk about him. She vowed to herself that from that moment on, she'd let Dee talk.

***

Summer ended, cool weather approached. Lizzy and Dee weren't spending as much time in the garden. Dee walked out there from time to time, to see if she could catch a glimpse of a butterfly. Still no sign.

They climbed in the Jeep and took rides out to the country, almost every night to talk. Sometimes they'd stay out until the sun came up.

They shared everything, from child hood memories, to the things people did in high school. In high school, Dee always had friends who weren't in the "normal" group -as Lizzy put it.

"Whatever happen to that guy they called Toad?" Lizzy asked. "He was so weird."

"Todd? I dated him…he wasn't weird. Ok he wasn't "normal" either. What is normal anyway?" Dee laughed.

"I guess you're right," Lizzy would say with a laugh. "I'm too righteous and rigid and that's not normal either!"

"What you see and how you see it, all depends on where you are standing," Dee added.

"Yes, and *you* are right." Lizzy almost felt the pop in her mind, as though a light bulb had come on in her head. She always thought of

23

the future, doing all the right things, and she never enjoyed the moment. What a wonderful gift Dee's perspective turned out to be.

One night, when they went on their nightly drive, they grabbed a twelve pack and headed out. Lizzy had finally become a beer drinker. That night Dee drove and they headed southwest. She had a special place she wanted to show Lizzy.

They drove for hours, though with conversations about the meaning of life and all the bizarre questions there wasn't any answer for. Lizzy hardly realized how far they'd gone.

The Jeep crossed over an old railroad track which looked as though it had been shut down for at least fifty years. An old two-story house stood behind a gigantic oak tree. Some cement stepping stones pushed up from the oak trees roots, and lay patiently as though they'd been waiting for them to place their feet.

The old house stood slanted, as if it had its head cocked. The paint had long ago peeled off, so she couldn't tell what color it had worn back in its day. On the second story, old bottles in framed out shadow box windows stood at attention, covered with dust. The bottom floor displayed old neon signs, desperately hanging in each window.

"I never showed anyone this place, except Raymond—and now you," Dee whispered. "There are ghosts in there," she cautioned.

"*Ghosts*?" Lizzy shrieked.

"Well, they say their spirits still walk the floors waiting for the next customer to arrive" Dee explained. "This town was a booming railroad stop at one time. This old house was the town tavern. Two women owned it and lived upstairs. Some say they were a couple which was not accepted at that time, not to mention it wasn't acceptable for a woman to own a business, let alone two women together."

"Wow," Lizzy said. "Oh hell, everyone in our town is starting to think the same about us." They both laughed.

Lizzy put her arm around Dee and walked her back to the Jeep. Lizzy glanced over her shoulder for one last peek, and saw two women figures looking out the window, smiling back at her.

"I definitely had too many beers tonight," Lizzy reasoned to Dee. "Let's get home."

***

When the first day of winter arrived, the yacht club business slowed down quite a bit. After the holidays, "snow bird" yachters started the business up again. Snow bird yachters were the northerners who came down to play in their fancy yachts for a few months because it was too cold in their northern and Midwest hometowns. The rest of the year their yachts just drifted sleeplessly at the dock waiting for their lover's return—almost like a love story.

Lizzy looked out at all the lonely yachts and imagined being out on one with Wrangler man. *No, Mr. Right. No, better yet, Mr. Yacht-Man.* She shook the dream from her head.

She had no clue what to do with her life. She wondered if she would ever marry or have children. Would she ever have the funds to go back to school and get her degree? She couldn't burden her parents because they had their hands full with helping to support Lynn and her kids. Besides, Lizzy wasn't even sure about college anymore.

So if she had no other plan, she would work, and work, and work. Lizzy shook her head again to get out of reality and back to her dream. Then Dee walked up and saved Lizzy from herself.

"Hey, wanna go armidilla huntin'?" Dee asked.

"What exactly is 'armadillo hunting'?" Lizzy inquired.

"Well it's really 'dilla huntin' but I didn't think you would know what I was talking about."

"Ok, what is 'dilla huntin?" Lizzy asked.

"Where you hunt ARMIDILLA!" Dee said almost laughing.

"Oh, I see," Lizzy observed. "Why?"

"The golf course at Rivertown wants my friend Johnny to go get rid of them 'cause they keep eating up the grass." Dee said with a smirk on her face.

"You don't kill them, do you?" Lizzy asked with a frown.

"Nope. We don't—Johnny does. We just scare them out of the bushes!"

"That's horrible!" Lizzy exclaimed.

"You always said you wanted a cowboy. That's the kind of stuff they do. Johnny's a *real* cowboy," Dee teased, then added, "Naw. He makes a trap, traps them, and then lets them go. Out on his daddy's property," Dee informed with a smile. "Come on. I want you to meet him. He is as righteous as you," Dee said as she walked away.

Lizzy took off her apron, hung it up and clocked out for the day. She yelled goodbye to Dottie and followed Dee out the door to meet the cowboy.

***

"Johnny, this is Lizzy," Dee said when the girls arrived at his house and got out of the Jeep.

"Nice to meet you ma'am," Johnny drawled. He tipped his cowboy hat as a greeting and turned just a little pink in the face.

"Hello," Lizzy answered with a smile. "Nice to meet you, too."

He glanced at his watch. "Let's go get in my truck and head to Rivertown before it gets too late."

The trio jumped in the big truck and headed off. Johnny drove, Lizzy sat in the middle, and Dee had the seat by the door. Lizzy noticed that he smelled good, not like she thought a cowboy would smell. *Is this what being a cowboy's woman feels like?* Lizzy wondered.

At the country club gates Johnny told the security guard why he was there. The guard flagged him through. The sky had a pinkish-purple dusk glow to it; too dark to golf, but still light enough to see.

Dee and Lizzy hopped out when he parked and met him at the tailgate. Johnny showed them how to set up the traps.

When they had most of the traps in place, Dee started whispering her best Elmer Fudd impression. "SHHHHH be very, very, quiet. I'm huntin' for a wabbit," Lizzy choked back a giggle and looked up to find Johnny. She busted out in a hysterical laugh-a laugh she couldn't stop.

Dee looked up to see what was so funny and busted out laughing, too. Johnny had tripped and fallen while holding on to a trap and had landed over the top of a rabbit hole. It must have scared the rabbit right into the trap.

"Look here. I done caught me a rabbit," Johnny chuckled. Carefully, he put the trap to the side, got to his feet and brushed himself off.

Dee and Lizzy continued to laugh. Lizzy laughed so hard her cheeks felt sore and when she looked at Dee, she noticed that her eyes watered too. *We must look a mess with our runny, red eyes.*

But Lizzy knew Dee needed a good old fashioned laugh. She hadn't laughed like that since before Raymond died. It had to feel good. Lizzy felt lighter watching her friend laugh without a care for the first time in so long.

Lizzy's momma always said, *"Laughter heals the heart."* Dee was healing she figured, and so was she.

Now Johnny was a real nice guy from a good family. He was a cowboy, but Lizzy felt no attraction to him as a mate. She knew that was Dee's intention. Lizzy liked the idea of Johnny in her life, thought he was super-sweet, but she couldn't get her heart to react. Maybe they could become close friends, though.

After the hunting trip Lizzy and Dee kept in contact with Johnny. After he took a job as a mechanic at the shop across the street, they saw him almost every day. He yelled to them from across the street as they left for work.

"Have a nice day at work ladies. I hope you make millions. I *really do*!" he'd holler with a tip of his hat.

Dee would yell back, "Shhhhhh...Be very, very quiet! We're huntin' for a rabbit!"

In their own way, Lizzy and Dee were letting him know their special friendship would last forever- because he gave them the gift of laughter.

CHAPTER SIX

Dirt-road Dreaming

Get out of your head and get into your heart...think less feel more-

Osho

As spring approached, the sun brightened the land, and more birds chirped their hopeful songs. Each day Dee and Lizzy spent more and more time in the garden as Lizzy tried to absorb all that Dee taught her. And, they watched for Johnny across the street as he worked.

"It really is a shame I don't get that tickle in my tummy for that boy," Lizzy remarked as she sipped her beer.

"Can't say I didn't try," Dee said. She sipped her beer and gave Lizzy a smirky smile.

"He really is a wonderful guy," Lizzy continued as if Dee needed convincing.

"I know. That's why I tried hooking you up!" Dee bellowed in indignation.

"I wish he could find himself a nice girl. One that treated him like gold." Lizzy sighed and took another sip.

"Shhhhh … be very, very quiet. We're huntin' for a rabbit," Dee taunted and then burst out in hysterical laughter. Lizzy joined in.

The girls spied Johnny walking across the street from the shop. As he walked toward the swing Dee grabbed a beer and tossed it to him. Johnny wasn't paying attention, until it was too late. The can hit him right- square in the nose and blood spewed everywhere.

"Damn, Dee! I thought you girls liked hanging out with me," Johnny cried as he held his nose.

"Oh, my god. I am *so* sorry. I thought you saw it coming," Dee confessed.

Lizzy was appalled. Neither she nor Dee would hurt anyone, let alone hurt Johnny and she felt as horrible about the accident as Dee did. Johnny left without his beer, though he accepted a baggie with ice cubes in it before he went home.

For the next week, Johnny walked around with a huge band aid on his nose. Not that the accident was funny, but every time the girls saw him and the band aid, laughter overcame them. They nick-named him the Headless Horseman.

Of course, they didn't tell him because both of the girls adored him and wanted to spare his feelings.

Johnny started stopping by the house a couple days a week. Then it turned into every day-even when Dee and Lizzy would go *dirt road dreaming*. (That is what they called it when they would take their ride out to the country where the farms were.)

The girls enjoyed his company and he knew every dirt road imaginable, how to get there and how to get back. He drove most of the time because Lizzy and Dee enjoyed drinking their beer.

One time, they went to Danny Johnston's farm to play in the mud. The farm sponsored the local mud bogging event the town held once a month. Being it was April, a time of an overabundance of rain, they ended up getting Johnny's truck stuck in the mud. Water swirled up over the hood, seeped through in the doors. They had to get out and get out quick, no easy feat since both Lizzy and Dee had had too many beers that night.

"Oh shit. My truck!" Johnny exclaimed. "How the hell am I going to get my truck out of there?"

"We'll get it out," Dee said with a bit of a slur. "Right?" she asked Lizzy who wasn't too sure what she could do about it.

The women tried to push the truck out but it wasn't budging. The harder they pushed, the madder Johnny seemed to get.

After several futile attempts, Dee and Lizzy felt every drop of alcohol they'd consumed and they started to laugh. They laughed at the mud that covered them and the truck. They looked at Johnny's angry expression and burst into new gales of laughter. That fact that Johnny always makes them laugh anyway, wasn't helping, thought Lizzy.

When their laughter subsided, Lizzy realized she didn't have any idea where they were or where town was from the farm. The darkness was black as pitch with the truck under water, but it wasn't quiet. Every night creature for miles seemed to be calling to them.

"Dee, you know where we are?" Lizzy asked in a hushed whisper.

"Not a clue," Dee replied with a giggle. "Johnny knows. Don't worry."

"He probably isn't ever going to speak to us again," Lizzy said. "He's probably going to leave us out here with his poor truck."

Johnny came up behind them and snapped on his key chain flashlight. He wasn't smiling.

"We need to follow the power lines. It will get us to the main road," he said in a low voice.

But his seriousness caused Lizzy and Dee to snicker and fall behind a few steps. They didn't want to make him mad or hurt his feelings, but they just loved the fact that when he was around, *"Shit happened."*

"Sometimes, even when bad things happen, good things come out of it," Lizzy's momma would say. Now Lizzy knew Momma was right. Although she had lost Lee and Dee had lost Raymond, they both had Johnny.

With Johnny walking ahead of them, Lizzy and Dee took the opportunity to talk about Lee and Raymond. When Johnny had joined in on their dirt road dreaming trips, they had stopped discussing the subject because they didn't want him to feel uncomfortable.

"I miss Raymond so much it hurts here, in my chest, and its spring. Where are the damn butterflies?" Dee slurred her words and tripped over the roots in the ground or her own feet. Lizzy didn't know which.

"We just had too many beers is all," Lizzy replied slowly. "I *missss* Lee, too."

"At least he's still alive!" Dee snapped. Her voice sounded drunk and angry. They staggered along for a minute in silence.

"You are right." Lizzy sympathized. "Oh shit, I don't see Johnny any more. Or the flash light!" Lizzy put her hand over one eye, so she could focus.

When Lizzy stopped in her tracks, Dee plowed into her back. They tripped over each other and fell to the ground. Once again, they started laughing, realizing that the beer caused them to have beer-goggle eyes. They rolled around in the mud. They had no idea where they were, no idea where Johnny was and no idea how they'd get home, but being drunk, they didn't really care, either.

Johnny found them that way when he tracked back to all the laughter. "Wallerin' like pigs in the mud," he mumbled to himself.

Lizzy and Dee blinked up at him when the flashlight beam hit their eyes.

"What in the gosh-darned world are you two doing on the ground?" Johnny said as he shined the flash light in their faces.

"No idear," slurred Lizzy. She looked at Dee who shrugged. "Glad you came back for us, though," she continued. She was delighted that he seemed to be in a better mood than when they'd started out.

"The hard road is only fifty yards from here," Johnny stated.

The girls struggled to help each other to their feet. Once they were standing up, Johnny shook his head and pointed to their left.

"Let's get to it and head towards town. I can get the tow company to come get my truck out. Good thing I'm a mechanic, 'cause it's going to take a lot of labor to get all that water cleaned out the engine," Johnny mumbled as he walked toward the hard road.

"We will help," Dee and Lizzy slurred in unison.

***

The next morning, despite headaches and mud that refused to come out from under their fingernails, Dee and Lizzy busied themselves drying out the interior of Johnny's truck. Johnny worked hard on the engine. Lizzy thought she'd never been as happy as when the motor finally purred.

"Good as new," Johnny said, wiping his greasy hands on a shop towel, then stuffing it in his back pocket.

"I can't believe you didn't just leave us out there!" Lizzy said.

"Yeah, our drunk asses wallerin' around like pigs in the mud!" Dee chimed in. "Must have been one hell of a sight." She rubbed her temples with her fingertips.

Then the three roared with laughter, almost as loud as the engine of the truck.

"Good times. Damn good times," Johnny said. "Don't worry, I'll get ya back. Besides, I still got a little trick up my sleeve for you, Miss Dee."

He glanced from under the hood with a sneaky look on his face. "Not only did I have to wear a band aid on my nose for a week or more, but I had to explain that a *girl* did it." Johnny walked over to Dee and wiped a smudge of grease on her nose.

"Hey guys, wanna beer?" Lizzy offered to change the subject.

***

Johnny came over every day after work. His truck purred like a kitten. Life was grand and before too long, it seemed as though he would never go home.

Some nights, he slept over on the couch. About a month slipped by, just long enough for Dee to forget about Johnny's warning about "the trick up his sleeve."

One night he put plastic wrap on the toilet. Of course, he warned Lizzy of the prank, then went to bed on the couch. Dee got up in the middle of the night to use the bathroom and got the surprise of her life. Lizzy almost fell out of bed laughing when Dee's hollering woke her up. She stood in the doorway of her room to watch.

"Damn it.... It's on, Johnny!" she yelled from the bathroom. She came out and kicked the couch as hard as she could. "Did you hear me? You Headless Horseman! It's *on*!" Dee screamed in his face.

And that marked the beginning of the official battle of the better pranks. Dee got Johnny. He got her back. Occasionally Lizzy got caught in the line of fire. Both women enjoyed having him around. He kept them laughing and on their toes.

Lizzy and Dee missed Ripley. Their old friend stopped by now and again after closing up the hardware store, to see who'd gotten whom lately. She was doing so well at the store that her daddy was considering retirement. He promoted her to manager which left her doing well financially. She talked about saving money to put a down payment on a house.

Dee and Lizzy were both ecstatic for her. They remembered back at how anal she'd been about the dishes in the sink, and almost at the same time they'd say, "No dirty dishes at that house."

Although Dee stayed busy thinking up new pranks to play on Johnny, she still checked her garden daily. Still no butterflies. The flowers bloomed, the bees pollinated, but the butterflies didn't return.

One night the threesome took a dirt road dreaming ride. Dee told them about her dream of owning her own business someday.

Johnny shot back with, "Doing what, slinging beer? Better have lots of band aids there."

Dee just gave him a nod which meant, "It's on!"

It wasn't always fun and games, though. Sometimes when Johnny came around, he would "serious up" with them and try to give them lessons on finding a good man. The do's and don'ts.

They questioned him about how men thought and felt about things. What type of things did men look for in life? How did men feel about relationships? Did men recognize the difference between friendship and love?

He didn't have all the answers and didn't pretend to, either. "All I know ladies, is I love *this* friendship," he replied one night.

Lizzy and Dee realized that Johnny was destined be one of those lifelong, unforgettable friends. They enjoyed having a guy around, too.

"Hey let's get some pizza," Lizzy said. She came out the door into the garden juggling three beers from the fridge.

"Okay," Dee said.

"I'm buying," Johnny said. "And one more lesson ladies -always ask to see his checking account balance before you settle down. Enough of Men 101. Let's eat."

As Lizzy watched her friends finish their beers, she thought about how good her life was now, even if she didn't have all the answers she thought she should have. Food always seemed to make things right. She remembered her momma's saying, *"The way to a man's heart is through the stomach." Good thing I can cook, then.*

They jumped into the Jeep and headed up to the new pizza place which had only been open a week. It stood next to the new strip mall that was in the process of being built. Their small town was slowly growing and so were they. As they went in to the pizza place, they ran into a girl they all had gone to school with.

"Hi guys, how are you? Oh, you look good, Johnny." Nickie's voice purred.

Dee and Lizzy looked at each other. They knew she was flirting with Johnny and they realized that he didn't even notice.

"We're great," Lizzy said. She didn't know how long she and Dee stared at Johnny to see if he noticed the come-on.

"My parents just opened this place," Nickie said. "Dee, it's nice to see you aren't wearing so much black these days." Nickie was trying to be nice but the girls could tell it was hard for her.

Lizzy straightened her back, ready to defend Dee at first. Then she realized Nickie was referring to their high school days. "We came in to try out the pizza," Dee said. Lizzy bet that Dee was trying to change the subject.

"Come on ladies, let's sit" Johnny said. He held out his arms for them to link onto and escorted them to the table.

Nickie came over to the table, the whole time staring at Johnny, and took their order. Never once did she make eye contact with Dee and Lizzy.

"I think someone's got a crush on you, Johnny," Dee said.

"I told you ladies, I love our friendship and would never do anything to jeopardize that." Johnny mussed with his cowboy smile.

"It's not *us*!" said Lizzy.

"It's her, you Headless Horseman!" Dee said and pointed to Nickie who was behind the counter taking a to-go order.

Johnny turned to look and said, "Ohhh."

Just then, Nickie looked up to see if Johnny had noticed her. At that point, Lizzy and Dee knew Nickie was hooked. They knew he deserved better but they weren't going to stand in his way.

They finally got their pizza and dug in. When they got to the bottom of their slices Dee said, "Did you know that if you put salt on pizza crust it tastes like a pretzel?" She salted her crust as serious as could be, then took a bite.

Johnny and Lizzy looked at each other and burst out laughing. Johnny said to Lizzy, "That's why we love our Dee...Always recognizing the simplicities of life!"

They shook their heads. Dee looked up as though she had no idea they were even talking.

As they were at the counter getting ready to pay, Dee pointed to the door. "Look."

Lizzy's sister Lynn walked in. "I went to the house," she said. "You weren't there. Then when I drove by I saw daddy's Jeep so I...Grandma is in the hospital. Not doing well. Said it may be a heart attack or...they don't know ...still doing tests on her," Lynn said, panting.

"Okay. Okay, calm down. Are Momma and Daddy there? Where are the kids? All right let's go!" Lizzy said without any time for Lynn to answer.

"Will you guys take the Jeep back to the house?" Lizzy asked Dee and Johnny.

"Sure." Johnny answered.

"Let me come with you," Dee volunteered. "You don't mind, do you?" Dee asked Johnny.

"No. No. Go on. I'll get your Jeep home," he offered.

Lizzy glanced over her shoulder as she walked out the door and realized they left poor Johnny and his wallet, alone with Nickie.

CHAPTER SEVEN

Memories and Ghost

Make new friends, keep the old, one is silver, the other gold

Lizzy's momma met Lizzy, Lynn and Dee as they walked through the emergency room entrance way.

"How is she? What are the doctors saying? Is she going to be all right Momma?" Lizzy asked without taking a breath.

"They are moving her to intensive care right now," Lizzy's momma said.

"When can we see her?" Lynn butted in.

Lizzy looked over her mother's shoulder and saw her father with his hands to his face. Lizzy's daddy, not being much of a talker, looked as though he was talking to someone now. Then Lizzy realized he was praying. Her daddy was on the verge of losing his mother.

"Oh no, Momma. Is Daddy going to be all right?"

Her father looked up. When he saw them, he wiped his face so they couldn't see he was crying. He got up and headed towards them.

"Oh Daddy, have you gotten to see her?" Lizzy and Lynn asked as they wrapped their arms around their daddy.

"I did but she wasn't conscious. They didn't let me stay with her long. They needed to get her hooked up to a bunch of machines. A nurse forced me out of the room."

Both the girls cried hysterically into his broad chest. Lizzy's dad was a big man. He was six and a half feet tall, two hundred and fifty pounds but was kind and gentle. Lizzy always seemed to know what her daddy felt, or said because of the secret *expression language* they shared. Fear flooded her heart because of what she read on his face. He was unable to hide it very well.

"Daddy are you going to be all right?" Lizzy asked.

"I'll be fine," he said. A tear rolled down his cheek and he wiped it away as though hoping no one would see it. But Lizzy saw it. Dee caught a glimpse of it. They looked at each other.

"Let's go have a seat. I want to talk to you girls," Lizzy's father said. He took both of his daughters by the hand and led them to the couch in a little room that looked very dim and quiet. *Probably set up for families with members that were dying,* Lizzy thought.

"Your grandmother is dying. There is nothing they can do for her," he said.

"Are you sure?" Lynn asked with a raspy whisper.

"Yes. I'm sure," he responded.

He bowed his head as if to regain his strength. He cleared his throat and finished explaining in almost a whisper. "They are setting her up in a special intensive care room. They will slowly give her medication to make her comfortable. The doctor doesn't believe she will make it the week. They are surprised she wasn't complaining of pain sooner. He did say she will be coherent but only a short time. As the pain increases, so will the medicine."

Lizzy's daddy put his head down and they sat together in silence. The room stayed quiet, real quiet for at least a half hour. Everyone just stared out to nothingness. Hypnotized by pain. There wasn't a word out of her daddy all evening. No expression either. Just a blank stare. Lizzy's momma and Lynn decided to get coffee in the special break room for the families of the dying.

A nurse with a clip board peeked her head in the door. "She is all set up. Awake. You can see her now."

Lizzy's father stood up, breathed deeply, and took his first step to say good bye to his mother. Lizzy and Dee stayed back to give him privacy and the time he needed.

"Coffee any one?" Lizzy's mother asked, balancing a cup of hot coffee in each hand as Lynn followed. "Where is your father?" she asked looking around the room.

"Seeing Grandma. We thought he needed time alone first. Besides, I heard the nurse say it was best to only have two at a time," Lizzy answered. "Momma, I'm worried about Daddy."

"Lizzy honey, he will be all right. It may take some time. He will be all right," she said with a worried look on her face. Lizzy couldn't remember a time when her mother was speechless. Her worry intensified and she caught her bottom lip with her teeth. *This is really bad ...*

Lizzy watched her daddy leave out of the doors of the intensive care room. He walked right past the small room that they were in, went down the long corridor and out the double doors to the outside.

Lizzy started to follow but her mother grabbed her arm. "He needs his time alone honey, don't worry. I'll make sure he is all right. He needs time alone to sort out his grief. He doesn't want us seeing him upset. I promise I'll make sure he is all right."

Lizzy figured her momma knew how to handle the situation because she'd lost her mother when Lizzy was in grade school.

"The babysitter can only watch the kids for another hour. Do you mind if I go see her next?" Lynn asked Lizzy.

"No, go. Go right ahead." Lizzy answered.

"Momma, will you go in with me?" Lynn asked, turning to her mother.

"Of course I will," Lizzy's momma answered as she patted her back.

Dee looked over at Lizzy. "Are you okay?"

"Yes," Lizzy answered. She rolled her lips under her teeth to keep from crying.

Lizzy was a lot like her father—wasn't much with words. She found it hard to express her feelings or to explain things that mattered to her. She kept most of her feelings inside. After a half hour Lynn and Momma returned to the room.

"Has he come back?" Momma asked.

"No, not yet," Lizzy said, getting to her feet. She felt as tired as she had when she'd left Lee behind and returned home. In some ways, maybe it was sort of the same.

"Ok, it's my turn. Dee, do you want to come with me? It's okay if you want to stay out here. It's up to you," Lizzy said.

"Yeah, I'll go with ya," Dee answered.

They headed out of the small room toward the special intensive care unit. Lizzy paused, took a deep breath, and then walked through the double doors.

***

Lizzy and Dee walked into the room. Lizzy's grandma sat up in the bed while the nurse moved the wires and tubes around her back. Then she laid back down. Surprise flooded Lizzy when she saw how thin and frail her grandmother had become. Her grandmother was always a plump woman and Lizzy loved that most about her. When her grandma hugged her, how comfy her grandma felt.

"Show me the pretty face, my sweet Lizzy," Grandma said.

Her grandma always said that to her when she was a little girl, when something upset her.

"Hi grandma. How are you feeling?" Lizzy asked with a forced smile.

"Oh honey, I'm fine. As well as can be expected. Doctor says I'm doing better than most, so I believe I'm pretty fortunate."

"Oh grandma, this is my friend, Dee," Lizzy said and pulled Dee's arm towards her.

"Are you Dorothy's daughter? You are the spitting image of her," Grandma said.

"Yes. You knew my mother?" Dee asked.

"I did. She was a student in my fourth grade English class. Oh, she was a dreamer. Always intrigued with the ironies of life. Excellent student."

Excitement brightened Dee's face, like she had just gotten a taste of a delicious treat and she wanted another bite. "You really knew my mother?"

"I sure did... and honey you are her."

Lizzy knew that was a gift Dee would treasure forever. An over whelming smell of roses floated through the air and Lizzy's grandma stopped talking and followed it with her nose. Then suddenly she asked, "Lizzy sweetie, are you going to go back to school?"

"Someday," Lizzy announced. She tried to change the subject. "Dee wants to open some kind of business. I may help her with that until I can get enough money to start back."

"Oh, a business. I knew two girls that I was dear friends with once, they opened a business ... Don't tell your father about this ... It was a tavern. Some accused them of having a brothel. When that didn't stick, the rumor became that they were lesbians. That one didn't stick either." Grandma took a breath and continued.

"See, back in those days, women did not own a business-much less a man's business. Women would only work in them—but these girls did it. They were very successful at it. Any one that really knew them, loved them." grandma smiled and looked into the air.

Dee butted in and looked at Lizzy. "Those are the women I was telling you about. The old house I showed you. I love that story."

"Oh honey, its more than a story, they were real. I was friends with those girls. Very close friends. I was about you girls age, just turned old enough to drink. I would go in around closing time. We would drink beer. I didn't like beer much. I just did it because I could." Grandma whispered.

"I would help them close up and then we would sit around listening to music and try to write love songs. Of course, the next day we would read the songs we wrote. We realized the beer made it sound better the night before. We definitely weren't ever going to be song writers." Grandma chuckled. "Some nights we would dance, pretend we were famous singers. Oh gosh. One night, we left the tavern, headed east to watch the sun come up. When we got to the ocean, it was beautiful. We even sat out on the rocks and pretended to be beauty queens. Don't tell your father..." she whispered again to Lizzy. "We all even went skinny dipping in the ocean. Oh, we had so much fun." She drifted off smiling. The smile turned to a sad expression.

"They both died a few years back. Some say they still walk the floors of the tavern," she said as she took a deep breath, "waiting for the next customer to arrive. Those were some of the best years of my life. A few years later, is when I met your grandfather and then I had your dad. I would stop by to see them now and again. Then life just got in the way. We all had a bond, something special, something that some people live a life time and never feel. I can see that in you girls. That same magic."

Lizzy suddenly realized something about her grandma. *Grandma is human*!

"Oh, grandma that is such a beautiful story. I'm so glad you told me," Lizzy said.

"Me too." Dee said.

"I felt like I was supposed to tell you that story, and I'm glad I did, too," Grandma said with a wink.

Lizzy thought back to the time she saw the women in the window of that house. *To think, grandma knew them.*

"Wow," Lizzy said out loud not realizing it.

"Yes, it was some of the best times of my ... " she said as she took a deep breath, closed her eyes and slowly drifted off to sleep.

The nurse came in. "Oh, it's about time that medicine kicked in. I thought I was going to have to give her another dose. Your grandma is an amazing woman to hang on for this long and she hasn't complained of pain one bit. The doctors can't understand how she's still alive."

Lizzy bent down and kissed her grandma's forehead. The smell of roses soon faded.

That night, Lizzy's grandma died and the nurses reported that she died with a beautiful smile on her face. Lizzy loved the story her grandmother had shared with her and loved how it gave her grandmother life, even though she was dying.

Lizzy was content to believe her two friends came and got her grandmother to go see the sun rise. That night Lizzy dreamed of her grandma sitting on a beach letting the sun shine on her face and the waves gently touch the tips of her toes.

When she woke, Lizzy knew her grandmother was where she needed to be.

***

On the day of Lizzy's grandma's funeral, Lizzy found Dee in the garden waiting for her so they could drive together for the service. Her heart felt like lead and she was in no hurry to say her formal goodbyes. She sat on the swing next to Dee and took a deep, cleansing breath.

"Wow," said Lizzy. "What fragrance is so strong out here today?"

Dee inhaled. "That's the gardenias. Aren't they something?"

"They are. Any butterflies?" Lizzy asked.

"Nope, not a single one. No one has seen them in months, now. The bees are here, the flowers keep blooming, but no butterflies."

For a couple of minutes they sat in comfortable silence, then Dee elbowed Lizzy and pointed at the sky.

"Did you see that eagle up in that pine?" she asked.

Lizzy nodded and got to her feet. "Yes, I have. He's been up there a few times. There's probably a nest around here somewhere." Lizzy looked at Dee "You ready to go?"

Dee stood. "I am. I have to say, I have lived here my whole life and never saw an eagle around here, but you've seen him a few times." Dee looked perplexed. "Don't you think that's odd?"

She shrugged and turned toward the driveway. "Maybe he is the one eating up your butterflies," Lizzy said. "You know, when I was a small girl I believed the bald eagle was God in disguise watching over the world. You know, because they were almost extinct and it was rare to see one," she said as Dee cranked the car. "I don't think they

42

are even on the endangered species list anymore, so we are more likely to see them these days than back then."

"Wow, you know a lot about that kinda stuff," Dee responded.

"Another thing that Grandma taught me. She was a school teacher." She wiped away a sudden, renegade tear. "God, Dee, I miss her. I know she's in a better place, but I hurt inside knowing she won't teach me anymore. She won't hug me anymore. That safe, quiet, strong place is gone for me, forever." She was quiet a long minute. "The better place? Is that transition? I mean, when Raymond died, is that what you meant?"

Dee stared straight ahead as though she was navigating a traffic jam. "Well, kinda, I guess." She acted as though she didn't want to explain. Lizzy didn't push it, just waited like she'd learned to do with Dee.

"You know, I ache missing him and if I just had a sign like I did...." Dee suddenly stopped speaking and changed the subject.

"Are we going to be late if I stop to get some roses to put by your grandma's grave side? I would like to do it, from my mother. She would have wanted to do that." Dee asked quietly.

"No, we should be fine. Momma and Daddy are already there. Grandma would love the roses from you and your mom," Lizzy replied. She twisted a wrinkled and nearly-shredded tissue in her fingers and looked out the window.

"You know that story my grandma told us about the two women and all the fun they had? I wanna believe she is with them again. On the beach watching the sun rise every morning."

"So, believe it," Dee said. "You know, that's the kind of place I want to open. You know, like in her story—a pub. Like in Ireland, with beer and food, and family friendly. Gotta have good food."

"Oh, if anyone could do it Dee, it would be you," Lizzy said with a slight smile.

When they arrived at the funeral home, Lizzy saw her mother and father standing near the door greeting people and thanking them for coming. She noticed her father's expression, lost and in pain but trying to hold it together for everyone else. *Poor Daddy. Grandma is in a good place, not in pain anymore, but he's hurting so bad my heart is breaking for him. How will I grieve when my mother is gone?*

"Hi, Momma. Daddy," Lizzy said as she wrapped her arms around her father's waist.

She could smell his musky manly aroma with a hint of old spice. She inhaled his scent as though to imprint it on her soul. His hands rubbed her back gently.

"We were in there before any one arrived," Lizzy's momma said. She continue to hug her father hoping to squeeze the sad out of him.

"She looks beautiful; you should go in and pay your respects to her honey. We will be in right before the service starts," Momma continued.

"All right. Is Lynn in there already?" Lizzy asked.

Momma nodded. "Yes. She could probably use some help with the kids."

Lizzy slowly released her father. With a sad smile at him, she and Dee headed inside. When Lizzy walked to the front, she noticed that beautiful smile on her grandmother's face. She remembered that smile from when grandma was telling her story. Lizzy then knew for sure grandma was fine and her tears became tears of joy and peace.

Lizzy only heard part of the service. Her father was unable to stand and talk to those gathered there, but Lizzy knew of their love for each other. She wiped at her tears even as she smiled with her memories. Her mind drifted back to the times she'd shared with her grandmother. She began to realize how glad she was that she'd had such a wonderful woman to love and care for her.

After the service they went to the grave side where Dee was able to leave the beautiful roses for Lizzy's grandma. Lizzy's heart was learning to understand the circle of life. The Phoenix and the butterflies.

CHAPTER EIGHT

Fortune Teller

The first step toward change is awareness. The second step is

***acceptance.*-Nathaniel Branden**

As seasons slowly changed there was still no sign of butterflies. Lizzy noticed Dee becoming uneasy. She knew how badly Dee needed a sign that Raymond was still with her-just like the sign Lizzy had received from her Grandmother.

When Lizzy pulled into the driveway, Dee was in deep thought as she pulled weeds in the garden.

Lizzy stood in the kitchen doorway, unwilling to startle her friend. "I have to know how Raymond is. I feel like I'm losing my mind," Dee mumbled to herself, but loud enough for Lizzy to catch them. Suddenly, she had an epiphany. "The witch's town."

Lizzy rested her hand on the door, feeling as though she was eavesdropping, but stopped as Dee stood upright and spoke to a tall plant with bright yellow flowers.

"That's it. I know what I need to do," Dee said. "All I need to do is convince Lizzy."

Lizzy couldn't stand it. She knew Dee was really struggling with Raymond's death these days. Once peaceful with the world around her, Dee was on a collision course with it. She walked into the garden and she hadn't heard Dee talking to herself again.

"Hey," Lizzy said with a bright smile. "Dottie wanted to know if you would fill in for Tuesdays shift." She plopped into the swing and pushed off with one foot.

"Yeah. Sure. I need the money anyway," Dee replied. "I didn't hear you come in. Did you have a good day?"

Lizzy nodded. "It was fine. How are you doing today?" She got to her feet and began to wander through the brilliant garden. *Still no butterflies ....*

"Hey," Dee called. "I wanna talk to you about something."

Lizzy turned and walked toward her. "What's up?"

"I know this might sound crazy, but I want to go see a medium. Over in 'the witch's town.' And I want you to go with me," Dee said, her eyes almost begging Lizzy to understand.

"Uh....um....why? And what in the world is the Witch's Town?" Lizzy asked confused.

"It's a spiritual town where mediums and spiritualists of all sorts live."

"Oh, yeah. I remember during high school some kids used to go there around Halloween. Sounded like a pretty scary place, really," Lizzy said. She pulled her bottom lip between her teeth. She wasn't sure she wanted to go near the place.

Dee gave her a tiny smile. "Well, the people who live there thought it was as much fun to scare the daylights out of the wise-ass kids as the kids thought it would to go there." She looked at the bundle of weeds in her gloved fist. "I need to know Raymond is all right. I need to know something! I keep looking for signs and I'm not getting them. Please Lizzy! It would mean a lot to me."

"Dee, I'd do just about anything for you, you know that. And, I'll do this, too. But I want you to know, I don't believe in that stuff. It scares me."

"I'm not asking anything from you but to go with me. Besides it will be fun. It's best not to take things you don't understand too seriously," Dee said. "Take it how you want, but I feel like it is something I need to do."

"All right...all right. How about tomorrow after work?"

"Sounds good to me." Dee smiled as she crossed over the hibiscus plant and hugged Lizzy. "This really means a lot to me," Dee said with both hands gripping Lizzy shoulders.

"I know it does. I've never done it before, but you're right. I don't have to take it so seriously. These people do believe in God don't they?" Lizzy asked. "I don't know that I want to get into Satan worshippers or something."

"For me to know and you to find out. Just kidding. Yeah, some do," Dee answered.

The next morning as Lizzy got ready for work, she wondered about the new adventure she and Dee planned for that evening. She intended to step outside her circle or her box of beliefs, whatever it was called.

At any rate, the more she thought about her new experience, the more it excited her. *Dee's right, I don't have to take any of it seriously. Treat it like a game of sorts.*

But what if the witch brings up Lee? Lizzy wanted to go for Dee, but she'd be totally messed up if that happened. She'd just be sure not to tell anything about herself.

By the time her teeth and hair were brushed, she was genuinely exciting, even if she didn't believe in mediums. Or did she? *Sometimes mediums are fakes.* Oh well, I won't take it seriously, Lizzy thought.

Mediums were an unknown entity and that scared Lizzy. Her religious upbringing didn't lend her strength since like most traditional religions, hers taught that mediums and witches were the work of the Devil. She wasn't sure she believed that, either.

She finished getting ready for work and headed out. Dee had the sunrise shift which meant she waited on the "early birds" who got up to watch the sun come up and then take off on their fancy yachts.

When Lizzy arrived at the club, Dee met her at the door. Her eyes twinkled with excitement.

"Dottie said we can leave early," she said.

Fear clutched Lizzy. *You'd think she was asking me to jump off a cliff with her.* Of course, Lizzy knew she would if it meant that much to Dee.

"Okay. I'm not going to take it seriously," she said. Then she realized how stupid and scared she sounded. *Like a little child being forced to go into the funhouse or something.*

"I believe ... Lizzy, you'll be just fine," Dee said.

After their shifts were over, they got into the Jeep and headed to the Witch's Town.

They hopped off the interstate and drove down a long winding road, then slowly pulled into a small town that looked almost as though time had left it behind. The little old cottages were cute colorful boxes with wooden porches. Some even had rocking chairs out front.

It didn't look "witchy" or evil at all, to Lizzy. Actually, it seemed quite welcoming and comfortable. She felt an overwhelming feeling of peacefulness and goodness. She wasn't scared at all.

At Dee's direction, she pulled up to a little cottage which had a garden filled with beautiful statues of angels, pastel-clothed fairies and a bright green leprechaun. It was so pretty Lizzy couldn't believe anyone would refer to the town as the Witch's Town.

"This is the place I feel is best for us," Dee said, then looked at Lizzy. "With the spiritual, you're supposed to go with your first instinct," Dee explained. "Did you know that the human being is the only living thing on this earth that does not operate on instinct?"

"Wow, I never thought of it that way, but I guess I can see that. We want to figure everything out first. Be logical," Lizzy replied.

Dee walked over to the garden and looked about. "Nope. None here either. No Butterflies."

Lizzy looked up and saw a sign in the window that said: "Madam Lafage, Medium, Psychic, Spiritualist and Healer. The next line underneath read, "Reverend of Spiritual Concealing."

"I want you to go first, Lizzy. I'd like to sit in the garden and concentrate on Raymond before I go in."

Lizzy tucked her keys in her small purse and cleared her throat. She wasn't going to let Dee see how nervous she was. "Oh. Ok. Through that screen door?"

Dee gave her a crooked smile. "Yes. Then ring the bell."

Lizzy headed up the cottage walk and climbed the long wooden steps. *Why am I so nervous?* "Just don't take it seriously," she whispered aloud.

She took the first step toward the screen door, pulled it open, and rang the bell. The door opened slowly, creaking the whole way. A sweet, cute, petite, silver haired old woman stood there.

"Are you here for a reading?" the women asked.

"Yes, ma'am," Lizzy replied softly.

"Well, come on in, sweetie."

Lizzy walked into the little cottage and looked around. In the small living room a crocheted blanket was spread across an antique couch that was once deep burgundy velvet. The afghan looked just like the one her grandmother made.

A small wood burning stove stood in the corner of the room waiting patiently for the cooler temperatures of winter. House plants hung around the sunny parlor as if they wanted to be noticed. A china cabinet held beautiful crystals, and a cross with Jesus on it stood at attention. The cabinet occupied the entire wall closest to the kitchen doorway where the little woman stood.

"Come on in here Sweetie, and sit," Madam Lafage invited.

This is not scary at all. It's so normal, not at all evil, Lizzy thought to herself.

"Sweetie, there is nothing to be scared of. Go ahead, sit. Would you like a cup of tea?" the little lady asked.

"No, thank you," Lizzy answered.

"Okay. Shall we begin?"

Lizzy sat down at the table. She admired with her hands the beauty of the pink flowers cross stitched onto the linen table cloth. She looked at the amazing stones lined up like soldiers awaiting a battle. A beautiful rose quartz, as well as turquoise-colored stones sat next to a deck of strange looking cards.

Madam Lafage bowed her head, thanked God for her gift, and then she asked for His hand to guild her in giving Lizzy a reading that would help guide her through her life journey.

As Lizzy listened to the prayer, she relaxed. It sounded so beautiful—not scary at all—almost angelic. The little woman asked the angels to guard Lizzy.

The medium told her there were two women watching over her and the third was enjoying the beach for a while. Chills crawled up and down Lizzy's arms. She knew the three women that the medium referred to. Then the madam suddenly changed expressions.

"Ye-ha ride 'em cowboy. Does that mean anything to you, sweetie?"

Lizzy laughed out loud.

"I like cowboys. I have a poster of a cowboy in my room. I guess he's sort of an imaginary boyfriend." Lizzy chuckled and shook of her head. *Oh boy, how did she get that one?*

"Oh honey, you'll get your cowboy, but he won't be what you expect. Yes, you'll get your cowboy," The woman explained with a warm smile.

Lizzy finally got up enough nerve to ask about Lee. "There is someone in my heart, I can't get out."

"Sweetie, your heart will heal. That time for you has passed. There were dark clouds over the moon with that relationship. Your next will start on the moon that is bright and full ... golden, you could say." Then out of the blue she looked up. "Do you smell roses?"

Lizzy replied, "No ma'am, I don't."

"You will. You will," Madam Lafage said still looking as though she was distracted.

"Who is Ray? No, Raymond?" the madam questioned.

"He was a good friend that passed," Lizzy replied all choked up. *Oh boy ...* Her stomach twitched.

The medium continued. "He has a lot of work to do. He says to watch over her. D...her name starts with the letter D," the madam said.

"D...E...E...., that is her name," Lizzy said. "That's who he wants me to watch over."

The old woman continued as though Lizzy hadn't spoken. "Pay very close attention to animals, insects, and nature. They will show you signs that you are on the right path that God has chosen for you. There will be a man that will give you something—something that will help you and Dee start on a new path." She paused, turned her head as though she was listening to someone that Lizzy couldn't see. "Learn who people are, their character, you might say. Watch, listen, and absorb. Listen to life's stories."

The little lady looked toward someone or something in the far distance. "Do you have any more questions for me, my sweet?"

"Will I ever go back to school?" Lizzy asked.

"Some day!" the madam said and she giggled but added nothing else. Then she bowed her head, thanked God for her ability to read, blessed her angels, and got to her feet.

Lizzy sat still for a long moment. She wanted to stay, for her time to continue. Then she remembered that she'd come to this place for Dee and now it was Dee's turn.

She thanked Madam Lafage with a warm smile and paid her for her time. Leaving the women in the bright kitchen, she walked through the living room to the screen door and onto the porch. Dee was in the garden, deep in thought. The door slammed behind Lizzy, making Dee look her way. "Well whatca think?" Dee asked as she walked toward Lizzy.

"Amazing. I am just blown away. I can't believe these people are called witches," Lizzy said. "She is waiting for you. Go!"

Dee hurried up the steps and disappeared into the house.

Lizzy walked around the garden and tried to remember word for word the things the madam had spoken to her.

Dark clouds over me and Lee, Lizzy thought.

I will someday go back to school—

Raymond wants me to watch over Dee—

I'll have a cowboy someday—

What could a man possibly give me and Dee? And what man? How will we know?

All the questions rushed through her brain along with a little disappointment that Lee clearly wasn't in her future. Some part of her still held onto that old, tired fantasy.

"Wow," Lizzy said as she shook her head. The experience was so much more than she ever imagined, so much more spiritual than she could ever dream. She'd overcome her fears and had a wonderful experience. Again she thought about how much she'd learned, how much she'd grown since she'd come back to town and moved in with Dee.

A hummingbird zoomed by her head. She remembered Madam Lafage's words about paying attention to nature. What had Dee taught her about the hummingbird? She sat in one of the two rockers on the porch and closed her eyes.

A hummingbird symbolizes many things. Because it's so fast, the hummingbird is known as a messenger bird and according to legend, is capable of stopping time. It symbolizes love, joy, and beauty. The hummingbird can fly backwards, symbolizing that we can look back on our past. This bird also advises us that we must not dwell on our past; we need to move forward. The hummingbird hovering over flowers while drinking nectar, teaches us that we should savor each moment, and appreciate the things we love.

A hummingbird has a spiritual significance. The hummingbird is a symbol of resurrection because on cold nights it almost appears dead, but comes back to life again at sunrise when the sun warms the earth.

Hummingbirds enlighten the heart of all. When we get hurt, that causes us to close our heart, until it gets a chance to heal, then our heart is free to love again. When the Hummingbird appears in our lives, our life becomes a wonderland of delights in flowers, aromas and tastes. We have learned to laugh and enjoy creation, and can appreciate the magic of the present moment and the magic of being alive.

Lizzy opened her eyes. The garden was vibrant and even more beautiful than it had looked when she first arrived. Bumble bees and dragon flies performed their acrobatic ballet amongst all kinds of flowers. Lizzy felt an overwhelming feeling of acceptance: of change, of life, of beliefs, and of her fate.

The sun flowers danced with the breeze and the fragrance of the honey suckle floated around her nose, so strong she thought it was magic. Lizzy remembered Madam Lafage asking if she had smelled roses. *What does that mean?* She looked around again. *No butterflies here, either.*

"I hope Dee spotted one, at least," Lizzy said aloud.

"Spotted one what?" Dee asked as she approached from the door.

Lizzy bolted upright. "You are done already? Time just flies out here."

"Yeah, it does. Seemed like that to me, too," Dee said, her words sounding distant. She seemed lost in thought with what the madam had told her.

She started towards the Jeep. "I've been chasing butterflies and its roses I needed to find," Dee said shaking her head in disbelief.

"Roses?" Lizzy asked automatically. But she didn't want to pry or to jinx her own reading. *Is this like a wish? It won't come true if you tell someone?*

Dee answered her, though. "Yes. The smell of roses. I don't have not one rose bush in that garden. But then, if I did, I wouldn't know if it was him or the bush, would I?" She stomped to the Jeep, her frustration evident.

Lizzy, unsure if Dee was talking to her or to herself, just followed and listened. Dee seemed a little unhappy with what the madam had told her.

Lizzy kept secret that the madam mentioned the smell of roses to her also.

CHAPTER NINE

Cooking up the Future

Worry never robs tomorrow of its sorrow. It only saps today of its

***joy*-Leo Buscaglia**

Lizzy wasn't sure what Madam Lafage had said to Dee, but she knew Dee was different, almost as if she were a lost dog looking for her owner.

Dee remained withdrawn and reclusive the next couple of weeks. She burned incense that smelled of roses, as well as something she called a *sage bundle*. It was to clean out the negative energy, Dee told Lizzy. She explained the sage bundle was "ceremonial sage the Indian tribes burned for centuries" for cleansing.

She also drank a tea made of anise hyssop which was supposed to ease frustration and confusion.

Dee stopped going to the garden. She said she didn't want the other essences of flowers to distract her from the smell of roses. Lizzy tended the garden for Dee and paid more attention to nature as Madam Lafage suggested.

The bees talked to her as they buzzed around her and pointed her to the flowers that needed the most attention. There was still no sign of the butterflies. Lizzy guessed that wasn't important to Dee anymore, so Lizzy tried to stop looking for them also. But she realized she missed them, too. The butterflies looked beautiful flying from flower to flower "*pollinating*", as Dee would say. Lizzy tended the garden then returned inside to cook something to get Dee's mind off of whatever crisis she was currently caught up in.

Dee's magical herb book laid on the table. Lizzy picked it up and read it. It contained many tea recipes with edible herbs which intrigued Lizzy. She thought maybe it would enhance her cooking.

Lizzy then turned to the kitchen and decided to cook something to help Dee snap out of her funk. *Cooking is like writing, if you put your heart into it, the outcome will only pass on to those who feast on it.*

Lizzy pulled a whole chicken out of the fridge and placed it on the broiling pan. The book advised that "salt that is pure" would protect, so she coated the chicken with sea salt.

Then she remembered the sage for cleansing. She looked on the spice rack and found some sage and sprinkled it over the chicken.

"Now that is for cleansing," she said to the chicken. "So, I protected. I cleansed. Now I need to add love," she chatted. *What is love?*

The roses. On the kitchen table were roses in a vase. She took a rose bud out, removed the insides and chopped them finely, then sprinkled them on the chicken. She scattered the petals at the bottom of the pan then placed it in the oven.

Lizzy remembered that she and Dee had started some seeds in the fall which were doing well—the squash and zucchini were baring fruit. She grabbed a couple of each and took them inside. She then picked up the "magical herb" book and read how squash and zucchini blossoms were edible and they also promoted cleansing of the heart. She rushed back out to the garden to grab some blossoms.

"We could *both* use some cleansing of the heart," Lizzy said to the zucchini and squash plant. "Thank for the fruit you bare for us and thank you for the blossoms."

Dee came in to the kitchen and inhaled the air through her nose. "Wow that smells amazing. What is it?"

"I was trying some new recipes I made up. I used some herb ideas from your book and veggies from the garden," Lizzy said, proud and smiling.

"The Magical Herb book?" Dee asked, looking pleased that Lizzy was taking interest in her weird beliefs. "Yeah. I never knew so many plants and flowers were edible and hold a lot of vitamins and minerals. They can be used for flavoring. I guess the magic part is just an extra!" Lizzy said, excited about her new found knowledge.

After about an hour, the timer clucked that supper was ready.

"Come on, let's eat. I'm dying to try it," Dee said. She grabbed some plates from the cabinet to set the table. Lizzy pulled the chicken from the oven and the aroma was unlike anything she'd ever smelled. Dee sniffed the air "I smell roses," she said. A smile brightened her face. The first smile Lizzy had seen in weeks.

"Yes. I seasoned the chicken with the inner pieces of a rose bud and used the petals in a tea to baste it with," Lizzy said excitedly. She turned to look at Dee.

Dee's smile slowly straightened. "I'm sure it will be delicious," Dee said, trying not to show her disappointment.

The girls sat at the table and finished every bite.

"Wow, that really was good, Lizzy. Thank you. You always make me feel better about this world—remind me not to take it so personally," Dee said.

As Lizzy started to clear the table, Dee grabbed the roses from the vase on the table. Lizzy watched and realized that Dee was looking too hard for Raymond. Roses and butterflies. What was Dee looking for? Lizzy wasn't even sure. All Lizzy knew is she had a wonderful friend that she treasured.

Dee would give her the world if Lizzy asked. It killed Lizzy to know Dee was wasting so much of her time in search of someone that was gone, but she said nothing.

***

Dee took the roses out of the house, walked across the street to Johnny who was working under the hood of a car. She handed the roses to him.

"Wow Dee, I didn't know you felt that way about me," Johnny said. His lips curved to a smile.

"Very funny, Johnny. I just don't want to force things to happen. I want them to happen when it's time to happen." Dee said.

Johnny had no idea what she was talking about.

"I hear you and Nickie have been hanging out. Give them to her. She would like that." Dee said.

She didn't care much for Nickie but she and Lizzy knew Johnny enjoyed the time he spent with Nickie. She looked directly at him.

"You know, I'd kill that girl if she ever hurts you. You know that don't ya, Johnny?"

"Yes Dee, I know. But don't worry 'bout me. I'm a cowboy. If I fall off, I get right back on!"

Dee returned to the house, went into her garden and sat on the swing.

"Thank you for the garden, Dee," Lizzy said when she joined her in the garden. "I've enjoyed working out here and learning about the insects and plants. Look over there," Lizzy pointed to a hose attached to a timer. "It waters itself. More time to enjoy it all," Lizzy said.

 Dee replied, "You are right. We should spend more time enjoying, less time taking care of—" Then Dee smiled. "Let's pull an angel card."

"Angel card?" Lizzy asked.

"Yeah," Dee said. She walked back into the house and returned with a deck of beautiful cards. Angel pictures graced one side while the opposite side contained sayings. Dee shuffled the deck and picked one, then passed the deck to Lizzy. Dee's card read:

I offer up to God all my anger, sadness and fears. I offer my past and my future. I stop doubting God. Thus, I free myself totally, for I know that God will put everything in place for me. It does not matter what happens, it will be the best for my soul.-Mario Duguay

Lizzy's card read:

I am creative. I do not get stuck in a routine, but put my habits aside and open myself to new experiences. Now, every day is

The girls sat in the garden until long after dark, cards in hand, the silence wrapped around them like a friend.

***

Lizzy and Dee were delighted when Ripley stopped by to see them after work one night. She was so excited about something that she couldn't sit still.

There was a new guy in town. Ripley always stayed one up on the new hotties because she worked at the hardware store. This new fellow lived with his grandmother while he looked for work in the construction field. Since the town was slowly up-grading by building Jiffy stores, a strip mall, and possibly a fast food restaurant in the near future, it was the perfect place to find work.

"Oh, he is such a cutie!" Ripley gushed. The three of them sat on the swing in the garden and sipped their beer. "I am going to ask him out," Ripley added.

"You, ask *him* out?" Lizzy questioned.

Dee followed with, "There goes Ms. Righteous again."

The three laughed. "Yeah, I am going to ask him on a date. I don't have time to wait for him."

Ripley, always the type to take control of any situation-even the dating scene, thought Lizzy.

"You know, I could never ... Good for you, ask him out," Lizzy said, realizing she was still stuck in her box of old fashioned ideas. "Good for you!" Lizzy said again.

Lizzy admired and envied the fact that both Dee and Ripley didn't care what the rest of the world thought. Lizzy constantly worried about everyone's opinion. She hated to disappoint anyone, even if it meant doing something she didn't want to do.

"I could see me having his babies," Ripley announced.

The three of them laughed until tears flooded their eyes.

CHAPTER TEN

Changing Tide

He spreads his wings over them, even as an eagle spreads over her young. She carries them upon her wings-As does the Lord his people!-Deuteronomy 32:11

Fourth of July was a day to celebrate for everyone who was anyone. Lizzy, Dee, and Ripley loaded up the Jeep and took the top off. They headed east, intent to drive as far as the road would take them.

On the way, the girls waved and flirted with a motorcycle rider. He became so distracted by them he almost crashed his bike. The girls laughed and drove on.

"Oh boy, we didn't mean for that to happen," Lizzy cried.

They took the road to the beach. Lizzy knew it was the same beach where her grandmother had made such fond memories.

Fair-skinned Dee wore a big straw hat and a long sleeve shirt that shaded every part of her body to prevent becoming red as a lobster.

Ripley's complexion was very tan, so she never worried about sun burn, but always carried every sun screen known to man in a huge beach bag.

Lizzy's complexion was light-medium tone. As a girl, she grew up around water and the beach. Every summer, Lizzy's family would stay on the beach side until it became time to return home to prepare for school to start. She and Ripley loved the beach, the sand between their toes, the smell of the air, and the taste of salt on their lips.

Dee hated it. *All* of it.

"This is the life," Lizzy squealed. She lounged in her beach chair and let the bright sun warm her face.

"Did you need to have the umbrella too, Dee? Don't you think the hat did the trick?" Ripley taunted with a giggle.

"I told you, I burn up as red as a lobster," Dee said through clenched teeth. Dee rolled her eyes at Ripley with pursed lips.

"I have sunscreen!" Ripley said, grabbing for her beach bag. "This stuff is great," she continued, digging in the bag for the best one she had.

"Never mind, Ripley. I *have* sunscreen on. It doesn't help a damned bit!" Dee ground out. She took a breath and then forced a smile.

"Well, maybe the long sleeve shirt you have on will help. Aren't you hot?" Lizzy chimed into the conversation.

"I'm fine. How long are we staying again?" Dee pleaded in a calmer voice.

"Till the fireworks tonight," Lizzy said.

"Yeah, till tonight," Ripley joked with a grin on her face.

"Oh, gee. Tonight, fireworks, red as a lobster," Dee mumbled.

"Oh come on," Lizzy pleaded. "We'll go up in a little bit to the sports bar on the strip, have a drink and check out the action. Ripley and I just want to get some sun first... Maybe, swim a little. That's why we're here, isn't it?" she asked, trying to sooth Dee.

"Yeah, I'm not much for the sun, but I will tough it out—just for you two. You hear?" Dee drawled.

Lizzy tore off her sunglasses and pointed toward the water. "Look. Isn't that Johnny walking on the beach? He's with Nickie. They're holding hands. Oh my God!" she shrieked.

"That's why he hasn't come by lately. She done snatched him up from us," Dee moaned as she fumbled with her huge straw hat.

"Well, he does look happy," Lizzy replied.

"Till she takes him for everything he's got," Ripley said, adding her two cents.

"I do miss hanging out with him. He used to always drive our drunk asses around. And now I have no one to pull any pranks on any more," Dee lamented.

"It's him. It's him," Ripley declared. She pointed in the opposite direction from where Johnny and Nickie were. She jumped to her feet, her posture straightened like a ballerina getting ready to perform. "The new guy. The hottie—you know, the one I was telling you about," she added, her gaze never wavering from the form of the young man in her sights.

"Did ya ask him out yet?" Dee purred. "Well, here's your chance. He's walking this way."

Without a word, she left the girls and met him half way to their chairs.

Lizzy and Dee strained to hear the conversation.

Ripley stopped him. "Hi, remember me? The hardware store."

He smiled. "Yeah, how are you? You know, I been wanting to come in and thank you for hooking me up with that job," the "hottie" responded. "Walter—my name is Walter. Wait, Ripley, right?" he asked.

Lizzy watched her friend's face light up. "Yes, my dad owns the hardware store," Ripley replied.

"No wonder you knew so much about tools and construction. I was really impressed," he said, nodding his head.

Ripley dug her toes in the sand. "Yep. My whole life has revolved around that stuff."

"Would you like to join me in my walk?" Walter asked.

"Sure, hold on, let me tell the girls where I'm going," Ripley said. She turned back to Lizzy and Dee, who hadn't missed a word.

"Go. Go. Don't worry 'bout us," Lizzy commanded.

Dee wrestled the ocean breeze for her hat. "Have fun," she mumbled to herself. "Till tonight," she added.

"Is being here on the beach really that hard on you?" Lizzy asked. She was beginning to wish she hadn't made Dee come. Friends didn't make each other do things they didn't like to do. She'd just thought it would be terrific for the three old friends to spend time together.

Dee looked away, then back to Lizzy. "Not really. Just wanted to make her feel like shit. Another one bites the dust," she said.

"I love to see people in love and happy. Especially when it's new," Lizzy responded.

She dropped the subject. She remembered Dee with Raymond and how beautiful it had been to watch them together. With the hurt of Lee's betrayal behind her, Lizzy had to acknowledge how moving it was to watch love emerge for her friends. But it was probably still hard for Dee.

As the day progressed, the beach piled up, loaded with the locals. People from every town fifty miles inland paraded in the sand. It was like a high school reunion. All the surrounding counties came to the celebration too.

Umbrellas of all kinds lined the beach. Several couples walked along the water's edge holding hands. Lizzy was lazily watching them, struggling to keep her eyes open, when a familiar body caught her eye. Her heart stopped. *NO! It can't be!*

But there he was—*the other L*. Holding hands with a girl. She heard a strangled sound escape her throat—an overwhelming burning in her heart as though it was about to catch fire.

Dee shot her a puzzled look, then she followed Lizzy's stricken gaze and noticed the couple only a few yards away from them Lizzy groaned. "That's Lee. What in the hell is he doing here?" Was he visiting his grandparents? Why hadn't she thought of that?

She tore her gaze away and pleaded with Dee. "God! Don't let him see me."

Without hesitation, Dee motioned for Lizzy to join her behind the large green and white striped protection. "Hide under my umbrella. And you guys made fun of me for bringing it. See? It's protecting you as well as me," Dee chuckled.

Lizzy dove into the shade, dropped face down in the sand, buried her head in her crossed arms and held her breath. "Oh my God, oh, my God, oh, my God, please keep walking …."

"You can come up for air, girlfriend. They're gone," Dee said.

Lizzy felt an overwhelming pressure in her chest—one that had been dormant for almost a year. Okay, so maybe she wasn't quite "over" him yet. She sighed and looked at Dee. "She was very pretty, wasn't she?"

"Didn't notice. Now him? He looked about ten pounds heavier than he did in high school," Dee said.

Lizzy sat still, willing her heart to slow down, the heat had subsided and her breath to return. The tightness began to ease. She got to her feet and brushed some of the sand off the front of her.

"Hey, let's go have that drink now," she said. "I've had enough sun. I want something tropical with a lot of alcohol."

Dee grinned, then got to her feet. "It is about damn time. I was on the verge of turning red—"

"As a lobster!" Lizzy finished. "I know," she mumbled.

Dee swung her arm around Lizzy's shoulder and they climbed the dunes toward the strip. They settled on the barstools, showed their ID and placed their order.

After a few tropical drinks, Lizzy realized this was the first Fourth of July the *double L's* weren't together. The summers her family had stayed at the beach, he often came along even though they were teens then and Lizzy's parents made sure he stayed on the couch in the living room of the beach house.

She remembered him holding her during the fireworks and how it felt so dream-like. But this year he would be holding *that* girl—not her. Then she gave her head a shake. *At least Lee is still alive.*

She looked over at Dee and realized how lucky she was to have her friendship. They were going to be there for each other no matter what.

***

The fireworks lit up the sky in brilliant burst of red, white, blue and gold. The bright flashing colors mixed with the sound of the pops and bangs and whistles were similar to how Lizzy's thoughts had been lately.

Some beautiful, with showers of twinkling light. Some just loud, with small snaps to follow. Lizzy looked over at Dee and put her arm around her. "Thank you Dee, for being here for me."

Dee smiled back and nodded. "Welcome."

After the fireworks ended, they met with Ripley who was designated to drive because the two of them drank way too many of those tropical beverages.

***

The next morning, Lizzy awoke with pounding head from the sun, the stress and all those tropical drinks she'd indulged in. Her body was sunburned and slightly dehydrated. Lizzy staggered to the kitchen to start a pot of coffee and found the coffee already made.

"I love that Ripley. Always on top of things," Lizzy murmured. She poured her first cup of coffee for the day and popped two aspirins in her mouth.

They'd arrived home late last night and Ripley had stayed over on the couch. After Raymond's death, Dee had changed Ripley's old room into an art room, so she could get back to painting, something she loved, but had all but given up.

Lizzy stepped out the front door, stretched, and headed for the swing in the garden. Ripley and Dee had beat her to it.

"Good morning, ladies. It's a beautiful day," Lizzy declared as she squeezed between the two of them.

64

"Yes it is," Ripley gushed. "Did you see his hair? Walter, that's his name. His hair. Oh my god!" she went on. "He has the most beautiful blonde hair with curls any woman would die for."

Before Lizzy or Dee could comment, she hurried on. "We're going out on Friday and he's the one who asked *me*. I was just about to ask him but he stopped me from talking and asked me out. Can you believe it?" Ripley exclaimed, her face glowing.

"That's so great. Did you see Lee?" Lizzy asked. She took a sip of her coffee and look up at the top of the pine tree.

"Look, it's my bald eagle!" Lizzy cried.

Dee and Ripley turned their heads to look at the top of the tree. "Sure is. You know, maybe he is, the butterfly snatcher?" Dee asked and looked around the garden.

Ripley giggled. "They don't eat bugs. They're scavengers. They eat small animals, fish. Not bugs."

"Butterflies are not bugs. Well, at least not to me," Dee insisted humbly.

"I read somewhere, that with some cultures, it is believed the eagle takes our prayers on its wings and delivers them to God. I've always been intrigued with eagles. I have some kind of attachment. I've always felt an eagle was God incognito," Lizzy said, smiling up at the beautiful bird.

"See what I mean? An eagle is something more than a bird to you, and a butterfly is something more than a bug to me," Dee added. "It's not just a bug!"

"Point taken," Ripley answered.

After they sat in silence for a while, Ripley answered Lizzy's original question.

"I saw Lee and talked to him, too. I wasn't going to tell you, but I'd rather you hear it from me. The girl… Well, they are getting married in the fall or so he says. Lizzy, he knows we're close and knew I'd come straight back to you and tell you. So please forgive me. I know it hurts, but you need to know."

Lizzy nodded her head in agreement, but said nothing. What could she say? Lee was getting married—to someone else. His life was on track, in order, he had a plan and none of that included her.

She could feel her heart shattering into a billion pieces, like the shards of glass from a broken mirror. She fought back tears and curled her lip under her teeth to keep it from quivering. She looked up to her eagle and prayed to God to give her strength and knowledge. What path should she take? Within a couple of minutes, the eagle took flight and disappeared over the treetops.

Roses? Lizzy turned to Dee. Lizzy noticed Dee never smelled them, which was probably for the best, because Dee had just started coming around from her obsession with the smell of roses and the butterfly thing.

"You know, I'm so glad I have you guys in my life." Lizzy wept. She got up from the swing and walked towards the house.

"Are you all right?" Dee asked with concern in her voice.

"Lizzy please, be strong!" Ripley ordered, her voice shaky.

Lizzy stopped, but didn't turn to face them. "I'll be fine. I just need some time."

Lizzy hurried to her room, closed the door, flopped onto her bed and cried into her pillow. There was nothing she *could* do, but cry.

<h1 style="text-align:center">CHAPTER ELEVEN</h1>

<h2 style="text-align:center">Road Trip</h2>

***If you surrender completely to the moments as they pass, you live more richly those moments*-Anne Morrow Lindbergh**

Dee knew that Lizzy only knew one response to her pain and that was to work as much as she could. The days passed and in time, Lizzy seemed to feel better about the fact that Lee was going to marry another woman.

But Lizzy had been a good friend during her grieving time and Dee wanted to do something special for her. She made the arrangements, put away some money and waited for the day when she could surprise her.

Lizzy woke that morning and headed for the coffee pot, as Dee entered the kitchen.

"Hey, sleepyhead, pack your bags! We're going on a road trip," Dee said with a grin.

"But, I have to work," Lizzy explained.

"Nope, Dottie gave us the week off with pay." Dee smiled. "We haven't taken any time off, and we were due for our paid vacations. She said we had to use it or we would lose it."

"Are you serious?" Lizzy asked.

"Yup. I thought we would head south to a nice "beachie" place," Dee suggested.

"What? You *hate* the beach," Lizzy said as she stirred milk into her coffee.

"Well, maybe you and Ripley are rubbing off on me. Besides, I'm bringing my umbrella. Already packed it in the Jeep," Dee said with a wink. A sly smile crept over her face.

Lizzy laughed. "Wow. This will be my first vacation as an adult. Except when Ripley helped me move to the foothills. Guess you could've considered that a vacation." Lizzy thought for a minute. "Ok. Let's do it. Tropical drinks too?" Lizzy asked. Her thoughts turned to clothes she would need to pack.

"I think it will do us both some good," Dee added. She turned, picked up her suitcase and walked out the door. Lizzy would catch up before too long.

"Hello, my darling Dee!" Johnny yelled from across the street.

"Hey, Johnny. Nickie must not be around today!" Dee taunted. She missed his company but still enjoyed teasing him whenever she got the chance.

"Naw. She went to the west coast to see her Aunt Norma. She's real sick. How's my other pretty lady, Lizzy doing?" he hollered back.

"She's good. We're going on a road trip. To where, we don't have a clue. I guess where ever the roads take us," Dee said.

"I'll keep an eye on your house and make sure the garden gets some water, if you want," Johnny suggested as he wiped his greasy hands on a shop rag.

"Gosh Johnny, that would be great. That's why I still love you, buddy." She smiled at him and headed into the house to see if Lizzy needed any help with her bags. When she walked into Lizzy's room, she found Lizzy sitting on the bed staring at her suit case. She was amazed how fast she'd packed.

"Wow, you are done already?" she asked.

"Yes. Sounds stupid I guess, but I kept everything easy access, just in case Lee called and wanted me back," Lizzy said on the exhale of her breath. "Now, I see I did it to be spontaneously swept away on a beachie vacation," Lizzy said with a laugh. "I'm really needing this. It feels good—exciting and so adult like. Almost like my grandma's story. Thank you, Dee."

"What are friends for? If you are coming with me though, you are gonna need nerves of steel. You know that don't ya?" Dee said. She stepped away from the bed and grabbed one of the suitcases.

Lizzy stood, took a deep breath and grabbed the other suitcase. "Let's get the hell outta here!"

***

"Boiled peanuts!" they called at the same time and laughed.

The old fellow selling the peanuts was always glad to see the girls, because he knew they were a sure sale. Peanuts in hand, they jumped on the interstate and headed south as they ate boiled peanuts, and felt free as birds. Dee drove for a couple hours and noticed a sign for a winery.

"Look," she said, "I've always wanted to do those tours."

"Well Miss Spontaneous, let's do it!" Lizzy said.

Dee pulled off the interstate and followed the long curvy road with signs to the giant arrow which read: "Winery just ahead." As they pulled into the parking lot, they noticed the tractor tours heading to the orchard.

"This is going to be so cool!" Dee said excitedly. Having an adventure again is wonderful, but so is having a friend along with me.

They got out of the Jeep and walked into a tiny gift shop. Bottles of wine, books about wine, and gift baskets of wine, crackers and cheeses lined the walls. Dee headed to the desk which was right in the middle of the store.

"We would like to take the tour please," Dee said to the lady as she pulled money from her pocket.

"That's five dollars each," the woman said. "Next tour is in five minutes. Pick up is out front."

Dee nodded. She and Lizzy shuttled out front and awaited their tour. When the tractor pulled up they jumped into the back trailer where the benches were lined up. The tractor moved out after the last of the people boarded. As the tractor drove though the vineyard, the guide talked about the different types of grapes, the soil, the sun and

69

the water that made them grow. He also explained the kind of wines made from which grapes. Dee was fascinated by every word that came out of the mouth of the guide.

When the tour ended, the guide took them to the barreling area where the grapes were smashed, drained, and put into barrels to ferment. *I never imagined this much effort went into a bottle wine.*

They followed the guide into a room with a very classy bar area and taste-tested the wines. The dim lighting that bounced off the glossy oak bar top accentuated the bottles of colorful wines that were set on the glass shelving. Every station of the bar presented each type of wine. The classy lady behind the bar explained how to sample, by smelling, then slowly rotating the wine in the glass to allow it to breath, then sipping and rolling it around the taste buds and finally spitting it out.

"Spit it out?" Dee asked. "Why would I spit it out?" *Silliest idea I ever heard.*

Dee was excited to learn about the wines. They tried them all. She was feeling the effects of the alcohol, though. When that part of the tour came to a close, they exited out to the gift shop.

"I have got to get one of those books on the different types of wine. I just love knowing about that kind of stuff," Dee told Lizzy.

"Like your herb books and my cooking books, I guess. I'd like a couple of those wines, myself," Lizzy replied.

So they walked through the gift shop and looked at all the books. Dee found two she wanted to get.

"What was the wine I liked?" Lizzy asked Dee. Since Dee learned every wine they tasted, Lizzy was confident Dee would know.

"It was the chardonnay and the white zin," Dee said confidently.

"I see a white zinfandel, but not zin," Lizzy said as she searched the shelves.

"That's it. 'Zin' is short for zinfandel." Dee laughed at Lizzy.

They made their purchases and walked out to the Jeep.

"Wow. It's later than I thought," Lizzy declared.

"We should head back toward the interstate and find a hotel," Dee said.

So, day one of the road trip ended at the Days Inn, right at the ramp of the interstate.

***

They woke the next morning, loaded the Jeep and headed back down the interstate. Lizzy glanced at Dee, hair whipping in the wind as they got closer to the coast. She felt so alive she was almost giddy. She and Dee were not only surviving life's roller coaster ride, they were having fun at it.

Lizzy spotted a sign as they approached the oceanfront area. "Now that's what I would like to do. Sail," Lizzy announced.

"Well, if that's what floats your boat, then that's what we shall do!" Dee announced with a laugh.

"It looks like it's about twenty miles ahead. We'll need gas by then. So, why not?" Lizzy added.

"I brought my giant straw hat, sunscreen and a long sleeve t-shirt, so I can enjoy myself," Dee said.

"Sounds like you are going to have a blast!" Lizzy countered. She appreciated that Dee was going to make the best of the beachie stuff that Lizzy loved. And, she'd do it with a smile, too. *They don't make friends any better than Dee.*

After fueling up they followed the sailing signs. They pulled up to a brightly colored pastel shack with a palmetto fan roof. Out front sat all kinds of water sports equipment wind surfing gear, paddle boats, and ski equipment. Lizzy climbed out of the Jeep. She looked on the board out front of the building to see the times for sailing and the lessons.

"Looks like they only do the lessons on Tuesday and Thursdays," Lizzy explained.

"What about wind surfing?" Dee asked.

"Really? I thought I was pushing your limits with the sailing," Lizzy stated with a chuckle.

"Hell Lizzy, I told you. Nerves of steel. That's my motto for the week."

"Okay, let's do it!" Lizzy exclaimed.

"Okay," Dee agreed.

Lizzy entered the wicker swinging doors, headed over to the tiki-looking counter and addressed the gold-brown blond gentleman standing behind it.

"We want to wind surf. Oh, and we've never done it, so we'll need lessons too. How much?"

The gold-brown man smelled as good as he looked. *Like coconut*, Lizzy thought.

He leaned over the counter. "Fifty a piece for one hour and I'll be your instructor. My name is Jamie." He stuck his hand out to shake hers.

Wow, he's hot enough to be model material, she thought to herself. *Surfer Man.*

"Okay, when can we get started?" Lizzy asked as she pulled a hundred dollar bill from her purse.

"As soon as my brother returns from his nine o'clock lesson," he answered.

"There are some restrooms on the other side of the building, so suit up. I would say I'll be ready by then," he said as he looked at his watch.

They fumbled through their suitcases to get all their swimming attire. Of course, Dee pulled her giant straw hat out.

"I don't think you'll be able to do it with that hat," Lizzy said carefully to Dee.

"The hat is coming!" Dee spoke in a for-certain voice.

"All right already. I get it. I get it," Lizzy said and shook her head.

Once they were suited up and Surfer-Man-Jamie came out of the shop, they prepared to head to the inlet.

"The inlet is the best place for beginners," he told them.

Thank God, Lizzy thought, *inlet sounds much more Dee's speed than the ocean.* They loaded up a beach buggy with the boards and sails and headed to the inlet. Once they arrived at the inlet they unloaded and set up the boards with sails.

The inlet water looked flat and glassy. Once again Lizzy could see this made Dee more comfortable with the situation she had put her in. *Surfer man* Jamie gave instructions and helped Dee onto her board.

"Miss, you may need to lose the hat," Surfer-Man-Jamie said to Dee.

"THE HAT IS STAYING!" she insisted.

Once he got Dee up on the board and showed her the way to move the sail with the wind, she was off.

"Oh ... my God, I am doing it! I am *really* doing it," she yelled. She fought the hat the whole time.

The instructor helped Lizzy onto the board. *Wow how good that felt to have his hands around my waist,* Lizzy thought. *I could get instructions all day and be just as happy about how I spent my fifty dollars.*

The wind caught the sails and the board started to move, interrupting her fantasy.

"Okay, you're off!" Jamie yelled out.

Lizzy was wind surfing—just like sailing. *Oh boy this tastes like heaven!* The water and the wind worked together to glide her to new places. Lizzy looked out and caught a glimpse of Dee. She was smiling, had lost the hat, and still sailed across the water. *She looks really, truly happy!*

When their hour was over, they headed back to the surf hut, talking over each other while they tried to explain to the other how much fun they'd had.

"We have to do this again!" Dee exclaimed when they arrived back at the surf shop. "I've never felt anything like that. I was an eagle, and a flying fish," she said through her laughter.

"I need a hat, though," she said. "Maybe a smaller one?"

They stopped in the surf shop next to the surf hut and shopped for Dee's hat. Lizzy bought a necklace made of shells to remember their wind surfing experience.

With the afternoon slipping away, they headed back toward their adventure. They got back on the interstate and were off again.

For the perfect ending to their second day of adventure, they found a hotel on the beach with a bar that specialized in fancy frozen tropical drinks with umbrella's in them.

The sun started to set and they watched it slowly slip into the West, silhouettes of trees lined the earth, while they sipped on their drinks.

***

The next morning, Lizzy sat on the balcony of their room in her big comfy bathrobe and watched the sun rise and shine over the ocean. While she sipped her coffee, Dee joined her.

"You are up early," Dee commented.

"I know. I just feel so alive here. I love the beach, always have. The smell, the feel. All of it," Lizzy replied.

"I will have to say, it's rubbing off on me, too. I get it. I get it," Dee said as though she was admitting it to the world and to herself.

"I always believed that when the sun is shining, it means God is smiling at me," she said. She stared at the bright sun light as though soaking up every drop.

"Wow, I never thought of it that way. I like that. Maybe our next adventure, I'll lose the long sleeves," Dee said as though she'd had an epiphany.

"You know, studies show sunshine produces vitamin D and helps with depression," Lizzy said.

"I believe it, 'cause I feel pretty damn good myself," Dee said. "Therapeutic."

"Thank you, Dee," Lizzy said.

"For what?"

"Giving me this vacation, friendship, all of it," Lizzy said.

"Well, you're welcome. And thank you for the friendship and a reason to *go* on a vacation. I haven't had anyone in my life to share a vacation with. Raymond was only in my life a short time. It would have been nice to have done this when he was here," Dee replied.

"He would have loved it, especially when you lost that giant straw hat during wind surfing." Lizzy chuckled.

"You are right on that! Okay, the hat was a little big. So what? And I believe he was there and here. Right here." Dee pointed to her head. "And especially here," she continued as her hand covered her heart.

"You are absolutely right," Lizzy said. She understood what Dee meant.

"My grandma and her friends are with us too. Right here and here," Lizzy said pointing to her head, then her heart.

"That's right!" Dee agreed. "Hey, let's rent those jet skis and try that out. I've always had a thing for motorcycles. They're like that, but on water." Dee pointed to the rental tent where the watercraft waited.

"Really?" Lizzy squeaked with a huge smile.

"Yeah, told you. Nerves of steel," Dee answered Lizzy, this time more confident than ever.

The girls suited up, and headed down to the beach to rent two jet skis for the day. They spent the day out in the ocean on the skis, enjoying the most wonderful feeling of being one with the water. Dee lost the long sleeve shirt so she could feel God smiling on her.

After hours of being on the water, they headed back to the room and dressed for dinner. A fancy sushi restaurant sat across from the hotel.

"Have you ever had sushi?" Lizzy asked Dee.

"Nope. I think it's raw fish, or something," Dee answered. "We going to try it?"

Lizzy looked at Dee and laughed. "Why not? Let's go!"

They crossed the street and pulled open the door. As they entered the restaurant they sniffed the air and waited to be seated.

"What should we get? I can't tell which would be good," Lizzy said looking at a display on the wall.

"Here, look at this. It tells you which ones are cooked and which ones are raw," Dee said as she handed Lizzy a menu.

"Hey, did you know sushi originated from the Japanese? They would preserve their fish in fermented rice until it was time to eat. It says it right here," Lizzy shared as she pointed to the menu. "Today's sushi is now made from vinegared-rice, but that is how it evolved," she read as they were escorted to a table.

"That's pretty interesting." Dee remarked as she sat.

"The history dates back to the sixteen hundreds," Lizzy added as she plopped down.

"Let's just start with the cooked stuff," Dee implied in her serious voice.

"What happen to Ms. Nerves of Steel?" Lizzy said with a slight giggle.

"You're right. Let's try one of everything."

And so they did. After leaving the sushi restaurant they headed back across the street to the hotel.

"That was really good. Maybe, that's what we should open up back home. A sushi bar," Dee said.

"Yeah, I liked it too. Not the real fishy-tasting ones though," Lizzy said. "I can't cook sushi, it's raw."

"Gosh, those were my favorite—the fishy ones," Dee said.

"I could tell. You ate almost all the raw ones," Lizzy noted.

"They were raw?" Dee stopped, then started to walk again. "See? Nerves of steel," Dee stated and they both laughed.

It feels great to laugh so much. I'm so glad we did this. I wonder if there's anything that can't be healed with laughter ....

"Let's get a good night's sleep and see what else we can encounter on this adventure," Dee said.

"Sounds good to me," Lizzy agreed.

***

The next morning they woke just as the sun had finished rising to the sky. Lizzy had her coffee and Dee a hot herbal tea. They loaded up the Jeep and headed for the highway. They were off again.

After an hour or so of driving, they passed a billboard which displayed an old castle, open for tours of a special kind.

"Wow, that sounds creepy," Lizzy almost whispered.

"Sounds totally cool to me. Let's do it!" Dee said. Excitement filled her voice.

"Then that's what we shall do," Lizzy said mimicking Dee's mantra.

They turned off the interstate and headed toward the castle. As they pulled in they caught a glimpse of the castle through the trees. Aged but beautiful, the magnificent stone structure peeked through.

In the lot, they parked the Jeep and headed for the door. Out front of the castle swans swam lazily in a slumbering pond. The circular driveway wrapped around the pond as though to contain it.

Beautiful trees with blooming flowers stood guard on both sides of the castle entrance. Five rows of steps led up to the huge wooden double doors with large golden handles. The steps stretched the whole length of the castle.

They entered through the massive doors and stood in a stone rotunda that seemed to glow. Granite floors flowed all the way to the stair case built from a glossy oak. Two Italian-looking guys were doing repairs to the granite flooring over to the left of the giant room.

"Déjà vu. I just had déjà vu. I feel like I've been here before," Dee whispered.

"Me too," Lizzy agreed, totally understanding where Dee was coming from.

77

"Have you ever felt like you are exactly where you are supposed to be? Like you were supposed to do this or be here? I'm supposed to be here. Right here, right now," Dee insisted.

Lizzy agreed again with what Dee was feeling. They walked to the front counter and read the history of the house. It had been built in the early eighteen-hundreds by a man who was an author of famous writings of that time period.

"He built it for his family to keep them safe from all the evils of the real world. He kept his family so safe that when they came of age to leave, they did. Some say he became so heartbroken from it, he died of loneliness. It is rumored he still walks the halls looking for his family. The state took it over in the nineteenth century because no one took responsibility for the outrageous taxes."

"Wow, that's so sad," Lizzy empathized after reading the brochure.

"Yeah. He loved them so much, he lost them. All of them," Dee replied.

Lizzy got a whiff of roses. She turned to Dee to see if she noticed it, and for a split second Lizzy thought she did, but Dee never mentioned it.

They did the tour and the whole time Lizzy thought of the "Lonely Man." She could feel his loneliness, almost as though it was hers.

When they headed out the doors, Lizzy looked back and felt a strong sense that the castle actually had a happy look to it. The castle looked as though the "Lonely Man" had enjoyed their company and the time they had spent with him.

They got back in the Jeep and headed towards home.

CHAPTER TWELVE

The Beautiful Butterfly

"Love is like a butterfly. It goes through stages." - Anonymous

Dee woke up the morning of the one-year anniversary of Raymond's death. She showered, brushed her teeth, and snuck out in a hurry, trying not to wake Lizzy. They had the day off and planned to go to the local annual rodeo, later.

Dee slowly pulled into the cemetery, got out of the car, and walked to Raymond's grave. She sat down beside his headstone.

"I miss you," Dee sobbed with tears in her green eyes.

She placed her face into the palms of her hands to cry. Once she calmed down, she thought back to the things they had done together.

The nick names they called each other, the conversations they'd had. Raymond told her she represented his caterpillar. One day, she would cocoon herself, and then change into his beautiful butterfly. It felt so real—the memory—as though Raymond sat there with her. She could feel him. Not physically, but the presence of his energy. She lost track of the time, resting in the presence of Raymond.

She lifted her face from her hands. A bright blue morpho butterfly in a slow bouncy flight landed on her shoulder. Dee had searched for butterflies for a year and when she no longer searched, it appeared.

Raymond had finally showed her a sign. The sound of beautiful music came from each flutter of the butterfly's wings. The two shimmering shades of blue, danced upon her shoulder. White snaps of bright white light twinkled around her, as the butterfly fluttered its reflective wings. Darting towards her, like a child wanting to play chase, she knew at that moment what she had to do.

"I have to convince Lizzy to open that pub, just like the women in that story," Dee announced to Raymond's headstone and then to the butterfly.

"I should have known you would be a morpho," she said to the butterfly as it land on her finger. "Morpho meaning changed or modified—metaphor for Aphrodite—the goddess of love—and rare," she chuckled.

"Thank you Raymond. I love you and always will."

***

Dee returned home excited, full of energy, and ready to tell Lizzy of her plans. She bounced into the house with a smile on her face.

"What's up?" Lizzy asked.

"Let's get to the rodeo," Dee said. "I'll explain later."

They arrived at the grand event and watched the cowboys riding the bulls. Dee knew Lizzy had a thing for cowboys. Lizzy's poster of Wrangler Man, the closest and safest relationship since Lee, sparked her love of cowboys.

Lizzy dated some but apparently never felt what she needed to feel, because she never dated any of them more than once or twice. Dee hoped that her friend would mend and find that special cowboy, but sometimes she wondered. Maybe neither of them was going to have a love that lasted a lifetime.

"Let's get some BBQ," Dee said to get Lizzy's mind off the cowboys and probably Lee.

They strolled towards the aroma of sweet, smoky barbecue which was different from the stench of the manure and saw dust over by the grandstands.

They got their order and sat at the picnic tables to eat. The local Cattlemen's Association donated the meat for the event and their wives prepared all of the side dishes.

"Good stuff," Dee pointed out as she wiped her mouth and threw the napkin in the garbage can.

"Unbelievably good." Lizzy followed and did a two-step to catch up to Dee. "Do you think I could cook something like that?"

"Damn right you could," Dee replied. "Come on let's go have a beer." *Maybe that will give me the right words, so I don't scare Lizzy off with the idea of owning a bar.* Dee thought to herself.

***

After leaving the rodeo they stopped at the convenience store on the way home, and picked up another six pack of beer.

Lizzy had finally acquired a taste for beer, but to enjoy it, she liked it really, really cold.

She was hoping that Dee would talk about her morning trip to the cemetery to visit Raymond's grave, but every time Lizzy mentioned it, Dee just told her everything was all right.

The ladies sat in the garden and sipped their beer as the aroma of the honeysuckles and gardenias drifted through the air. Suddenly, without any shift in the breeze, the scent switched to the strongest and sweetest scent of roses Lizzy had ever smelled.

Dee doesn't have any rose bushes, though. Lizzy looked at Dee who obviously had caught the scent too.

"I want to talk to you, Lizzy. It's about something..."

Lizzy was sipping at her beer but lowered the amber bottle when she realized Dee looked serious.

"Okay, what is it?" Lizzy asked concerned.

"I want to open a pub, here in town. Just like the one in the ghost story of the old women. The one your grandma told us about. I want you to be my partner," Dee stated without looking at her.

Lizzy froze, but she tried to hide it with a smile. *It's got to be the beer.* That tickle in her tummy, the one she once felt for Lee, was back.

"Can I be in charge of the kitchen?" Lizzy chuckled.

"I'm serious!" Dee proclaimed. "It's what I'm supposed to do. You know … my fate."

Dee stared down at her beer bottle and started to peel the label. "Please don't think I'm crazy like they said back in high school." She took a deep breath and continued. "Raymond told me … it is my destiny. He showed me … that you should be my partner."

"Why? How?" Lizzy asked.

"I can't explain. Did you smell the roses?" Dee asked as she looked up.

"Well, yes. I did," Lizzy answered.

"Then it *is* you. You're supposed to do this with me," Dee insisted.

"Well then, I guess, I'll have to be your partner, because you and I smelled roses."

Lizzy giggled as they clanked the beer bottles together.

The next day, Lizzy recalled their conversation in the garden and thought the alcohol caused the talking, like it did any time they had too much to drink.

She got out of bed with a sigh and headed for the coffee pot. When Ripley lived with them, Ripley left just enough for Lizzy to have a cup before going to work. But Dee didn't drink coffee and that meant Lizzy had to make it and she dreaded it.

Just as she hit the brew switch, Dee walked in. In her hand waved five or six loan applications, all from different loan companies and different towns.

She was really serious. A flutter tickled her tummy again. Lizzy smiled. *Oh, boy!*

***

For the next month, Dee and Lizzy filled out application after application for loans. Each loan consisted of a thirty-year loan and in the end they would be paying four times the amount borrowed. All were denied.

"I figure it's going to cost us about sixty-thousand to get the kitchen up and running—and stocking it with food, beer, and of course wine," Dee said. "If we could just get thirty-thousand, we would be fine."

Lizzy turned to Dee and asked, "What do you mean, only thirty? Where is the *other* thirty coming from?"

"I been meaning to tell you. My mother, when she died, she had a life insurance policy," Dee started to explain.

Lizzy interrupted. "Oh, no!" she nearly shouted. "You are not going to use that money. Your mother did that because she wanted you to use it wisely, not on some harebrained idea for a business!"

"There goes Ms. Righteous again. Let me explain first. I had it put into my will to give to you. When you came to the hospital and said the things you said, you made me want to live. You gave me life— something to live for. If my mother was here, she would completely agree with my reasoning. You should have that money, not me. I tried to take the precious life my mother gave me." Dee took a breath and put her hand up to stop Lizzy from interrupting her again.

"Just listen to me. I know now that you won't leave me alone about that, so to make you happy, and I know my mother would agree, we'll use it to start a business together. End of story." Without waiting for Lizzy's argument, Dee shoved through the screen door and went into the garden.

Lizzy followed on her heels, ready to argue. As she stomped out the door to the garden, she noticed the garden was alive with butterflies fluttering from flower to flower. Several were enjoying the nectar of a brilliant rose. *That wasn't there yesterday!* Lizzy forgot her anger. She was mesmerized by the life of the garden.

"Wow! Where did they all come from?" Lizzy whispered to Dee. "Isn't it late in the year for them? Wow, they are so beautiful!" she stammered as she looked about with child-like wonder.

"Yes they are. No more chasing butterflies or the smell of roses for me. I'll have them in my life every day and right here at home! Do you understand now, Lizzy?" Dee questioned. "I have everything I want. Now I want us to do this business. Together," Dee insisted.

Lizzy nodded. "I get it. I really think I am starting to understand you, which is a little scary to tell you the truth." She gave Dee a wide smile. "Well, I could ask my parents. I don't think operating a bar is what they imagined their "righteous" daughter would do for a living, though," Lizzy volunteered still mesmerized by the garden.

"It's not just a bar. It's going to be a pub, like in Ireland," Dee reasoned. "A place for people to meet, have good food to eat, ice cold beer and the best wines. This town is perfect for this."

Lizzy knew her parents wouldn't like her involved with selling alcohol. For them, it was the fruit of the Devil. There'd be no sugar-coating thick enough to explain it to them so they'd be happy—or supportive about it.

She looked up in the pine to see if her eagle was perched up on a limb. He wasn't. She sighed and took a giant sniff of the wonderful smells of the garden and walked back into the house. She'd worry about it later.

The next morning, Lizzy got ready for work and assessed the best way to approach her parents. She decided there was no "best way."

"Just get to work and worry about this later," Lizzy muttered to herself. She went out front door and headed to the Jeep.

Johnny shook her out of her fog. "I hope you make millions today, Miss Lizzy!" he yelled from across the street.

"Me too, Johnny!" she replied, then murmured to herself, "me, too."

But even work didn't chase away her trepidation. There was no getting around it. She was a people pleaser and the people she wanted to be proudest of her were her parents. The idea of approaching them for the money to open a bar almost made her sick to her stomach. She could picture her father's expression, the one he wore when she told them she was leaving college to chase after Lee. The one he wore when he said goodbye to his mother. But how could she disappoint Dee? Tears filled her eyes and she dashed to the ladies room to pull herself together.

As Lizzy reset two tables with fresh linens and silverware, Doctor Anthony Burger, a long-time member walked into the clubhouse.

A down-to-earth man, he was referred to in the community as a man of "new money." He was raised by his grandparents that were very poor. He made his way through school on scholarships, grants and anything else available. He appreciated his fortune and he was always warm and friendly to everyone he spoke to. He called every female, "miss" and he never raised his voice.

Most of the yacht club members came from what was called "old money" that was handed down from generation to generation. Those people never worked a day in their life. Lizzy smiled at the direction her thoughts took as she wiped down a table from the "old-money" members who'd barely left a dollar tip after running her ragged.

Satisfied the table was perfectly set and ready for the next customer, she shook her head. *It'll be a long time to thirty-thousand dollars on tips like these....*

She approached Dr. Burger with a smile she didn't feel. "Hello, Doctor. How was your water adventure today?"

"It was lovely, Miss Lizzy," the doctor replied. He looked at her closely. "Is there something bothering you, missy?" he asked. "You don't seem quite yourself today."

She figured her bloodshot eyes were a giveaway and sighed. "Just wondering how to approach my parents about borrowing money. I'm worried," she confided.

He looked about the quiet dining room and motioned for her to explain.

And explain she did, without giving him a moment to offer an opinion. From her search for a purpose in life and Dee's suicide attempt, right on down to the life insurance money and her parent's religious aversion to the evils of liquor. When she was done, her eyes were once again filled with tears.

"I'm so sorry, Doctor. I can't believe I just dumped all that on you. You must think I'm an idiot," she said, trying desperately to smile.

He waved his hand as though to dismiss her concerns. "I asked you to explain, remember? And you did a thorough job of it, missy." He opened his napkin, placed it in his lap and with no change in expression, he said, "Don't ask your parents just yet. Let me see what I can do. I might have a solution for you and Dee."

Lizzy was so relieved she almost wept for joy. No matter what Doctor Burger came up with in the long run, for today she could tell Dee that there might be a way to get their start-up money. She wouldn't have to ask her parents who would most certainly refuse her the loan, even if they had it to loan and she wasn't sure they did. The doctor cleared his throat to get her attention.

"Miss Lizzy, are you and Dee working tomorrow?"

"No, we both work the same shift, Friday." she said.

"I will see you and Miss Dee Friday then, missy."

"Doctor Burger, thank you so much. Thank you for listening and for wanting to help us find a solution."

She took his order and thanked him again, this time with a smile that was warm and genuine.

Cool, two more days to mull it over, Lizzy thought to herself.

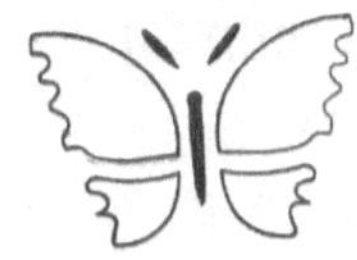

CHAPTER THIRTEEN

The Eagle Lands

A friend loves at all times - Proverbs 17:17

For the next two days, Lizzy and Dee waited to see what Doctor Burger would come up with. Out in the garden, Lizzy looked up at the tall pine and saw her eagle looking down on them. She said a prayer that Doctor Burger would have a solution to their problem.

Dee kicked her feet back and forth under the swing. "We filled out every application known to man, and were denied by every loan company in three counties and *he* might have a solution? Does he own a bank, maybe?" Dee said with a frown.

Lizzy shook her head. "He told me to hold off asking my parents for the money—that he might have a solution for us. I don't know what he meant. It was such a relief to me to have a couple of extra days to get my pitch right for my mom and dad, I almost cried," she said. "Maybe he has pull at some of these banks. Maybe he knows some way to do it a little cheaper. I honestly think we should hear what he has to say tomorrow."

"I know, you're right. I just think we're wasting time," Dee moaned, still kicking her feet. Then she stilled her legs and sat up as she looked across the street to the auto shop. "Hey look, it's Johnny and Nickie. He's such a good guy. That Nickie better be treating him good!" she growled.

"He looks happy," Lizzy acknowledged.

Dee peered at them, then resumed her swinging. "Yeah. He does look happy. Just miss him, is all," Dee said.

Lizzy looked around them. "Hey, wanna have garden soup for dinner?"

"What's that?" Dee asked.

"A little bit of everything in the garden, in a fresh chicken broth."

"Can we at least get some meat with the broth?" Dee begged, unsure of what might be in store for supper.

"Absolutely," Lizzy answered with a grin. "There's some chicken breast in the refrigerator. I'll cook that up and add it. I can use the broth from that."

Lizzy got up from the swing, picked some squash, zucchini, scallion, basil, lemon grass leaves and parsley, and then headed into the house. After getting the soup started she decided some carrots and celery would complement the herbs and give the soup more consistency. The soup's aroma drifted out to the garden through the screen door. Lizzy watched from the window as Dee took a whiff.

"Wow! That girl can cook good stuff out of anything," Dee said to the butterflies.

The essence of the soup must have made its way across the street and to the mechanic shop because Lizzy could see Johnny and Nickie turn towards the house.

"Smells like Lizzy is cooking a dandy supper for you tonight, Dee!" Johnny hollered from across the street.

"It's garden soup, with chicken in it. I think," Dee yelled back.

Dee got up from the swing and headed into the house to see how much longer she would be tortured by the smell of dinner. Lizzy had the table set.

Dee pointed to a plate with triangular biscuits on it. "What are those?" she asked.

"Scones. Like they make in Ireland. Irish pub, remember? I'll need to know how to cook that type of food. I've been practicing for my big debut in our business adventure. It's my Aunt Laurie's recipe. She gave me a couple other ones, too. Taste one, see how I did," Lizzy ordered.

Dee took a bite. It crunched like a biscuit.

"Wow, they are good and it's going to go good with the soup. Just that hint of sweetness, sort of moist like a cookie. Very nice, Lizzy. If we don't get that loan, we should consider selling your cooking out of the house to raise the money," Dee said chuckling. Lizzy laughed too.

Lizzy spooned the soup into Dee's bowl and then into hers. The soup steamed but the fragrance made it hard not to sip just a little, even if it was too hot to eat. They dipped the scones in the bowls until the soup was cool enough to eat.

"This is a lot better than peanut butter and jelly with canned chicken noodle soup. That's all Ripley and I *ever* ate around here," Dee muttered with her mouth full.

"I know. That's what made me realize I needed to cook or I was going to starve!" Lizzy said, smiling. "I do like cooking, that's for sure."

After they were done eating, they cleared the dishes and washed them, remembering Ripley's pet peeve about dirty dishes...Lizzy sure missed having her around.

***

Friday morning, Lizzy got up, had her coffee, and waited for Dee. The days they had the same shift they rode together to save gas.

"Ok, I'm ready. My uniform is getting snug on me. It must be your cooking," Dee confided as she tucked her white collared shirt into her black slacks.

"Me too," Lizzy said as she grabbed her keys from the table. They headed out the door. Johnny yelled from across the street.

"Have a wonderful day at work ladies. I know it's gonna be a good one for ya!"

"Thanks, Johnny. Right back at ya!" Dee said. She looked at Lizzy. "Wow. He yelled something different to us today. Nickie must be close by."

"You'd better get used to the idea of Nickie being in his life, Dee. Looks pretty serious to me," Lizzy said, looking over her shoulder to back out of the driveway.

"I guess," muttered Dee. "I sure hope the good Doctor shows up."

They arrived at work, punched in at the time clock and headed towards the kitchen. Dottie stopped them to let them know that Doctor Burger was waiting in the dining room to talk to them.

She winked at them. "Go ahead girls, I'll cover for you."

Lizzy was so nervous her legs wouldn't move, almost like she was trying to walk in a deep mud hole. One look at Dee's face and she knew her friend was just as anxious as she was. Lizzy took a deep breath and forced her body to move forward.

"Okay. Let's just see what he has to say, right?"

"Right. Then go from there," Dee said.

They grabbed each other's hand and walked through the swinging kitchen door into the dining room of the yacht club. Doctor Burger sat at the back table with what appeared to be a stack of papers. The girls slowly moved closer until they reached the table.

"Hello Miss Lizzy and Miss Dee. Have a sit, missies," he said. He pointed to the two seats across from his. Like school children who'd been sent to the principal's office, they lowered themselves into the chairs.

He turned the papers to face them. "This is a contract. Take a look at it. Take as long as you like. If you are interested in this agreement, we will get together and get it notarized. And, I'll write you a check for the money."

Lizzy and Dee just stared at the papers. They turned to each other and stared. Then they looked back down at the papers. Lizzy thought they must have looked like little robots.

The doctor chuckled. "I told you, read them over at your leisure and my number is on there. If it sounds like something you are interested in, then I'll arrange for us to get them notarized. I'll file them at the court house myself."

They both were speechless at first, and then as though stuck by a pin, both women said, "Thank you!" at the same time.

"Don't thank me until you have the check in hand," he said, and then stood. "You have my number so give me a call. Okay?" He gave them a little salute and moved away from the table. "Have a wonderful day, Missy and Missy," he said as he nodded his head at each of the young women. Then he exited the club house.

Lizzy was still speechless, but the butterflies in her stomach had returned. She was afraid to open her mouth for fear they'd fly out of her mouth. *Holy cow, this is really going to happen....*

Dee spoke first. "What do you think this big stack of papers says?"

"I have no idea, but we are going to have to read them eventually," Lizzy said.

Dottie broke the spell. "Girls ... time is up. Got to get to work," she said, looking out through the swinging kitchen door.

"We'll read it tonight, when we get home," Lizzy whispered as they both stood.

"Okay," Dee agreed. "I still can't believe this ...."

***

After work the girls said their good-byes to Dottie. They walked to the parking lot but Lizzy had no idea where she'd parked that morning.

"I think we parked in the back of the lot," Dee pointed out.

"Oh yeah. Guess I picked a bad day to fight my predictability. I don't even remember getting here this morning, talk about being distracted. There's some good points to being predictable, I guess," Lizzy remarked and they laughed.

"Let's not look at this contract until we're in the garden. I want to see if my eagle is there, first." Lizzy said.

"Yeah, I would like to see if I smell roses and if the butterflies are there," Dee agreed.

"Deal!" the girls announced at the same time. They nodded at each other.

Once they arrived at the house they headed to the garden and sat down onto the swing. Dee sniffed the air and looked around, sheaf of papers clutched in her hands.

"Ok, it's all here," Dee declared.

Lizzy slowly glanced at the tall pine only to find an empty branch. At that moment the eagle swooped down and landed on his branch and looked down onto the two of them.

"Ok, let's read it," Lizzy said with relief in her voice. *Roses, butterflies and my eagle.* Everything had to be right.

They held the pages then slowly started to read.

"The payment will only be five-hundred a month?" Dee exclaimed. "The loan companies wanted nine hundred a month. Five hundred is like making a car payment. We could do that easy even if we don't keep it open. It's only a five year loan. The banks were thirty. There has to be a catch," Dee cautioned.

Dee read some more. Lizzy sat speechless and relieved at the possibility that she wouldn't have to involve her parents at all. Dee read and read and read.

"He is only charging us one percent interest. Still not finding a catch," Dee analyzed. "This is too good to be true. You know what they say about that stuff." She looked around the garden, then up at the eagle who still peered down at them.

"Or is it? Hey, remember when we went to Madam Lafage? She said we would get a loan from a man with the initials AB, was her words to me. At that time I thought it was your father because his name is Abraham. I know now, that "AB" stands for Anthony Burger," Dee said, finally disclosing some of what the madam had told her.

"Oh my God, Lizzy. We are really going to do this aren't we?" Dee squealed.

Lizzy couldn't keep the grin off her face. "My dearest friend, I do believe we are!" Lizzy almost crushed Dee's fingers in her hands. "I'm scared shitless!" Lizzy said with a quiver in her voice.

"Holy cow, Ms. Righteous, watch the language. But it's not only you. Me, on the other hand, I'm scared shitless too!" Dee squealed. They wrapped each other in a hug and held on tight.

Dee took a big whiff of her roses and an inventory of her butterflies. Lizzy looked up and blew a kiss to her eagle. She could have sworn the eagle winked back at her.

They held the contract for hours just smiling at the world around them—the world of their magical butterfly garden. Every so often they turned to each other not saying a word, just smiling. Each one knew the other was high on the idea of actually opening the pub and making Dee's dream a reality. On the same note, what if they failed at this?

As though Dee read her mind, she looked Lizzy in the eye. "Even if it doesn't work out for us, we owe Doctor Burger every dime back he lends us. No matter what," Dee insisted.

"I agree—one hundred percent!" Lizzy agreed.

"But, we aren't going to fail. I know it." Dee began to rock on the swing. "Our friendship is always going to come first. We need to agree on that. Money and success can ruin people," Dee said. "It's friendship that's going to get us there. I would never have even tried to actually do this if I didn't have you in my life," Dee added.

"I would never thought I would do it, period!" Lizzy proclaimed and both girls laughed.

They laughed so loud Johnny heard them from across the street. He yelled out them, "You ladies must have made your millions today!"

"Not yet Johnny, but pretty damn close," Dee shouted back and they laughed some more.

"Hey, let's go check out that old house. Where that tavern was," Lizzy suggested.

"That old house?" Dee said with a grin.

"Yes. Definitely. That's where it all started! Maybe I can visualize grandma as a young girl, writing her songs!" Lizzy said. "Yes ...yes. Let's do it!"

Lizzy cranked the Jeep, yelled out a goodbye to Johnny and they headed south west to the old house.

Time flew by, just as it had the first time Dee had taken Lizzy there. The ride felt like they'd entered a time warp.

They arrived at the old house which still appeared to have its head cocked at the girls' arrival. They pulled up closer to it this time than the last. Lizzy realized her grandmother's story made her feel closer to the old place.

"Let's go in this time. I want to see if there is still life left," Dee said.

"I would absolutely love to. I want to picture my grandma young and dancing around inside," Lizzy said.

As they sprinted up the steps of the house, the house stopped slouching and straightened its posture. The paint wasn't peeling and the dusty old windows were shiny clean.

When they opened the doors, they heard music and people laughing—and saw the two women behind the bar. A young beautiful woman, just barely old enough to drink, turned to see them enter and nodded her head, as though she waited for their arrival.

She returned her gaze to the women behind the bar and gave them the okay sign. The women welcomed Lizzy and Dee and offered to show them how everything was done.

Without understanding or caring, two friends from today and two friends from yesteryear bonded in a season outside of time. After a time, Dee walked over to the wall and removed an old rusted sign that read "Old friends....nice to see you....new friends nice to meet you." She turned to the bar-owners who nodded and smiled at her, indicating the sign was hers to keep.

Lizzy and Dee walked out of the house, walked down the steps, turned and looked over their shoulders. They saw the business owners and Lizzy's grandmother standing in the window watching them, their spirit-faces smiling the whole time.

Lizzy and Dee got back into their vehicle and the magic disappeared. The old house with the peeling paint, sagging stairs and slouching roof line returned.

Lizzy drove them back home. She understood only that she'd never understand what they'd experienced, and yet she didn't question that they had experienced it. It was message from the universe that they were on the right track. Though they talked little, Dee seemed to agree.

CHAPTER FOURTEEN

New Liaisons

*A person can hear, but a friend listens for the meaning. A person can look, but a friend sees the heart. A person can know, but a friend understands your dream - **Anonymous***

The next morning they called Doctor Burger who arranged to meet with them at his office that afternoon. He promised to have a notary there to verify the signing. They only had to get through the next few hours but Lizzy thought that was as hard as waiting for Christmas morning, with all its treasures just begging to be revealed.

"What time is it now?" Dee asked for the third time since the phone call that morning.

"Almost noon. Just a couple more hours," Lizzy said a little more patiently than Dee.

"What should we do with the check?" Dee asked Lizzy.

"We will have to hold on to it until Monday when the banks are open," she answered.

"We will need a business checking account," Dee advised. "And, a place to rent, coolers, a register—"

"Whoa, slow down, one step at a time, Dee," Lizzy pleaded. "Go relax in the garden and stop overwhelming your brain with all the to-do's."

"You're right. I need some fresh air," Dee confessed as she walked towards the screen door.

Dee saw Johnny across the way and Nickie was nowhere to be found, which she found odd.

"Hey, Johnny!" she drawled.

"Howdy, Dee. No dirt road dreaming today?" Johnny hollered back.

"No, this is the day that our dreams come true," Dee sang out.

He wiped his hands on a shop rag and headed across the street. "So tell me, what are you girls up to today?" he said as he sat on the swing next to Dee.

"Remember me telling you I wanted to open a pub? Well, Lizzy and I are going to do it. We are *really* going to, just do it," Dee revealed. She could hardly believe the words she'd just said.

"Really?" Johnny asked, his eyes shining.

"We've got the loan. Monday we'll start a bank account, find a location, and apply for licenses.... Well you understand," Dee said, apologetically. She knew he wasn't much of a detail man, but she couldn't seem to help herself. The excitement seemed to be oozing out of her pores.

"I am so happy for you girls. I always knew you both had something special. I really do hope you make a million!" he affirmed to Dee grinning from ear to ear.

"What are *you* so happy for?" she asked.

He looked at the garden for a moment, then glanced back at her. "I'm getting married, or at least, I'm going to ask her to marry me, tonight," he announced as he pulled a ring from his pocket and showed Dee.

"Wow! It's beautiful, Johnny. She is a lucky girl to have you," Dee admitted then gave him a hug. About that time Lizzy came out of the door.

"Johnny is getting married!" Dee bragged.

Lizzy threw back her head and laughed. Then she stood in front of him and patted his shoulder.

"Wow, Johnny. Congratulations!"

"Well, she hasn't said yes yet, but she tells me she loves me. And I figured, I'm just going to ask her tonight and see what happens."

He showed the ring to Lizzy. "It's so pretty," Lizzy praised. "I wish you and Nickie all the happiness you can stand," she said. Dee could see the lost look Lizzy gave the ring.

"Ladies, you are the first to know. Got to get back to work before boss man see's I'm over here," he announced. He tilted his hat to them and headed back across the street.

"Pretty ring." Lizzy sighed.

"I could tell that you thought so." Dee answered knowing her friend was envious.

"Well Miss Dee, wanna head out?" Lizzy asked.

"We still have a couple hours, don't we?"

"Nope. He called and ask if we could come a little earlier. His afternoon appointment canceled."

"Hell yeah, I'm ready!" Dee exclaimed as she scrambled to her feet and jogged to the door.

"Then off we shall go!" Lizzy giggled, poking at Dee's side.

***

They pulled into the parking lot of the doctor's office. The girls sat in silence for a minute. Then they looked at each other.

"Let's do it!" They said at the same time.

They got out, walked up the sidewalk, and entered the doctor's office.

"Hello ladies. Do you have an appointment to see Doctor Burger?" the receptionist asked looking over the top of the tiny glasses that sat on her pointy nose.

"We do. Lizzy and Dee from the yacht club," Lizzy announced. Dee nodded.

"Please have a seat. He will be with you in a moment," the receptionist said.

Lizzy kept taking deep breaths to calm her stomach which switched back and forth from butterflies to nausea. She looked at Dee who was a bit pale, too. *Are we really going to do this?*

A tall lady dressed in a nurse's uniform opened the door. "Right this way, ladies. Go straight back to his office and have a seat. He'll be right with you."

Lizzy and Dee glided down the hall to the office and opened the door. A giant, shiny maple desk sat in the middle of the room. At least twenty framed certificates hung on the walls. Three large, dark leather-cushioned chairs sat patiently around the desk, waiting for their arrival. They sat.

Lizzy could hear her heart pounding and wondered if Dee could, too, but she didn't dare ask. Dee sat and looked at her hands which were clasped so tight that her knuckles were white.

Doctor Burger entered the room. "Hello, Miss Dee. Hello, Miss Lizzy. Are you girls ready to make this big step?" Doctor Burger asked.

"I believe we are sir," Lizzy said, her voice cracking.

"Well, let's get started. You read over the contract. Do I need to make any changes?" Doctor Burger asked.

"No sir, I believe you can't possibly be any more generous," Dee admitted to Doctor Burger.

He nodded, then turned and pressed a button on his desk phone. "Mrs. Howard, we are ready."

A minute passed, then the woman with the little glasses who was behind the desk when they arrived, walked in. He opened the contract, signed his name, and then passed the contract to Lizzy, then Dee, to sign their names.

Mrs. Howard stamped each place with a large stamp. Doctor Burger sat down and wrote out a check from a giant check book. He ripped it out and handed it to the girls.

Nether girl reached to take it. They looked at each other and said, "Okay, we'll take it together." And they did.

"Thank you so much," Lizzy said, fighting tears again.

"Yes, thank you, so much," Dee added.

"So ladies, I probably won't be seeing you girls at the yacht club much anymore," Doctor Burger mentioned with a smile.

"Well, we're going to stay as long as we can. Until we get on our feet," Lizzy said.

"Since we work different schedules, we'll just have to rotate the pub hours," Dee said with it all figured out.

"It's going to take some adjusting. It will work out for you, though, I know it. Miss Dee and Miss Lizzy." The doctor stood, nodded and left the office.

The girls stood from their seats still hypnotized by the check and walked out of the office to the parking lot. Dee held the check while Lizzy drove.

"We are really gonna do it," Dee whispered.

"I do believe we are," Lizzy replied. She looked at her friend and thought she'd never seen her happier. Her heart felt like a hummingbird, fluttering at a million miles an hour.

They returned to the house, parked in the driveway and again sat staring at the check.

"We have to call Ripley and tell her what we are going to do," Dee finally said.

"I wonder if Walter is still in the picture?" Lizzy asked.

"Of course, that's why we haven't seen her," Dee said.

They got out of the Jeep, walked to the garden, and sat on the swing.

"Wow, thirty-thousand dollars. Who is crazy enough to lend two girls our age, thirty-thousand dollars?" Dee asked out loud as she looked down at the check in her hand.

"I guess Miss Dee, he believes in us. I'm going to go get the mail, Missy." Lizzy chuckled, then got up from the swing and walked to the mail box. She got the mail and laughed at two of the envelopes. She tore them open.

"After reviewing your application we would like to inform you that you qualify for the amount of funds you were seeking," Lizzy read.

She put it to the side and then opened the next. It read something very similar.

"Wow, we really *do* have angels behind us," Dee said. "Can you imagine? It would have taken us thirty years to pay that back. With the doctor's loan, we'll be free and clear in five, maximum."

"Everything happens for a reason, you always tell me that. I believe it now," Lizzy said to Dee. "Now all I have to do is tell my parents what we plan on doing," she said, feeling her stomach start to flip flop all over again. She wasn't going to let Dee down, so she'd just have to figure out how to be an adult about it. It was time she stopped trying to live for everyone else.

"Just blame it on me," Dee said. "Anything that they think is wrong, blame it on me. I am the unpredictable one." The girls laughed. "Let's go to the hardware store and show Ripley the check. She doesn't get off until six," Dee said.

"Ok, let me put this mail in the house and we'll head up there," Lizzy said and disappeared into the house. Seconds later

Lizzy came out the door.

"Ready?" Lizzy asked.

"Yep, if I watch Miss Nickie any longer, I'm gonna puke. She looks at him like he's a loser. She is so fake!" Dee hissed. Then she yelled across the street where Johnny and Nickie were standing. "Keep it real!"

"I think Miss Dee, she thought you were being nice," Lizzy said as they got into the Jeep.

"I was being nice. That's not what I wanted to say, at all." Dee growled. "She better treat him right. I'm the only one who gets to play tricks on him."

CHAPTER FIFTEEN

Hardware as Accessories

"When we do the best we can, we never know what miracle is wrought in our life, or in the life of another."-Helen Keller

Lizzy and Dee found Ripley helping a customer in the hardware store.

Once Ripley finished, she walked over to them. "Sorry I haven't come by. Between the hours I'm working and seeing Walter, I haven't had much time left to even shave my legs. I *do* miss you guys."

"Oh Ripley, we completely understand. We came to tell you some good news," Lizzy said in a rush. She could barely get the words out, her heart was beating so fast just at the thought of what she and Dee were really going to do.

Dee nodded. "Remember how I always wanted to open a pub? A pub like they have in Ireland? Lizzy and I are actually going to do it!"

"Really? How? Are you for real?" Ripley squeaked.

"Yes ma'am, we are," Lizzy said, knowing she was grinning like a Cheshire cat and not caring at all. "We've gotten a loan from a private investor."

"And some money from my mother's life insurance," Dee added.

Lizzy felt her smile freeze. "I told you we weren't going to spend that money, Dee! Your mom wanted you to have that in case of emergency," she snapped.

Dee glared at her. "Yes, we are!"

Lizzy took the check from her pocket and thrust it at Ripley. "Hold this check. I'm about to rip it into tiny pieces. Money is *not* going to come between our friendship. No money!" Lizzy fumed, stomping her foot like a child. She couldn't risk it—wouldn't risk it. Her friendship with Dee was the one thing she valued most in the whole world.

"All right already. There has to be a solution," Ripley said gently. "Start out with this money here," Ripley pleaded, shaking the check at the two of them. "Then use the other as a safety net. Emergency money. Just in case business takes longer to turn a profit," she suggested.

"I will agree to that if Lizzy does. It's a good compromise," Dee acquiesced.

"I will only if… If we don't absolutely need it. Then and only then. Otherwise Dee keeps it for herself. I don't want her money, just her friendship," Lizzy insisted with tears welling up in her eyes. She looked away from them both so they didn't see how close she was to tears.

"*Deal*!" Dee barked through barred teeth.

"Well then, that's settled. You two hug on it," Ripley said with a grin.

Dee and Lizzy turned to each other and hugged. Then they started sobbing. They looked at each other, each swiping their tears with the back of their hand.

"Don't ever let anything come between us, Lizzy. Promise?" she sniffed.

"I promise!" Lizzy agreed.

Ripley patted each woman on the back and let out an exaggerated sigh. "I'm sure glad *that's* settled. Let's celebrate, ladies. I get off in fifteen minutes. I'll call Walter and tell him I am going out with my business-owner friends this evening. He'll understand." She giggled. Besides its good to keep them wondering a bit."

Dee and Lizzy waited in the Jeep for Ripley to finish. At first they just sat in silence.

"I meant what I said about not wanting anything to come between us, Lizzy. Not even this business."

Lizzy nodded. "I meant what I said, too. I don't want your money. I want your friendship!"

Dee spit in her hand and stuck it out. "Let's shake on it, Ms. Righteous."

Lizzy spit in her hand and put her palm in Dee's. She curled her nose at the slimy mess it made in her hand.

"This is *definite*ly a friendship," Lizzy said, wiping her wet hand on her jean-clad thigh. Then they broke into belly-busting laughter.

Ripley locked up the hardware store and jumped into the Jeep with Dee and Lizzy. "Let's go have a drink, beach side." Ripley suggested then added, "You guys look like you are in a better mood."

"Much better," Lizzy said as she glanced at Dee for confirmation.

"I would say, I agree," Dee said with a smile.

Ripley handed the check to the front of the Jeep. "Good, 'cause you'll need this!"

"Oh shit," said Dee. "You still had our check. I forgot all about it."

Once they arrived beach side, they found a cute little bar and grill right on the water. The sunset had left the sky streaked with pink and blue with swirls of purple.

"Now this is a beautiful ending in a salute."

"To our wonderful friendship!" Dee toasted.

"Yes. Wonderful friendship!" Lizzy agreed.

"Hear, hear," Ripley chimed in.

As the night went on, the three friends shared ideas on decor. And what to name the place, of course.

Lizzy wanted a country name hoping to draw in the cowboys. Dee wanted some kind of snake name like Copperhead, which sounded too rough and rowdy for Lizzy.

Ripley clapped her hands with glee. "You should name it "Buckets." Serve beer in buckets. Food in buckets. Hell, have everything in buckets. Bucket of fries, bucket of chili, and buckets of fun!"

Lizzy and Dee were dumbfounded. "I think she's onto something," Dee said after a half a minute.

Lizzy had that tingle back in her stomach. The butterflies that always signaled that things were right. "It does sound a lot better than our ideas. We would need to get all *different* size buckets. That will be my job, so I can figure out what types of food to serve." Lizzy replied.

Dee held her glass in the air. "Then "Buckets" it shall be!" she declared.

"We can't do anything until Monday, when the bank opens," Lizzy reminded them.

"Sure we can," Dee laughed. "We can go to all the junk stores in the next three towns. "We can find some old buckets to use for the decor."

"Count me out. I've got to work a double, tomorrow," Ripley said. "I'll be there in spirit, though. I *did* come up with the idea."

"Oh no, I have to work Monday. I *so* forgot," Lizzy moaned. "I'll call Dottie in the morning and see if she'll cover for me."

"I'm sure she will. You *never* call off from work, Ms. Righteous," Dee said with a laugh.

"Well ladies, we need to get going. I've got to get home and the alcohol is getting to me," Ripley said as she stood.

They paid their check and left, heading inland to get ready for the start of a new day.

CHAPTER SIXTEEN

Rosco's This and That

"Ask, and you will be given what you ask for. Seek and you will find. Knock and the door will be open."- Matthew 7:7

Sunday morning found Lizzy and Dee working in the garden. The butterflies flew everywhere, as usual. Bees were nowhere to be found and the fragrance of all the different flowers drifted in and out of all of the plants like colors for the nose.

Lizzy pulled the weeds in the garden, as Dee added the new top soil that had a fertilizer additive. In the area where the vegetables and herbs grew, a tiny green frog sat and waited on his lunch.

Lizzy looked up every so often to see if her eagle was watching over them, but he was missing. *Was he enjoying a day off or did he have other things to do today?*

Across the street it was as busy as it was during the week. Lizzy straightened and stretched her back, shaking the dirt off her leather work gloves. Were they trying to catch up on work from earlier in the week? They'd never been open on Sundays. Even the mechanic shop had cars there, also.

"Wow, I can't believe they are open on Sunday," Dee said, thinking the same thing that Lizzy had.

"I do know they hired extra help because they had gotten so much business after....." Lizzy started.

"Raymond's death," Dee finished. "You know that I believe he sent them there. He loved that place and the owners. So, I believe he sent them the business. But, you can say it—Raymond's death. It's really okay."

"I know. I don't mean to be weird about it. I just wouldn't hurt you for anything. I've always have been one to hide my feelings and assume everyone does the same," Lizzy admitted.

"Lizzy Girl, God didn't give us feelings to hide them. He gave us feelings to feel them," Lizzy remembered her mother say more than once.

"Hiding your feelings only puts them away for a period of time. Someone or something will eventually find them," Dee said.

"Well, I don't hide them. I write them. I write all of my feelings and my thoughts on paper. Then I throw it away, so no one can see it again, not even myself," Lizzy explained.

"I wrote Lee probably a thousand letters. How I missed him. How much I hurt. All that kind of stuff—until Raymond passed away." Lizzy looked up at Dee. "I decided then that I wouldn't write Lee anymore because I could have sent Lee those letters and you would never be able to send yours to Raymond." Lizzy went back to arranging the fresh soil around the base of the plants.

"I assumed you were like me. I'm still writing, but I'm writing my thoughts about life. About our new business venture, Madam Lafage's predictions. My future cowboy. What I want in a man. I think that list is so long it would be impossible to find that man, by the way. All I want is to feel those butterflies in the tummy again. I'm sorry I'm babbling on and on." Lizzy looked up at Dee.

Dee tossed a handful of weeds into the pile that was already two feet high. "Raymond's helping you get over Lee. That's his gift to you for saving me from killing myself." Dee stopped shoveling the soil and straightened. She took a whiff of the roses and smiled. "You have gotta love him!" Dee smiled.

Lizzy smiled back. *I think she's on to something. My writings have been full of hopeful things. No more tears.*

"Hey, when we finish up, let's go visit some garage sales. See if we can find some things to go with the 'Buckets' motif," Lizzy said to Dee as she picked the weeds up with the rake.

"Sounds marvelous, my dear," Dee answered back.

They finished in the garden and got cleaned up. Once outside again, they hopped into the Jeep. Lizzy fired it up and the engine made a horrible bang.

It scared the girls so much they jumped then ducked. They weren't sure if someone was shooting at them or if it was the Jeep that had made that god-awful noise. Then they slowly looked and noticed Johnny from across the street, laughing.

"Just a little bang to let you ladies know I was thinking about you," Johnny joked.

"You think you are going to get the last laugh, do ya?" Dee yelled.

"It's on, Johnny!" Lizzy screamed in her deepest voice.

Johnny's grin disappeared and he looked worried. Looking nervous, he tilted his hat. "Have a good day, ladies!"

Lizzy would have waved back, but she didn't dare take her hands off the steering wheel. She was still shaking. She glanced in the rear view mirror and backed out of the drive.

Lizzy and Dee crossed the county looking for yard sales or garage sales. No luck. As they entered the next county, they came across a large metal building—a warehouse of some sort. On the side of the building, painted in hand brushed red paint, a sign read, "*Rosco's This and That for Sale!*"

They stopped just to find out what "this and that" old Rosco was selling. A lot of antique farm equipment sat out front with stickers and prices on them.

"Bet we find some neat buckets in there, right?" Dee said, pointing at the building.

"I'll bet you're right," Lizzy agreed.

Sure enough, Rosco had every size imaginable. They had some buckets so large that Dee and Lizzy both fit inside them. A little old man with white hair and a white beard strolled out from the back of the warehouse with an oxygen tank on wheels. He reminded the girls of Santa Claus.

"I'm Rosco. This here is my store. I have anything and everything you need—a little of this, a little of that. You name it, I got it. If I don't got it, I can get it. At a good price too. Best price around." He took a breath. "So, how can I help you young ladies?"

Dee explained what they were looking for and what type of business they planned to open. They needed anything and everything for the place. The old man scratched his white-bearded chin. "I do have some old bar stuff in the back. Come take a look, but I'm not going to honey coat it—it's older than dirt."

The girls walked in the room in the back of the warehouse. It appeared to contain everything Dee had described to Lizzy that she wanted for the business.

From bottle coolers, to old beer mugs with little symbols stamped into them that resembled a bucket. Then Lizzy turned to the left of the room. There, abandoned in the corner sat all types of equipment for a commercial kitchen.

"If we get all of this stuff today, I don't know if it will fit. We don't even know where we're going to rent, yet. We don't—" Lizzy stuttered.

Dee interrupted her with a wave of hand. "How much for all of it?" Dee asked Roscoe.

"I've gotta get at least five. Five-hundred, that is." The old man looked as though he was sorry to have to ask for so much.

"We'll take it all, and two of every size bucket that you have out front," Dee said. Then she frowned. "What were you asking for the buckets?"

"I gotta get at least two apiece for them. They're antique and worth some money. I'm giving you a good deal," the old man said with more confidence.

"Hundred? Two-hundred?" Dee asked with dismay. Lizzy gasped.

"Oh no, dear, two dollars. They probably are worth the two-hundred, though. I ain't out to get rich, just make a living. Since you're cleaning out this back room for me, two dollars is a fair amount for me." Rosco answered.

"It's a deal," Dee announced. "We'll be back tomorrow to pick it up. Do you want the money now to hold it for us?"

He shook his white head, a warm smile on his face. "No ma'am, just your word will do for me. Tomorrow would be perfectly fine."

They all shook hands and the girls walked out the door to the Jeep. Lizzy looked over her shoulder to wave good bye, but he'd already disappeared. Lizzy wondered how he moved so quickly.

CHAPTER SEVENTEEN

Serendipity

"Reality is a product of our dreams, decisions and actions."-

Unknown

Lizzy had set her alarm clock, and despite wishing she could roll over and go back to sleep, she didn't. She knew they had a busy day. Lizzy stumbled out of her room half-asleep and headed to the coffee pot.

"Good morning, sunshine!" Dee chirped, even though it was a well-established fact that Lizzy was not a morning person.

"Yep. Yeah. Morning." Lizzy poured a cup. "Thanks for making the coffee for me. You don't even *drink* coffee."

Dee laughed. "I know. But I was up early—too excited to sleep, I guess. Besides, I'm starting to love the smell of it in the morning." She sat down across from Lizzy at the table. "Oh yeah, Dottie is going to take care of our shifts today, but tomorrow we are back to work until she gets some new girls hired and trained."

Lizzy took a sip of coffee and put the cup on the table. She looked at Dee. "I wanted to talk to you about that. I'm going to still work there a few days a week. To be on the safe side. I'm scared if I do quit, I won't be able to give you money for staying here, or to buy groceries. I cannot eat peanut butter and jelly sandwiches."

Dee thought a moment, then shrugged. "I understand what you're saying. You're right. We aren't going to be able to get the kitchen going right away. And, we still need to eat and keep the electric on," she added.

They sat for a while in comfortable silence. Lizzy was trying to wake up and put together a mental checklist at the same time.

Dee cleared her throat and stood. "I'll be back. I want to see if Johnny will let us borrow his truck. Then we can go pick up that stuff at Rosco's."

"Yeah, that's a good idea. See if we can use that trailer, too," Lizzy added.

After Dee pounded out the kitchen door, Lizzy kicked back thought about the huge step she planned to take. *How should I tell my parents?*

"I'm doing this for Dee and for me. Why am I so closed-minded? I have to change my way of thinking," she said into her cup of coffee.

Dee returned and barked orders. "We got the truck and the trailer. Good thinking, Lizzy. Go get ready to go and I'll meet ya outside."

Lizzy stood and gulped down her coffee so she could wake up faster.

"All right already," she grumbled as she put her cup in the sink.

As she quickly showered, the checklist solidified in her mind. The list wasn't all that long, but everything on it was very important. She dried her hair and got dressed in record time. Dee was waiting for her in Johnny's truck.

They went to the bank and set up their joint business account. With large grins, they handed over the check to the manager. Lizzy's butterflies were back and she imagined she was just a little bit more of an adult in that moment.

Then they headed to "Roscoe's This and That" to pick up all the inventory and equipment they'd agreed to the day before.

"What are we going to do with all the stuff till we find a spot?" Lizzy asked.

"Good question," Dee said. "Hey, pull into the hardware store real quick."

They pulled into the lot and Dee ran in. A minute later, she came out and jumped back into the truck.

"It's covered. We can store it in the hardware store's shed out back. Ripley said they just cleaned it out. She said there is more than enough room."

"Wow, Dee, good thinking!" Lizzy said.

They proceeded to Rosco's. As they pulled into the lot, Roscoe stood out front with his oxygen tank trailing behind him, like he was expecting them. They got out of the truck and before they could say a word, he greeted them. "Well how are you young ladies today?"

"We're good," Lizzy said. "Have a lot of work ahead of us."

Rosco nodded his head. "Good news. My grandsons are here and they're going to lend you young ladies a hand."

Two very good-looking young men with thick arms came out the door. Their teeth were as white as sugar sparkling on top of a sugar cookie.

"Lookie here, lookie here. We have help, and I want to say *help*!" Dee whispered.

Lizzy looked up, broke out in a sweat and wiped her forehead.

"They sure are pretty Miss Dee," Lizzy drawled so only Dee could hear.

"Yes ma'am, they are. This work may not be so bad after all," Dee said softly, watching the young men approach them.

"I get the one with the dimples," Lizzy said for Dee's ears only.

Dee said loud, "They both have dimples...."

"*Really!*" Lizzy burst out on a laugh. Dee laughed right along with her. Again, Lizzy had the sense that her life was exactly where it was supposed to be and it felt good!

They loaded the back of the truck with all the smaller purchases, first. Then they put the coolers and other large equipment onto the trailer.

After loading was done, Lizzy went over to one of the grandsons to make small talk. Dee went inside to pay Roscoe what they owed. She strolled back outside to talk to the other grandson who was sitting on a tractor tire drinking a bottle of water.

"Thanks for the help, she said. "It would have taken us all day to load this stuff up."

"You and that Lizzy girl owes us now," he said with a sheepish smile.

"Owe you what?" Dee asked.

"A cold beer at the bar you two are going to open up," he said. "By the way, I'm Brad and my brother's name is Jessie. Don't forget now, you owe us a beer. Brad and Jessie."

"That's a deal," Dee said, "Hey, we're going to need help getting the place going and we can pay, if the two of you are interested?" Dee asked.

"Sounds like a good deal to me, let me ask Jessie," Brad said, then hollered over to his bother.

"Hey, Jesse. The ladies want to hire us to help get the place set up. Wanna help them out?"

Jessie yelled back, "Sounds like a grand idea to me."

Jessie looked at Lizzy and she smiled. Dee glanced at Lizzy and saw she agreed with the idea. The girls climbed into the truck and headed out.

"They sure are eye candy," Lizzy gushed as they pulled away.

Dee laughed. "And we get to pay them, just to watch them work. I love this new business adventure."

"Me, too," Lizzy said, realizing that her heart skipped a beat when she thought of the handsome young men.

"I get Brad, the smart one," Dee said.

Lizzy raised her brows. "Fine. Jessie's got the better dimples any way."

The owners of the new town tavern were on their way.

***

Tuesday saw the girls back to work at the yacht club, distracted about finding a location for Buckets, but doing their best to honor their responsibilities.

114

At the end of a day that felt as long as forever, they drove toward home. As they pulled into town they noticed the new strip mall was almost completed. A man was going from one store to the next, putting *For Rent* signs in the windows.

"Pull in there!" Dee shouted.

"Holy cow!" Lizzy gasped, jerking the wheel hard to the left. "I thought I was about to run someone over." She followed Dee's pointed finger.

Dee jumped out of the Jeep and trotted over to the man. Lizzy watched them talk, saw the man nod with interest and in a matter of minutes, they shook hands. Dee jogged back to the Jeep.

"Well, we have the location and he said as soon as we get him the first month's rent, we can start moving in," Dee reported breathlessly.

"Really? That's so cool!"

"Let's go to the house and get the check book. He said he would be here for about another two hours," Dee said.

"Really? Really? I can't believe it. Just like that?" Lizzy stuttered.

"Come on girl, step on it. I cannot wait to get a start on the place."

They raced to the house, Lizzy mindful to avoid a speeding ticket or any children playing in the streets. Dee ran into the house, grabbed the check book, and then popped right back out the door.

She yelled across the street to Johnny on her way back to Lizzy. "Hey Johnny, can we use the truck and trailer again? Tonight?"

"Sure, as long I can use the Jeep to follow you two and see what you're up to!" Johnny yelled back.

"Please do. We may need your help!" Lizzy shouted from the driver's side window.

When they returned to the newly finished strip mall, the man was still out front.

"Wow, you are quick," he said when Dee stood in front of him. He was older, very distinguished in his white shirt, pressed khaki slacks, and brown leather loafers.

"Since I will be your landlord, I guess I need to introduce myself. I'm Jack Karen. It's nice to meet you ladies." He shook their hands. "I'll be back with a contract and your keys—just give me a few minutes. Everything's over in the office." He peered at them closely. "You look a little young to be starting a business like this. You are just barely old enough to drink, yourselves."

He glanced back and forth at the girls. "A little word of advice: always pay for your product. If you don't, you'll drink up your profit and start bad habits. Besides, it will keep you from becoming an alcoholic, too. If you can't afford it, you can't drink it!"

"Point taken and nice to meet you!" Lizzy affirmed.

"Yep. Thanks for the advice," Dee agreed. Then the girls looked up and saw Brad and Jessie pulling into the parking lot in an older model pickup truck.

"Look, it's our eye candy," Lizzy cheered. "I wonder how they found us."

Dee glanced at Brad's truck and shrugged. "With only one way in and out of town, guess they just recognized us standing here. And perfect timing, right? I wonder what they want?" she puzzled.

Dee walked over to their truck. "Howdy fellows! What brings you to our neck of the woods?" Dee drawled.

Lizzy watched from outside of the Jeep. *Hmmm.* They're either really thirsty for those beers, or they like us, Lizzy thought. *Long way to drive, though.* She walked over to stand beside Dee.

"Well, we aren't making a big deal of this, but you never paid us Yesterday," Brad said.

"Oh!" Dee said with a puzzled look on her face. "Oh, for helping us load?"

"No, for all the stuff. The stuff you bought yesterday," Brad said with some hesitation.

Lizzy could tell by the confused look on Dee's face that she wasn't sure what was going on. Lizzy wasn't sure, either.

"Oh," Dee said, a smile dawning on her face, "I paid your grandfather."

Dee and Lizzy stood waiting for Brad and Jessie to understand the bill was paid, as agree.

But Brad shook his head as though he had a buzzing in his ear. "That's impossible. He's been dead for ten years. The stuff was his, but we couldn't let it sit around anymore. That's why we've opened the shop back up. Been trying to get it all sold off."

Lizzy felt as though the ground was spinning. She'd talked to Rosco. *Laughed with him. Watched him shuffle around with that oxygen tank.* She turned toward Dee.

Dee gestured with her hands. "I can show you. I have the number of the check I wrote, right here." She opened the check book.

There it was, the check she had written to "Roscoe's This and That" for six-hundred and fifty dollars. She snapped the check book closed and turned red with embarrassment. For a long moment, all four stood still as statues.

Lizzy cleared her throat and Dee jumped. "I'm sorry. How much did you say we owed you?" she asked Brad quietly.

She opened the check book to write him a new check when he said, "Six hundred and fifty dollars."

Dee looked down and noticed that exact amount already written on the check. "Okay. Here you go," Dee said as she ripped the check from the book.

Brad took the check and stared at it.

"See? I had it written out already with yesterday's date," Dee noted, not explaining any more.

 Brad looked at her with a puzzled look. "I sure don't know what's going on, but I'm glad you got what you wanted. Thanks for the check." He folded it and put it in his pocket.

Brad motioned to Jessie to join him. "Hey, when would you ladies like us to come help you set up?" he asked.

"As soon as you can," Lizzy urged, "We're going to be getting a key for our place, today." She smiled at Jessie.

Jessie, Lizzy thought, was not the sharpest tool in the shed. He is nice to look at, just like my Wrangler man. Except Jessie is real flesh and blood and I can touch, smell, and look at him.

Now Brad on the other hand, is taller, good looking, a real ladies man; knows all the right things to say is the smart one. A rebel— perfect for Dee.

"Well then, looks like you'll owe us more than one beer," Brad teased. "Let me park this truck and when you're ready, we'll be waiting."

About that time, Mr. Karen joined them with some papers and two keys on a ring, which he handed to Dee. Dee handed them to Lizzy, then opened the check book carefully, as though she was expecting a snake to pop out.

"Whew! A blank one. Okay," she muttered. She looked at Mr. Karen. "Who do I write it out too?"

"Karen and Associates, LLC," he replied.

After all of that was done, Mr. Karen shook their hands, reminded them to heed his warning, and promised to check with them later in the week.

The foursome walked over and opened the door. Lizzy was almost lightheaded with the anticipation. They were really, really going to have their own business! She and Dee left Brad and Jessie standing in the doorway.

The building smelled of fresh paint and glue from the flooring.

Dee spun to face Lizzy and grabbed her by the shoulders. "Lets get the truck and trailer! We'll head to the hardware store and bring Buckets to life. Today!"

As one, Lizzy and Dee walked to the door. Dee took Brad by the arm and spoke softly. "I am *really* sorry. I thought I paid for our stuff before we pulled out with it. I guess with all the excitement, I just forgot."

Brad gave her a small smile. "I'm not sure what happened at all. But it doesn't matter. We're here and we can help you with this. Maybe that's what's important, you think?"

She nodded. "Why don't you and Jessie get something to eat and meet us at the hardware store in town, maybe in thirty to forty-five minutes? We're going to pick up the truck and trailer, again."

Lizzy and Dee jumped into the Jeep. Dee turned to Lizzy and asked, "Did you see the old man named Roscoe? Sunday when we were there?"

"Yeah, I sure did. Saw him, talked to him, and watched him shuffle through those old buildings. I'm confused," Lizzy answered.

"It is a puzzle," Dee murmured.

CHAPTER EIGHTEEN

Opening His Door

God opens doors no man can close and closes doors no man can

open.-Unknown

Lizzy and Dee pulled into the mechanics shop. Johnny walked out of the garage to meet them.

"The keys are in it. I hooked up the trailer for ya," he said to Dee.

Dee seemed not to hear him. "I have never been able to see spirits. Only knew they were there or I could imagine them. Now I actually have had a conversation with them?" she muttered.

"What's that?" Lizzy asked.

"Oh, nothing." Dee shook her shoulders as though casting off a spell.

"We will be at the new strip mall, the last store front on the end. You don't have to follow us too far," she told Johnny as she handed him the keys to the Jeep.

"We're going to stop at the hardware store and collect the equipment we bought yesterday, then we're going to get it all unloaded at the pub!" Lizzy added.

"So, you ladies are really going to do it?" Johnny asked tilting his ball cap.

Lizzy always loved him in his cowboy hat because that was the one he'd worn when she first meet him. He changed hats like some women changed purses. She winked at him.

"Yes, we are and nothing is going to stop us now," Dee said.

Lizzy's stomach lurched. She still hadn't mentioned any of this to her parents but would eventually. They had so much to deal with right now, with Lynn and the kids, and Grandma's passing, she couldn't bear to add another burden to their hearts. She knew they'd be disappointed she was going into the liquor business.

She shook off her thoughts and climbed into the truck. They had plenty to keep her busy and with Brad and Jessie probably waiting at the hardware store by this time, she had no more time for her silly worries.

"I'll be up to help out as soon as I finish up here," Johnny called before they pulled away. "Nickie will probably come along with me. You know she's a little jealous of the two of you," he warned.

"You did explain we're just good friends, haven't you?" Lizzy said.

"Yeah, she just don't get it, though. She'll get used to it. She has got too. I'm your friend till the end!" He replied.

Dee and Lizzy pulled out of the mechanic shop parking lot.

"I don't trust that Nickie. I can't pinpoint why. I'm trying to, but I still get them bad feelings in my stomach about her," Dee said as they turned the corner. "My intuition says she's going to hurt that boy."

"Remind me to dump a can of sardines on the engine when we finish with his truck," Lizzy said.

"Oh, you are *good,* Lizzy," Dee said with a smirk.

***

They parked behind the hardware store. Brad and Jessie were out by the shed talking to Ripley.

"Hey Rip," Dee yelled from the truck. "They are with us." The girls got out of the truck and walked over to the three of them.

"Walter and I will come help after I close up the store." Then Ripley turned to leave and whispered in Lizzy's ear. "Very nice eye candy. Even if they *weren't* here helping you guys, I was gonna give them whatever they asked for."

121

Lizzy giggled, knowing Ripley liked good looking fellows.

The four of them loaded up the trailer and the back of both trucks. The shed was empty again. Lizzy looked back before climbing into Johnny's truck and though it looked almost sad, as though it had lost its new-found friends.

The little caravan drove to the strip mall, which was only a block away. They pulled the two trucks in and Dee hopped out and looked at Lizzy.

"Let's turn the key together. It's like us giving birth. When we open this door, the Buckets will never be empty again," she said.

Lizzy thought for a moment. "Wow, I never looked at it that way. Then that's what we shall do!" Lizzy felt the familiar fluttering in her stomach and had a thought of thanks. She may have dreaded telling her parents what her new goals were, but she knew those goals were right.

They unloaded both the trucks and the trailer into Buckets. Dee had an idea of where she wanted things placed. Lizzy marveled at Dee's precision, as though she had a schematic in her brain.

"We need color. We should paint before we set up. I'll be back," Dee said, and then disappeared.

"Where is she going?" Brad asked.

"My guess? Back to the hardware store. She's going to get paint. Dee doesn't tip toe in the water, she jumps right in. That's my girl," Lizzy laughed.

Jessie turned to Lizzy. "What about you Lizzy? Do you tip toe or jump?"

She noticed a little pink in his cheeks that wasn't there before. Lizzy replied, "Tip toe, then wade, then get waist—deep, then if I'm comfortable, I go under. For me, it's a process."

Lizzy babbled on. "Don't get me wrong. I would love to be the type to just jump in. I admire that about Dee. All of this. I would never have done this. She just pushed me in and I'm glad she did. I'm having a blast."

Brad interrupted her. "Does Dee have a boyfriend?"

Lizzy hesitated, then said, "Yes." *That's not true, though.* "Well, he passed away about a year ago. She's not ready. Well, maybe you should ask her all of this stuff and not me."

Brad nodded. "I understand. If I can tell you, I really like her. I'll leave it at that."

"And I will, too. Please don't mention that you know about Raymond. I don't want her to think I was telling her business to people. It wasn't like that. I just thought you should know," Lizzy said carefully.

"That's a deal!" Brad said.

"Good. I don't ever want her to think I betrayed her in any way, shape or form."

Jessie then turned to Lizzy. "Do you have a boyfriend?"

She could feel her face getting warm. "Nope. Can't find anyone willing to tip toe with me." She laughed.

"Haven't tip toed in a while, but I could sure try," Jessie answered.

"I'm flattered!" Lizzy said. Tip-toeing will suit me—*he's very nice to look at, but there are no butterflies in the stomach.*

The sun set as Dee pulled into the parking lot and strutted into the pub toting two cans of paint and a hardware store bag. Lizzy met her half way.

"I've got two more cans in the back of the truck and some rollers. Let's get going on the paint," Dee said as she handed Lizzy the bag.

In a matter of minutes, all four of them were painting. A suitable beautiful pale metallic blue paint, almost the color of the oxidized buckets they'd bought from Rosco's.

"Wow, this is a perfect color." Lizzy complimented.

"Ripley helped me pick it out. She says it's the best on the market," Dee said.

An hour or so went by as the foursome painted in comfortable silence. Then the front door opened and in walked Ripley and Walter.

"Need some help?" Ripley asked, rolling up her sleeves as she walked toward Lizzy.

"Sure, grab a brush or roller and start on the back wall," Dee commanded.

A half an hour or so later, Johnny and Nickie arrived.

"Now this is going to make all the business in this small town look like peanuts. I might have to shower up before I come here," Johnny praised as he looked around the room.

Nickie gave him a look of disgust. "My dad almost chose this color for our pizzeria but my mother said it was too manly looking. However, it does suit *this* place."

Lizzy could not tell if Nickie was giving a compliment or criticism, but she was relieved to notice that she didn't really care, either. Was she outgrowing her need to please everyone? She certainly hoped so ….

Dee said, "You guys going to help or just stand there? Grab a brush!"

Johnny grinned at Dee. "Hell yeah, I wanna help." He grabbed a roller from the bag and sauntered toward an empty paint tray.

Nickie walked over to the bag with her nose crinkled up, got a brush, and looked like she'd rather have been picking up road kill.

"Nickie come over to this wall and help me with the small stuff," said Lizzy. "You were always so good at detail when we were in art class together."

Nickie straightened her back and regained her not-so-negative look and smiled. She looked over at Johnny expectantly. Now a proud look on her face, because of what Lizzy had said. Johnny tilted his hat at her, winked, and resumed rolling paint onto the new wall.

As the night progressed, everyone joined in the conversations that floated in and out of the room. Lizzy smiled at her friends. She looked at Walter and Ripley, Dee and Brad, then Johnny and Nickie. Lizzy then looked over at Jessie who was already looking her way. Lizzy nodded. She felt an overwhelming sense of appreciation for all of her new found friends. Lizzy knew Buckets would be a success.

It didn't take as long as Dee and Lizzy imagined to get Buckets set up and ready for opening day.

While many people referred to their favorite inanimate objects in the feminine form, Dee felt their business was guided by Him, and so they referred to the business as "him" or "he".

One night as they were working on the finishing touches, Dee told Lizzy that "Buckets" symbolized the buckets used throughout the ages for feeding and tending flocks. Two young ladies with dreams made "Buckets" shine. Now "he" could feed his flock again.

With Grand Opening only two weeks away, Buckets waited patiently for the licenses and final inspections to go through.

Brad and Jessie came around on a daily basis. Brad tried hard to get close to Dee but she couldn't respond to the energy he radiated. She wasn't ready to open herself to anyone.

Dottie, their manager at the yacht club, always counseled them that things meant to happen did so in their own, right time. Sure enough, she was right. Each night, Dee and Lizzy would get off from work at the yacht club, head over to Buckets and work on setting up. Brad and Jessie showed to meet them.

With opening day right around the corner, Dee gave Dottie her two-week notice at the yacht club. Lizzy kept working part-time, planning to stay until the business got on its feet.

Brad helped Dee use the old buckets to make tables. They hammered flat some of the larger buckets and decorated the outer part of the bar, with those. The giant bucket worked beautifully behind the bar as a beer tub, which was Lizzy's idea.

Behind the tub stood a beautiful book-shelf-type shelving that Jessie built of oak. With the rich brown stain and the mirror behind it, the piece really made a statement. The night he finished it, Dee had almost cried, she was so excited that everything was coming together. Buckets would be a wonderful place for people to meet.

Ripley got credit for the lighting idea which produced a sheer and calming look to the place. Johnny had some old wood from his barn that he sawed into wainscoting and put half-way up the walls to give it a warm, rustic look.

That night, they all stood back admiring each one's creations. Dee turned to Brad and wrapped her arms around him, hard.

"You, my friend, are worth the effort!" she said looking into Brads eyes.

She almost laughed at the look of surprise on his face. It was about time she let Raymond go and let someone wonderful into her life.

During the two weeks before opening, Dee spent as much time with Brad as she could.

She told him all about Raymond and losing her mother during her senior year of high school.

She told him about death of her younger siblings when she was a child. She also confessed to Brad that she had never met her father.

"I can't rely on people being in my life for long, you know. You might want to reconsider getting involved with me," she said without a smile.

"I will be here for you Dee, until you tell me to leave," he told her.

Dee put her hands on her hips. She had to make him understand. "Unless it's your time. You have no say in that. Then, poof, you are gone."

He didn't laugh. He opened his arms and let her walk into his hug. "Let's enjoy the now. Not be scared of the future," he whispered into her hair.

She stood in his embrace, enjoying the feel of him, the security of his heartbeat against hers. For a long time they stood like that, just enjoying the peace of those moments.

Finally, he released her and looked down into her upturned face. "How about you and me take a little vacation? Once Buckets is open, you won't have time for a long while. What do you think?"

And Dee agreed. With Lizzy willing to take on the inspections and final details before opening, Dee and Brad drove to West Virginia where he had an old family cabin in the gully on a small creek. The creek ran between two mountains. It was there he told her he loved her. They waded through the creek. He picked up a stone and placed it in her hand.

"I don't expect you to say you love me. This stone will be a reminder to you, that I love you and always will, no matter what," he promised with bedroom eyes.

Dee cared for him dearly but was not over Raymond's death. She worried that letting Brad believe there could be room for him, was unfair but agreed to enjoy the moment as Brad asked.

"I think you really love this guy, Dee. He's a good man," Lizzy said the night that Dee returned home. Brad had gone to pick up cold beer for everyone.

"I know he is. I haven't had time to sort it all out. I've been honest with him and he wants to wait until I figure it out. It'll be all right," Dee said, then turned and went into the garden. She sat on the swing and took a deep breath. She smelled the night blooming jasmine and sighed.

Lizzy joined her and they sat in the quiet, listening to the frogs and the crickets in the dark. They heard the front door shut and Brad called to them.

"We're out here," Dee yelled. He appeared with three bottles in his hand and handed Dee and Lizzy one each.

"You ladies look delighted with yourselves. What's the news?" he asked, taking a swig, then sitting on the top step of the porch.

"We can open tomorrow if we want too," Lizzy announced.

"We can?" Dee asked, surprised.

"Yep!" Lizzy replied. Licenses are hung on the wall, bar is stocked and I bought an open and closed sign this morning.

"Then that's what we shall do!" Dee assured as she turned to Brad, then back to Lizzy.

"Let's celebrate!" Brad cheered.

"Absolutely! Where has Jessie been lately? I feel bad to celebrate without him. He helped us out so much," Lizzy said.

"His ex-girlfriend, the one that really did a number on him—she's worming her way back into his life. Only because she knew he was spending a lot of time up this way," Brad remarked. "I'll let him know you guys were asking about him." Brad said as he turned to Lizzy.

"Please tell him how much he was appreciated! And he's welcome any time," Lizzy said and Dee nodded to agree.

They opened a bottle of champagne that Johnny had left for them, and poured each a glass to do a toast.

Before they could offer it though, they heard the door open again. Through the kitchen screen door walked Ripley and Walter, with Johnny and Nickie following a minute later. Johnny had another bottle of champagne and Dee laughed.

"This will be the last toast you'll drink out of my jelly glasses," she said. "Let's go inside where we can do this right."

When everyone had champagne, the seven of them brought their glasses to the air. Dee looked around with tears in her eyes.

"To wonderful friendships and to how powerful they can be. I thank all of you for making my dream come true!"

Then they clinked their glasses and sipped.

"It really *is* sad Jessie wasn't here," Lizzy muttered.

Dee knew that Jessie didn't interest Lizzy romantically, but her friend cared for him nonetheless.

Brad raised his glass.

"To steps down new paths and may they be everything imaginable and then some!" he toasted.

"Hear, hear!" they all cheered.

Dee looked at everyone and thought her heart would just about burst. A perfect moment. She understood what Brad meant. Still, she was excited for tomorrow.

Opening day!

CHAPTER NINETEEN

Buckets

Life has wonderful ways of making things happen that we need to

experience to find our paths

Sun came up and warmed the earth with her motherly glow. Lizzy marched her way to the coffee pot, then sat at the kitchen table awaiting her turn for the shower.

Dottie worked out the schedule for Lizzy to be off from the yacht club for a few days while she and Dee worked out the "Buckets" schedule. Lizzy was thankful for that. She sat at the table, excited to start a new way of life.

She thought back to the conversation she'd had with her parents. They accepted Buckets, same as they had Lee. Her decision. She knew that they weren't proud of the idea of their daughter owning a bar, yet they mustered all of the support they could. Her excitement about Buckets turned out to be all that mattered, even though part of her wanted to make her parents happy.

"I'm an adult now and this is my decision!" she announced to her cup of coffee.

The glasses from last night's impromptu celebration were still in the kitchen sink. It had been late when everyone had gone home. She laughed and marveled that she hadn't even stayed up to make sure they were washed first. Ripley would not be pleased, she thought with a grin. *Oh well.*

Dee's bedroom door closed.

"My turn to shower? Are you all done in the bathroom?" Lizzy yelled from the kitchen table.

"Yeah, I'm done. Hey, wear your black pants and white collared shirt. I want us to match," Dee hollered through her bedroom door.

"Yes, Miss Boss Lady!"

Lizzy chuckled her way to the bathroom. "She wants everything to be perfect, even me!"

After her shower, she strolled to her room and dressed. She came out of the room and Dee stood in front of her with something behind her back.

"I've got a surprise for you."

"Really?" Lizzy squeaked.

"I hope it fits," Dee said.

Dee threw her a collared white button up shirt.

"Wow, it is beautiful!" Lizzy grinned. Their "Buckets" logo was embroidered on the left side while Lizzy's name danced across the right side.

Lizzy ran to her room to change; then popped out of the room and twirled about as though she wore a beautiful ball gown.

Dee reviewed the itinerary for the grand opening and checked things off the list as they walked to the Jeep.

"I'll be up there as soon as I get off from work!" Johnny yelled from across the street.

"We hope so too, and see you when you get there!" Lizzy hollered.

"First beer is on me!" Dee yelled.

Their first stop: the bank to get three-hundred dollars in small bills and change to fill the register.

Everyone at the bank seemed as excited as Lizzy and Dee, and they each offered an encouraging word. The gift of their kindness warmed Lizzy's heart.

"Oh no! We're going to need to find someone to take care of our federal and state taxes and...." Lizzy stammered once they were back on the road. *What have we gotten ourselves into?*

"Relax, I've found a very reputable accountant and book keeper—Doctor Burger recommended her. I called her. She's willing to take us on as a client and she said to call her at any time if we have questions. We just need to document everything we do," Dee said.

They pulled into the parking lot and got out at the same time. Each drew a deep breath and exhaled, both stepped towards the door. Once again, Lizzy and Dee turned the key together and walked in.

They strolled to the register and turned the key again together. The silence seemed to solidify their commitment to Buckets and each other. They filled the register with the small bills and turned to each other.

"This is it!" Dee exclaimed.

"Yes, this is it. The start of a new journey!" Lizzy answered.

"Oh geez. The open sign!" Dee cried.

"I'll get it. You go get the grand opening sign to put out by the road," Lizzy suggested to Dee.

As Lizzy approached the door to turn the sign on, a couple walked in, holding hands. The man was a blond; so blond, it could be mistaken for white. The woman had short brown hair and eyes as blue as the sky.

"Are you open yet?" the man asked.

"We are now," Lizzy said with a laugh. She turned on the sign.

"Have a seat and one of us will be with you in a moment," Lizzy said.

The couple headed to the bar, then took seats there.

"You're our first customers ever!" Lizzy chirped. Then she realized they'd have no way of knowing what she meant.

"Today is our first day of being open more calmly."

"What can I get for you?" Dee asked as she stepped behind the bar.

"Bottle of light beer for me and a white zinfandel for my wife," the man said.

Dee opened the bottle of beer. Lizzy poured the glass of wine. As she passed it over the bar she remembered to put down the coasters that read, "Buckets, the coldest beer in town."

Dee beamed at the couple. "I'm Dee and that's Lizzy. Your names are?"

He lifted his beer and took his first sip.

"Now *that's* a good, cold, beer," he said as he looked at the bottle of beer.

Dee smiled because she'd read up on tricks to make beer super cold. The door opened again, another man, though this one walked in alone.

"Welcome" Lizzy said to the new customer.

Lizzy thought he looked like he needed a friend. He looked to be in his eighties and he carried a pipe of some kind.

"Can I smoke in here, Miss?" he asked Lizzy as he took a seat.

"Yes you can," Lizzy replied as she slid him an ash tray.

"I don't drink beer or wine. Do you have coffee?" the old man asked.

"We do. Give me one minute to make up a pot," Lizzy said.

She disappeared into the small room at the end of the bar where they had set up the coffee pot.

"Can you change that channel to the Price is Right for me?" the old man asked.

"I sure can!" Lizzy bragged.

She grabbed the remote and changed the channel. Soon the coffee beeped ready. Lizzy served him with a smile, of course.

The day progressed and people of all sorts came in. Each one pleased with the beverages of their choice. Many asked about the kitchen and how long it would be until it would be up and running. This excited Lizzy and she looked forward to getting it going as soon as possible.

Three hours before closing, having had a very busy day, Lizzy and Dee both mentioned their aching feet. Right about then, Ripley walked through the doors.

"Hey, just closed up the store. I had to come by and see how your first day was?"

Two guys sat at the bar who worked across the street at the gas station. Ripley turned to them. "Hi, I'm friends with the owners. My name is Ripley." She stuck out her hand and shook their hands. She wriggled onto a barstool near the register.

"I'll have a beer, please," she said.

The door opened again and in marched Brad, Jessie, and a girl they assumed was the ex-girlfriend Brad had mentioned yesterday. They too sat at the bar.

"Give us a bucket of beer please!" Brad ordered with a smile.

"You are the first to order a bucket. I was starting to think we picked the wrong name," Dee mentioned.

"No dear, you didn't. You need to mention that the buckets are special. People will buy them," he pointed out.

The guy at the end of the bar blurted, "We'd like to get a bucket too!"

Brad smiled. "See? I told you!"

The door opened again. Johnny and Nickie walked in.

"I'd like to have a bucket of a light beer, if you would, ma'am," Johnny drawled to Lizzy in his cowboy voice.

"Why surely, sir," Lizzy mimicked with a curtsy.

When they made "last call" and everyone said goodnight, Lizzy picked up a cloth and wiped down the bar with club soda, just like

Dee had taught her. It cut through the spilled beer and left the surface clean and fresh.

"We had one heck of day, didn't we?" she called to Dee who was straightening the tables and turning off the lights.

"We sure did. I think we had us a picture-perfect grand opening, Lizzy Girl

***

Each day that passed, more and more new faces came through the doors of "Buckets". Each told a different story. Lizzy and Dee listened to each and every word.

One gentleman in his sixties came in and told his story. A soldier, one of the few survivors of Hamburger Hill. He told them very little of the mission, but plenty of what he had witnessed. He told of how he lost his brother on that hill. Tears ran down his face as he told his story. He said it should have been him who had died.

Lizzy could see the love and guilt that he felt; could almost feel his pain for the loss of his flesh-and-blood. He was the one that survived. He was the one that had suffered the most. The man had lived his life to its fullest for himself *and* his brother.

"He is with me every step I step and breath I take. There isn't a day that passes that he isn't with me," the man lamented.

Lizzy glanced at the newspaper she read earlier that day. On the front page it read, "*Men of war remembered in memorial ceremony and families gather to pay their respects.*" In that moment, Lizzy knew each story came as a gift to her. A gift to embrace and learn. The article stood as her confirmation that conversations needed to be remembered and the stories cherished.

One particular gentleman came in on a regular basis. He was a short, slight-built man, very intelligent, his thick glasses making him look even smarter.

He was a retired professor. His hair was always a mess. Lizzy nicknamed him "The Professor." He told Lizzy that she represented a dolphin which Lizzy didn't understand, but of course remembered, every time he walked into Buckets.

"Why did you say I was a dolphin?" Lizzy finally asked one day.

"Oh dear, I am a faithful man to my wife," he said.

At first Lizzy thought he mistook her kindness as a sign of interest in him. She was certainly interested in him, but not in a romantic or sexual way.

"You are the same. When you find your mate, it too will be for life. Dolphins find a mate and it's for life," he said.

"Someday, I hope my husband says the same thing about me."

Lizzy wondered how The Professor could have come up with that analogy of her but the association with animals and nature opened her eyes a little wider to life and its forces.

Lizzy noticed that Dee also became very attentive to some who entered. She gravitated toward the older people who came in. Dee often told Lizzy, "They have lived a lifetime and the stories they tell are so much like the story your grandmother told us. Full of magical friendships and love. Do you think stories and memories get better with time, like wine?"

Since Lizzy had no idea, she decided to adopt Dee's question as her own. She would listen and learn all she could.

In the evenings, while cleaning up after closing, Lizzy and Dee often compared stories they'd heard throughout the day.

"Everyone has a story," Dee said. "Some are just trying to get out to live again."

"What a lovely way to say that," Lizzy said. "Their stories let them live again each time they tell them." She sighed and looked at Dee. "If I ever write a book, I want their stories to live again, too."

"I feel I've known some of them in another life. Many of them feel like they were put into my life for a reason," Dee told Lizzy. "To learn from or maybe to just listen to their story."

One night after closing, with the doors locked and the "open" sign off, a knock sounded at the door.

"Who could that be?" Dee wondered as she turned towards the door.

Jessie's terrified face peered through the glass. He kept banging on the door. Dee dashed to the door, unlocked it and jerked it open.

Before she could say a word, Jessie stuttered, "It's Brad. A bad, bad, accident. He rolled his truck. You have to come. They don't know if he's going to make it."

Dee fell to her knees and screamed. Lizzy came from behind the bar and scooped her up by her arms.

"Let's go! What hospital are they taking him to?" Lizzy asked Jessie as she locked the door and helped Dee out to the Jeep.

"Memorial hospital, off the interstate. Follow me," Jessie said through his tears.

Lizzy got Dee into the Jeep and headed to the hospital.

Dee babbled in shock. The only words Lizzy could make out sounded like, "Why me? Not again. I should have told him. Oh God. Not again. Why me?" Dee stared out the window into the darkness mumbling words.

They pulled into the parking lot of the emergency room right behind Jessie. He flew out of his truck, grabbed Dee's arm and dragged her to his side. They rushed through the doors.

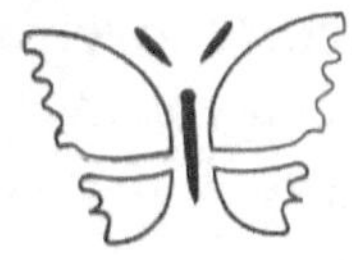

CHAPTER TWENTY

Déjà Vu

Every stage of life whether easy or hard, good or bad, is necessary.
It makes us who we are.

This cannot be happening ... not again. I just can't bear this. I can't lose him like this. She felt as though she was watching from somewhere very high in the air, wrapped in cloud that muffled the sounds and sights around her. Could she breathe? Could she move?

"Dee, Dee?" Jessie pulled at her. "He's right here."

She looked to her left and saw doctors surrounding a gurney. They stepped aside to speak to each other and she saw him. Mangled and bloody. She swallowed her scream and squared her shoulders.

"There's nothing we can do. He's in too bad a shape. Let the family say their goodbyes," one of the Doctors said to the others.

Dee walked up to Brad and smiled. She acted as though he looked as beautiful as the day they had met. He would always be her "eye candy" no matter what. She leaned down to his ear.

"Hi Brad. It's me, Dee"

A smile spread to his face. He struggled to speak. "Rock" he groaned to Dee.

"Yes Brad, the rock. I have it," she whispered, fighting back tears. Dee pulled the rock he had given her from her pocket and showed him.

He tried to speak again. "Remember the rock."

"I will always remember the rock," Dee whimpered. "I love you. I never told you because I was afraid to lose you. I pushed you away." She kissed his head. "I can't lose you without telling you. I love you!" she repeated, then kissed him again.

His eyes closed as her lips touched his forehead. The smile returned to his face and the heart monitor beep transformed into one long, relentless alarm until the nurse came in and turned off all of the machines. Dee didn't move, couldn't move.

"He's gone now. Please take your time..." the nurse said as she left the room.

Lizzy arrived just as Brad passed away. Jessie put his arm around Dee and they stood together watching Brad's still, battered body.

A peaceful silence filled the air.

After several moments, Dee looked up to say goodbye to Beautiful Brad as he moved toward the doorway.

"Rosco is waiting, my love," Dee whispered. Then she smiled through her tears and felt the warmth of love in her heart. She squeezed Jessie's hand. He just stood staring at her.

"Your grandfather is right there in the door, Jessie. He's got his arm around Brad and he's okay. They're walking toward the light," she said to him softly.

"You know Dee, you were the only girl he ever loved. Truly loved," Jessie admitted to Dee.

Dee looked at Lizzy who was hiding her face in her hands. *Poor Lizzy, she doesn't understand there is no hiding from this.*

"I know," Dee replied. "This rock he gave me tells me so. For the rest of my life, it'll be a gift he gave me because he knew I would need it someday." Dee put it back in her pocket.

Dee walked over to Lizzy. "Let's go home."

The three of them walked out of the hospital with their arms wrapped around each other.

***

Lizzy didn't get much sleep. How in the world would Dee survive yet another crushing loss? Another death of someone she loved? *Why are you so cruel, God? Why does she have to have so much pain? She's such a good woman ...*

The sun peeked through the window blind reminding her God wanted her to see the beautiful day He'd blessed them with. She pulled herself out of the bed and stumbled out of her room and went straight to Dee's room. There was no Dee to be found.

Oh God, please let her be okay ...

Lizzy walked out the kitchen door and saw Dee in the garden, smiling at the new flowers that she must have planted last night in memory of Brad. The flowers appeared to be the most beautiful passion flowers.

Dee turned to her. "This unusual flower grows wild all over the Southeast, especially here in Florida. I've always loved it because of its beauty and what it represents. The flower thrives with neglect in somewhat dry, sunny, or partial shade environments. The butterflies use the plant for shade. They call it the Passionflower or Passion vine because the floral parts that were once said to represent the Christian crucifixion story, sometimes called the Passion."

Dee pointed to the petals. "These ten petal-like parts right here represent Jesus' disciples, excluding Peter and Judas; the five stamens are the wounds Jesus suffered in his hands, his feet and his side. The knob-like section represents the nails; the fringy part, the crown of thorns. The name "Maypop," which is the fruit, comes from down here," Dee picked one. "The yellow fruits pop loudly when crushed." She crushed it to show Lizzy.

"Passiflora incarnata, that's the botanical name of the plant. The flower is a larval host and nectar source for many types of butterflies' native to our state," Dee continued.

"It's here in my garden to represent Brad. He was put in my life to teach me to always tell the people I care about, every day, what they mean to me. I didn't get that with Raymond. As for Brad, he was in my life for a short time, but he's the one that taught me to say it.

Lizzy, life is too short. I was too scared to tell him. I thought I would lose him. Then I was terrified to lose him without telling him."

Dee spun around and faced Lizzy. "Promise me, Lizzy ... even if you fight with someone—let them know you love them. Lizzy, I love you."

"Dee, I love you too!" Lizzy whimpered and flung her arms around Dee.

From what Lizzy could see, and she was paying a lot of attention, Dee took Brad's death well. The day of the funeral, they closed "Buckets" and taped a sign to the door that read: "Closed due to the loss of a loved one."

In smaller letters it read, "Tomorrow we will be open." Even smaller letters stated, "Our hearts to you. Love all. Dee and Lizzy"

Lizzy was relieved when they arrived at the funeral to find that Brad was not on display. Everyone who loved him would remember his handsome face and brilliant smile. She was happy that Dee would be able to remember her "eye candy" just the way he was when they'd met.

It was rumored that he'd been almost completely decapitated and his face destroyed, but Lizzy and Dee saw and heard different. Brad had lived just long enough to hear Dee say she loved him. He communicated to Dee to remember the rock. Lizzy and Dee knew and cherished those facts and ignored the rumors.

After the funeral, Jessie caught up to Dee and Lizzy as they were leaving.

"Dee, I wanted to give you something that I ran across. I thought you might want it." He handed her a picture.

It was a picture of Brad and Jessie standing with their grandfather in front of Roscoe's This and That Warehouse. Brad and Jessie were just barely ten-years old. Lizzy wasn't quite sure of the age but could tell they were young.

"I saw this photo. It made me remember something that's really important. All those buckets you bought. Brad, back then, would always be looking for ways to use them. We were just kids. He loved those buckets. Almost as much as you. It never made sense to me. It makes all the sense in the world now."

"Thanks Jessie," Dee said as she placed the picture on her heart. "It's a great gift. I'll put this picture up at Buckets. Brad will know that the buckets got some use."

Lizzy and Dee hugged Jessie. Then they hopped into the Jeep and headed for home.

"Are you all right?" Lizzy asked.

"I am. I actually am," Dee replied.

Lizzy believed her and they drove in comfortable silence. She remembered something her grandmother had read to her several years ago, when Lee had gone off on one of his trysts and Lizzy had thought she'd die of the heartache. As she drove, the piece played in her mind.

People come into your life for a reason, a season or a lifetime. When you figure out which one it is, you will know what to do for each person.

When someone is in your life for a REASON, it is usually to meet a need you have expressed. They have come to assist you through a difficulty; to provide you with guidance and support; to aid you physically, emotionally or spiritually. They may seem like a godsend, and they are. They are there for the reason you need them to be.

Then, without any wrong doing on your part or at an inconvenient time, this person will say or do something to bring the relationship to an end. Sometimes they die. Sometimes they walk away. Sometimes they act up and force you to take a stand. What we must realize is that our need has been met, our desire fulfilled; their work is done. The prayer you sent up has been answered and now it is time to move on.

Some people come into your life for a SEASON, because your turn has come to share, grow or learn something you have never done. They usually give you an unbelievable amount of joy. Believe it. It is real. But only for a season. They bring you an experience of peace or make you laugh.

LIFETIME relationships teach you lifetime lessons; things you must build upon in order to have a solid emotional foundation. Your job is to accept the lesson, love the person, and put what you have learned to use in all other relationships and areas of your life. It is said that love is blind but friendship is clairvoyant.

— Unknown

***

Lizzy and Dee returned home. Dee still held the picture Jessie gave her to her heart. As they pulled up into the driveway, Dee slowly brought the picture down. She took another glance.

Another picture appeared to be stuck to the back of it, almost like the picture had tried to hide itself, until that moment. The photo showed a picture of a silhouette of Brad and his grandpa fishing. Brad was very young, probably six or seven. His grandpa sported a pipe in his mouth. The two of them were fishing in the creek.

The creek Brad had taken Dee to. The creek where Brad told Dee he loved her and gave her the rock.

"Thank you, Brad," Dee said as she looked to the sky. "I love you, too."

She placed the two pictures over her heart and exhaled a smile.

Lizzy and Dee walked out to the garden and sat on the swing. They embraced the scent of the flowers, the buzzing of the bee's, and the beauty of the butterflies.

"Do you think they know we are thinking of them? After they're gone?" Lizzy asked.

Dee stopped the swing. "I don't think. I know!" Dee smiled and explained. "Instinct. Humans are the only creature of God's that don't operate on instinct. It's that feeling. It's that first thought. It's the butterflies in the stomach you are always looking for. I believe that is them pointing us in the direction we need to be," Dee said "It's the letting them know that's the important thing!"

"Wow Dee, I love how you look at life, death, and nature. I know you aren't religious, but you have something angelic about your thoughts. I love that about you!" Lizzy said.

142

They started to swing again.

"And I love that about you too!" Dee said with a smile.

Ripley pulled into the drive and jumped out of the hardware store truck Lizzy and Dee watch from the garden.

"Hi guys. I heard about Brad. He was such a good guy. I wish I would have heard sooner. I would have come with you to the funeral," Ripley said as she walked into the garden and sat on the swing with Dee and Lizzy.

"You aren't working today?" Lizzy asked.

"No. Haven't been feeling very good lately. Been throwing up a lot," Ripley groaned.

"You are pregnant," Dee reported with a smile.

"Yes, I am. How did you know?" Ripley asked. "I just took a test this morning and that's another reason I came over. I needed you guys. I don't know who to tell first. My parents or Walter."

Lizzy let out a little laugh. "Don't ask me. It took me weeks to tell my parents about Buckets because I didn't think they would accept the idea. I couldn't imagine telling them I had a baby on the way. It would kill them. Dee, your call on this one."

"Walter is the father and you both should approach your parents. He should be told first. The baby is part his," Dee said.

"Yes, you're right. Just because I know and he doesn't. Yes. You're right. I *so* love you guys." Ripley hugged the two of them.

Then she stood and stretched, as though a weight had been lifted from her shoulders.

"I'm going to tell him now," she said. She walked back to the truck. She turned and said, "You know. I love this baby. I'm going to keep it. I know it won't be easy. I'm going to give it my all. No matter who is—or isn't—behind me."

Lizzy and Dee both replied at the same time, "We're behind you!"

Dee and Lizzy turned to each other and smiled. "Momma always says, '*When there is death there is always a birth to follow,* and I guess she's right." Dee mimics Lizzy.

Are you my conscience?" Lizzy joked to Dee.

"Are you mine?" Dee asked back and the girls laugh together.

They looked up and saw Johnny coming out of the garage looking across the street at them on the swing. He crossed the street, off his hat and placed it over his heart.

"I heard this morning about Brad. I'm so... so sorry, Dee. If I can do anything for you girls you know I'm here for you."

"We're fine, Johnny. Just be our friend. That's all we need from you," Lizzy said.

"Always," he said, putting his hat back on. He turned to leave, then turned back around.

"Nickie said yes to my proposal. I didn't get a chance to tell you. We plan to marry next spring," he said with a sheepish grin.

"I'm happy for her. She's getting a good man," Dee said.

"Congratulations to you both. We're going to be invited aren't we?" Lizzy added.

"Hell. You ladies will be my best men. I hope you have suits to wear," he teased.

Johnny laughed an evil laugh as he walked away and muttered, "Dee and Lizzy in tuxedos. That'll be something."

"We really are lucky to have such great people in our lives," Lizzy admitted.

"Yes we are. Lucky. Very lucky," Dee replied.

CHAPTER TWENTY-ONE

Graced with Gracey

"When the student is ready, the master appears." - Buddhist

Proverb

The next day Dee opened up Buckets without Lizzy since she had to work at the yacht club.

Dee walked behind the bar with the picture Jessie had given her of Brad and Jessie with their grandpa. Dee placed it on the shelf behind the bar.

"There you go Brad. The buckets have a job to do now, and you, my love, can watch them work their magic," she said to the picture. Every day she'd start by saying good morning to the guardian angel of Buckets.

Dee was excited about Lizzy working her last week at the yacht club and the kitchen was almost ready to open at Buckets. All of that was forgotten due to Brads Death but the excitement returned as Dee turned the lights on in the kitchen. Buckets patiently waited on the final inspection from the state and of course the food distributors to come. Then Buckets could open the kitchen. Lizzy had already printed up a temporary menu.

"We'll start with a small amount of food items and work our way up," Lizzy insisted. At home, Lizzy tried different beer recipes and used Dee as her guinea pig. She came up with a beer bread to die for. The bread piped a light, crusty outside with a fluffy inside and just a hint of beer flavor.

Then, just barely warm, she would fill the inside of it with chicken seasoned with sage, sea salt, scallions, black pepper and a hint of lime. It was a sandwich that would "melt in your mouth," Dee told Lizzy. She smiled at her memories.

As she busied herself getting ready to open, Dee thought back to the day Lizzy tried beer batter on everything she could get her hands on. Lizzy invented a beer-battered chicken wing that would go well with beer. Dee also researched what type of beer and wines would go with certain types of food.

Dee neatened the pile of coasters and cut some fresh limes. Oh, and the stews and soups, also another specialty, with the scone recipe Lizzy had tried with Dee once. Lizzy even came up with a scone recipe that had beer in it. Dee giggled to herself about that idea, too.

"I'm almost as excited about the kitchen opening as Lizzy is," Dee babbled aloud.

She agreed with Lizzy about buying fresh potatoes from the local farmers to make their French fries, and cabbage to make their cole slaw fresh daily.

But what really excited Dee about opening the kitchen, was that the smaller buckets would get some use. Dee knew Lizzy was just dying to get her food into the mouths of the world. Just one more week and Buckets would be all they had planned.

The door opened and in walked a real old man sporting a well groomed beard so silver it shined, and he had no hair on his head.

"Welcome, what can I do for you today?" Dee asked as she placed a coaster on the bar in front of him.

"I would like one of your ice cold beers, please," he answered. "I hear you have the coldest in town."

Dee reached in the cooler and grabbed him a bottle, opened it and placed it on the coaster.

"Really? We're being talked about in town?" Dee asked, feeling rather proud.

"Yes ma'am, you are. Two young girls, in this kind of business, got to be talked about," he said. "Honey, I have lived in the town all my life. I knew your mother when she was alive. She was a looker. I used to own the gas station on the corner back in the day. Name is Henry. Henry O'Donald," he asserted.

"Well, Mr. O'Donald, I believe Lizzy and I went to school with both of your grandkids, Jan and George O'Donald," Dee remarked. "My name is Dee and I'm honored to have you as a customer. Please, the beer is on us."

"Oh no, dear, I have more money than I could possibly spend in my life time. Take my money," he demanded.

"No, next time," Dee insisted.

"Fine, I will be here every day to get one. Only one, ice cold beer, and every day until the day I die. My girl, I never break a promise," Old Henry pledged.

Dee turned back to him and smiled. "That's what I am hoping."

The door opened again and Lizzy's favorite customer, Mr.-Price-is-Right, walked in.

"How are you today? Would you like a cup of coffee?" Dee asked as she put a coaster on the bar in front of his favorite seat.

"Yes, please. Where is my Lizzy today?" he asked.

"She's working at her other job today. She only has to do it for about one more week. We'll then have her to ourselves," Dee added as she grabbed for the remote control. Then she glided into the kitchen to make a pot of coffee.

After the coffee finished brewing, she brought him out a cup, sat it onto the coaster. He took a sip. He shook his head.

"It's not my Lizzy's coffee, but it will do," he remarked.

Dee, not much of a coffee drinker herself, had Lizzy show her how to make his coffee. She was sure she did it exactly as she had been instructed.

Just then she realized that sometimes we have things that other see as our magic. *He obviously thinks Lizzy's coffee is her magic. Mine is my ice cold beer.*

The door opened again and Manny and Milly walked in. The couple, from Buckets first day in business, had been coming in quite regularly over time. Dee was quite attached to them and their stories.

As people came and went, the day passed quickly. Dee glanced up at the clock and realized Lizzy would be getting off from the yacht club soon to relieve her. She could get some dinner then come back and help close up.

As the day passed, Dee figured she had to have rung up over two-hundred dollars on the register. According to their accountant, *anything over two-hundred would be profit.* That thought excited her. Buckets was really going to make it. The door opened and Dee finished counting the drawer.

"Honey, I am sorry for your loss. I came by and saw the sign on the door yesterday," a female voice said as Dee faced the register with her back to the bar. She turned to see a woman. Dee could see she was middle aged but she still held her beauty.

"Hello, I'm Dee. What can I do for you?"

"I'll have a beer, in a glass, please," the woman said. "My Name is Gracey and I'm looking for work. Are you hiring?"

Dee grabbed a frosted glass from the freezer and pulled the beer from the tap.

"No we aren't, but..." Dee said, then stopped.

Ripley isn't going to be able to work nights now that she's pregnant and the kitchen will be opening—Lizzy and I will never have time off together and ... "

Dee made a decision based on instinct. "You know, we could probably could use some help," she admitted.

"I'm your lady. I'm a hard worker. I managed a pub over in Ireland for ten years when I was in my thirties. It was my uncle's place. I have tons of ideas." She glanced around. "This place reminds me of his place, so much. I guess that's why I was drawn to it. I moved here about a month ago to stay with my mother who's sick with cancer," Gracey continued.

"You are hired," Dee stated. "Finish up your beer and I'll show you around, if you have time."

Gracey smiled. "I've got all the time in the world."

Then Dee looked back over her shoulder. "Ireland huh?"

Gracey nodded as she sipped her beer. Dee suddenly knew Gracey had been placed there to show her things. Dee could feel a connection—the familiarity of Gracey.

***

Lizzy showed up at Buckets right after the sun had set. She walked in and noticed a woman with Dee behind the bar. Dee was showing her around. *Who is this?*

"Hello. Sorry I'm late. Dottie had me training a new girl at the yacht club," Lizzy explained. She looked at the other woman. "Hi, I'm Lizzy."

"Lizzy, this is Gracey," Dee said. "She ran her uncle's pub in Ireland, for ten years. I thought we could use her, since the kitchen would be opening soon. Ripley probably won't be working like we had thought."

Lizzy thought a moment, and then extended her hand. "Nice to meet you, Gracey, Ireland huh?"

"Yes, it's absolutely a place to see. You girls are awfully young to be in this kind of business. Are you old enough to drink?" Gracey asked.

"Yes. We're old enough," Dee stated with a giggle.

"But just barely," Lizzy chuckled.

"Dee, can I talk to you for a minute, alone?" Lizzy asked.

"Sure," Dee answered.

The door opened and three men in dress shirts and dress pants walked through the door.

"Okay, Gracey, let's see what you got. Remember what I told you," Dee coached.

Dee walked to the kitchen with Lizzy. The two of them peeked their head out and watched Gracey wait on the customers. Once Gracey finished they retreated back into the kitchen.

"Are you sure we can afford to hire someone right now?" Lizzy whispered to Dee, so Gracey wouldn't hear.

"Well, I originally told her we weren't hiring. Then I realized we would never be able to hang out together let alone get any rest at all with Ripley out of the picture now. The kitchen is going to add on more work and we can't work all the time. I don't know, it just felt like the right thing to do."

Lizzy nodded slowly. "I'm sure she could teach us a lot. She seems to be very good with people. I guess I'm just scared."

Dee smiled. "You know me, I go off of instinct and I think we'll be fine. Besides, she said she knows we've just opened. She'll work with us on her pay. The pub in Ireland did it. I know she was sent here by Raymond. Raymond would only send someone here that was going to help us."

Still whispering, Lizzy gave in. "I sure hope you're right," Lizzy whispered as she peeked again out at Gracey. That's when she spotted a butterfly tattoo on Gracey's shoulder.

"Okay, then, that's what we shall do." Lizzy was convinced as she turned back to Dee.

"Come on, let's have a seat and watch how she works. I'll order a pizza delivered and we'll have dinner here," Dee suggested.

"Sounds like a plan," Lizzy responded.

About forty-five minutes passed and the delivery guy saunters into the door with the pizza. Gracey pointed to the end of the bar where the two of them were sitting and continued talking to one of the gentleman at the bar.

"Great, I'm starving." Dee said as she paid the driver.

The delivery driver asked, "Thanks. How late are you open tonight?"

"Midnight, we close," Lizzy announced as she took a bite of her first slice of pizza.

"Cool, I'll be off in an hour. I'd like to try one of those coldest beers in town, I keep hearing about," the delivery driver said as he walked towards the door.

"Wow, we're being talked about, Dee!" Lizzy cheered with a mouth full of pizza.

Dee returned her smile, right before she took her bite of pizza. "So that's what I hear," she mumbled around a mouth full of food.

As the night progressed, so did the ringing of the register. Gracey did outstanding work. She even gave them advice on how she did inventory.

She showed them little tricks she had for pouring the perfect draft. By the end of the evening, Lizzy was convinced Gracey was there to teach them and show them the ins and outs of a successful pub. Gracey even shared some Irish stew recipes that Lizzy couldn't wait to try. Of course, she would add a few extra ingredients to make it her own.

The pizza delivery guy came back and brought four other people with him. They drank and laughed all night. Dee and Lizzy had a hard time getting them to leave at closing time, but they finally did. They also threatened to come every night after work.

"So far tonight was our busiest since we've opened," Dee praised as she read the register receipts.

Lizzy said, "We should take the night off more often."

Gracey piped up, "I'll work."

The three of them laughed as they shut down all of the lights. They closed Buckets together.

***

Over the next few weeks, Gracey worked out very well. Lizzy and Dee became quite fond of her. She helped Lizzy organize the food by putting things such as condiments close at hands reach, so the food would get out to the customers as fast as possible. She taught Lizzy how to precook some of the items so it wouldn't take as long to prepare the orders. The soups and stews were cooked in the mornings to get the aroma in the air for opening, a little trick Gracey had brought back from Ireland.

"You have to hit all of the senses: smell, sight, sound and touch." Gracey coached.

"Touch?" Lizzy asked, and then looked at Dee.

"Yes, like a good old pat on the back or a shake of the hand," Gracey suggested as she patted Dee's back.

Lizzy wasn't much for "touching" unless it was Dee or Ripley. So Lizzy had to work on getting more comfortable with the touching part of the equation.

Gracey showed Dee how adding salt to the coolers helped keep the beer and wine colder. As for the buckets of beer, salt in the ice helped the iced beer stay colder longer and frosted mugs only for serving the draft beer.

Dee and Lizzy were finally able to take time away from Buckets. Gracey was definitely a blessing behind the bar. The girls worked unbelievable hours and every day became busier than the last. The town definitely appeared to be talking. Even Lizzy's momma had heard about how great the place was through one of her social clubs.

The drinking atmosphere, not exactly Lizzy's parent's cup of tea, meant they weren't much for visiting her at work. Lizzy made it a point to stop by the house to see how they were doing and bring them her new daily specialty soups.

Ripley's belly got bigger by the day. Walter and Ripley decided to keep the baby and try to work together as parents. They didn't have plans of marriage. Ripley said she wanted them to marry because they *wanted* to, not because they *had* to. A child was coming and they both felt that they weren't ready for marriage.

Lizzy didn't really know how she felt about that, but Ripley and Walter sure seemed happy. And she was happy as could be that she and Dee would have a new life to love and nurture, soon. Maybe life just didn't get better than that.

CHAPTER TWENTY-TWO

Changes and Instincts

There are far better things ahead than any we leave behind. -

Unknown

Ripley's parents decided she could continue running the hardware store until the time came that she couldn't. They were considering getting someone to manage the store temporarily until Ripley returned and she was thankful for that.

As for Johnny, he was doing all right, but he and Nickie started having problems. She broke up with him one week and wanted him back the next. He started drinking a lot and would come in to Buckets at closing time to talk to Dee and Lizzy about the things that Nickie had been doing.

He even rode his horse into town one Friday night, drunk as a skunk. He tied it to Lizzy's daddy's Jeep just to come in and cry on their shoulder. Of course, Dee and Lizzy did everything they could to help him, but it was no use.

"He won't sober up long enough to listen to what we say," Dee said in frustration.

"The drinking is just adding to their problems," Lizzy moaned.

When he was around the bar, Dee teased Lizzy about him. "The Headless Horseman will never change. Shhhh, be very, very, quiet, I'm huntin' for a rabbit." Then they would laugh remembering the good times they'd shared before Nickie came into his life.

But for Lizzy, Johnny's behavior made her sad. Would they be burying him soon, too? She missed his easy laughter and warm smile. His eyes were dark and haunted and he looked like he was living behind a dumpster most days. He was her friend and she loved him, but he refused to listen to her or Dee. She could only hope that he'd be okay until he came to his senses.

Then one night, it happened. Lizzy and Dee were in Buckets watching the news, and there he was, the Headless Horseman, drunk again. This time he was arrested on his horse for riding it within the city limits.

The news report spread from coast to coast. The novelty of a young man being arrested for riding drunk and disorderly made his indiscretion a great headline. In his own way, Johnny put their little town on the map. He had to pay some fines and was put on probation.

But the good news was that as a result of his crazy behavior and the embarrassment it caused Nickie's family, she was forbidden to see him again and the wedding plans were called off. Lizzy and Dee watched Johnny emerge from his darkest days like a Phoenix from the ashes. Lizzy's fears for him quieted and he didn't touch a drop of alcohol after his arrest.

The summer was the hottest in years. Dee was dating again, not really settling down with any one person, but dating. Lizzy dated but never encountered those butterflies she had been looking for. Besides, she had a list longer than Buckets' register tape with the qualities of the man she wanted in her life.

"Men like that don't exist, Lizzy," Dee cautioned.

Lizzy figured maybe she was being so picky because she wasn't ready for a relationship. She was sure of what she wanted and what she didn't. She'd just wait and see if the right person came into her life. If she believed the fortune teller—and she did—she was going to find the right man. She just had to stay aware.

"I'll know when I feel those butterflies in my stomach. That means I'm ready for a relationship," she told Dee.

Besides, she'd heard Momma say a million times, *"If you don't absolutely love everything about your man, you don't need to settle with him...because you can't change him."* As she got older, she understood the wisdom in those words. She was content with her life and enjoyed the new love she had found for herself. Truth be told, what she really missed was the connection, the closeness of making love with someone she loved.

***

As the days passed, business improved by the day. Gracey endeared herself as a great asset to Buckets in more ways than one.

With Gracey working, Dee and Lizzy enjoyed personal time to hang out together. They could date if a gentleman appeared interested.

One hot, summer day while Gracey handled Buckets, Lizzy and Dee stayed home to tend the garden. They were catching up on their neglected house work, especially the laundry. The laundry had backed up so much that when they didn't have a clean outfit to wear, they'd treat themselves to a new one.

"New cloths make a woman, old ones keep her the same," Dee would say as they headed to the store. Lizzy wasn't so sure, but since Dee was usually right, why not go along?

They were honest with each other and in agreement about their money. They tried not to over-spend because their business was new and they didn't take their success for granted. They knew that it might not last and then they'd be paying the good doctor out of their own pockets, so they made sure their bills were up to date and their savings in good shape before spending on themselves.

Lizzy took a break from catching up the wash and walked out the screen door into the garden.

"Looks like neglect is good for the garden," she said to Dee with a smile.

Dee stood and stretched her back. "Yeah, I was afraid the weeds were going to take over, but everything is really doing well."

Lizzy dropped onto the swing and set it rocking. "Dee, do you think I'll ever feel the butterflies in my belly again? I mean, I'm dating but I don't *feel* anything," Lizzy said with a frown.

Dee stopped pulling weeds and glanced her way. "Sure, when it's your time, you'll feel it," she said in her counseling voice.

Lizzy sighed and rested her head against the back of the swing. "I sure hope so. If I am attracted to them physically, I'm not mentally. If I'm attracted mentally, I'm not physically. I want both, especially if I'm going to mate for life."

"Why not just mate, forget about the "for life" thing?" Dee said as she walked to join Lizzy on the swing.

"What about you, do you just mate?" Lizzy asked.

"No, I don't mate. I have sex," Dee blurted out. Then she laughed and poked Lizzy in the ribs. "Ms. Righteous, live a little. Quit trying to be so—proper. Do something *wrong* for a change. You might like it. I'm not saying harm anyone, or rob a bank, or even kill someone, Lizzy, but guys don't appreciate a good woman any more. They honestly don't care. Have you ever noticed that they fall for the girls that half the town has slept with?" Dee noted.

Lizzy grimaced. "That does seem to be the case around here."

Dee turned serious. "Some of the single guys that come in on my shift at Buckets have asked me if you were gay, and it's only because they don't know anyone who has slept with you. Besides Lee, that is. It's not that it's wrong or right, it's just not normal at our age and they think you and me are a couple. I just date to appear straight."

"I just want you to know, if I were gay, you would know it, because I would want to have a girl like you, Ms. Dee," Lizzy said with a laugh. It was her turn to poke Dee in the ribs.

"It's not funny! You're ruining my reputation," Dee said with a grin.

They looked up and saw Johnny coming out from the garage.

"He always knows when we're having one of our laughter conversations," Dee remarked.

Johnny waved but didn't say anything, which was not like him.

Dee yelled over to him. "How are you doing, Johnny?" Before he could answer, she continued. "We miss you!"

Johnny smiled from ear to ear and hollered back, "I'm good! I decided that I wasn't going to drink any more. That's why I haven't been to Buckets lately."

"We sell soda and coffee, too," Lizzy shouted.

"Then I'll stop up and have a soda or coffee with you one day. I just thought you ladies would be embarrassed to have a national drunk as a friend."

"*Never!*" Dee and Lizzy yelled back in unison. They looked at each other and laughed some more. "Hey, Johnny, Can we get an autograph?"

He smiled, then shook his head before he disappeared inside the garage.

"*Any* girl has got to be better than Nickie. I'm so glad she's out of his life. Oh hell, perfect example, good guy in love with a bad girl. She messed around in High School with half the football team," Dee commented.

"How do you know that?" Lizzy asked.

"I just know. Everyone knew; ask Ripley if you don't believe me," Dee said.

Lizzy shook her head. "People said a lot of things about you that weren't true, right? I don't like Nickie because of how she treated Johnny, but maybe the football team *wanted* her to mess around with them."

Dee stopped the swing and got to her feet. "That's a real good point, Ms. Righteous. I don't like her, but that's based on my instincts, not the stories. I was just using her to make my point."

"Honestly Dee, I haven't found anyone I would just want to have sex with. Just don't want to waste the time or energy on someone I'm not physically and mentally attracted to," Lizzy summarized.

Dee blew out a long breath of air through her lips. "I do understand that. I have regretted it several times in my life. I guess you just have to follow your instincts."

CHAPTER TWENTY-THREE

Magical Music Man

***Your world will not change if you don't change first* - Unknown**

Things were very good for Lizzy and Dee due to the fact, they put some money in savings and Doctor Burger got his payment, sometimes early. They made sure it was always a three-way split: Lizzy, Dee, and Buckets.

They also made sure Gracey earned good money. They felt she deserved every penny. Dee and Lizzy split the night shifts and day shifts so they both had a variety. Gracey filled in on the day or night so they could hang out.

One Tuesday, on Dee's shift, a nice-looking guy with an olive complexion, dark wavy hair, and a smile that yelled *Italian*, walked in toting a guitar case.

He looked around a bit then turned to the bar. "Does your owner have live entertainment play here?" he asked Dee.

Laughing to herself Dee answered, "No, but I suppose I could find out if the owner is interested."

Dee knew most people didn't believe she and Lizzy could be the owners of Buckets. Most bar owners were old retired guys who had money. Dee felt a strange connection to the young man. Almost the same connection she'd felt with Gracey.

The Italian-looking guy spoke again. "I haven't played in a while. Well, I play all the time but I haven't played in public in a while. I moved down here a year or so ago with my girlfriend. I do construction, since work is booming here. I've been too busy working to do what I love, and that's playing my magic to the public."

"Did you just say magic instead of music?" Dee asked.

"Yeah," he chuckled. "Sounds silly maybe, but I consider my music, my magic. All the songs I sing are my own music. I have about thirty, I guess."

Dee pointed out, "We could use some magic around here."

Hmmm. He thinks in terms of magic. Lizzy possesses the magic of the kitchen, mine is the ice cold beer, and Gracey's magic is her organizational skill. At that moment, she knew he needed to be there.

"You know," he started, "I've been driving by this place every day and had this pull to come see if you needed some entertainment. Today I just did it." He laughed, a sound that was almost musical in a rich sort of way. "Oh, my name is Joe. I play acoustic guitar," he concluded as he put his hand out to Dee.

She shook it and smiled. "Well Joe, have a seat. Let's hear what you got," she said.

He played his *magic* for about an hour and it sounded beautiful. Dee knew she needed to hire him. She watched the customers react to the music and knew her hunch would be right on the money—again.

"You my friend really *do* have the magic," Dee confessed on his last strum of the strings.

"How about this Friday night? Start about six and play till nine? Forty minutes on, twenty off. Food's on us, soda or coffee, too. If we're busy and the customers want you longer, we'll work with you," she offered.

He smiled. "Really? Sounds great!"

He packed up his guitar and drank down the beer a customer had bought him during one of the tunes he had played.

"I'll see you Friday. I've got to get busy practicing, so the owner wants to have me back," Joe said.

"Oh, good idea. Lizzy will be working that night. Yeah, I'll be here in and out that night, too," Dee said, realizing she probably should have told him she was one of the owners. They shook hands and he disappeared out the door with a wave, guitar case in hand.

Dee would be there during the busy part of the night. She knew in her gut it would be a great draw. *Oh, I need to advertise let everyone know about this Friday Night. Oh, and tell Lizzy too*. Uh-oh. Lizzy hated her spontaneous acts. "But she'll like this eye candy *and* his magic," Dee announced out loud.

Lizzy was due to relieve her and take over before the Tuesday pool league started up. Dee was still hearing the magical music echoing in her ears as she prepared the bar for Lizzy's arrival.

Lizzy and Dee started a league at Johnny's suggestion. It turned out to be something he could do to help out that didn't involve drinking. The league played every Tuesday night and packed the place. People came from three different towns, which was good. Buckets even had *other* towns talking, Dee noted with satisfaction.

***

An hour later the front door opened and in pranced Lizzy smiling, flipping her blonde ringlets back and forth like her ringlets were ready to work.

"Hi Dee, how was your day?" she asked.

"Really good. This guy—eye candy—came in and wants to play his magic here," Dee said.

"Magic?" Lizzy asked with a puzzled look on her face.

"I meant music. If you hear it, you would call it magic, too," Dee explained. "Oh yeah, he's playing on your shift Friday. Six to nine or later, if we're busy and he wants to stay."

Lizzy felt her temper rising. "You always just jump. No tip toeing, just jump," she scolded, shaking her finger at Dee. Of course, Dee's ideas hadn't hurt them any. Where would they be without Gracey? Or Buckets? She let out a breath and smiled.

"I'm sorry. That's cool. We did need to do some kind of entertainment on Friday. People are using gas to go out of town for entertainment, when they could just stay here in town. Good idea, Dee," Lizzy conceded.

"I felt like it was what we were supposed to do," Dee admitted.

"So far Dee, your hunches have been right on the money," Lizzy praised as she waited on a couple customers.

She noted with satisfaction how good she'd gotten at multi-tasking. She and Dee, both. They could clean counters and develop menus at the same time. She could pour a beer with the perfect head on it and talk up ideas with her partner. *How far I've come in so little time ....*

"Oh, by the way, I bought a computer today. To do the book keeping, flyers and whatever else they are good for," Lizzy reported as she checked the cooler boxes to make sure the bottled beer stock was sufficient.

"Sounds like I'm rubbing off on you. You know, the jumping part." Dee chuckled, then gave her evil laugh.

Lizzy smirked. "I felt like I was supposed to do it," she mimicked.

Dee tore the paper wrapper off a package of cocktail napkins. "Hey, that was perfect timing. We need flyers done for Friday's entertainment."

"Sure thing, boss. I'll get her done in the morning," Lizzy drawled as she salted a bucket and loaded it with ice.

The shift was busy, but images of the flyer kept popping into Lizzy's head. The idea of the flyer excited her. As soon as the lights were off and Buckets' doors were locked, Lizzy headed home to start work on her first artistic creation.

She stayed up for hours but she wasn't working until the night shift tomorrow, so she kept at it. She knew exactly how she wanted to do the flyer.

Learning how to operate the computer took the most time. Once she had the program running, she had to figure out how it worked.

After working it all out, she fought sleep determined to have the flyers for Dee to take to Buckets by morning. The Flyer read: *Buckets presents live entertainment this Friday night by aspiring new acoustic artist. All original masterpieces 6-9PM.* In the upper left-hand corner in a diagonally slanted box it read, *The Magic of Music.*

She sat back and cocked her head back and forth to see if it appeared eye catching. "It needs more color. Maybe black shadowing. Let's see. Oh, that's how you do it," she muttered as she clicked on different tabs in the program's menu box.

"Oh goodness. That made a big difference," she continued to babble.

As the printer spit out the colorful flyers, she picked one up to see the finished product. She absolutely loved her masterpiece. *How can I have so much feeling for a piece of paper?*

She took the first one she printed to keep in her journal. She could always look back at it in the future when she'd mastered the program and the art of flyer making. It would be fun to see how her skills had grown.

Next challenge is the menu. Since their clientele were a lot of the same people, Lizzy was going to change the menu up a little bit, sort of like stirring the pot when soup's been sitting too long.

"I really need to get some sleep. I'm brainstorming way too much," she convinced herself. She reluctantly shut down the computer and then got ready for bed. She walked to her room, slid on her nightie and wished Wrangler Man a good night, then turned out the light.

***

He was soft spoken. Golden-brown eyes ... but his face was fuzzy ... so fuzzy. She couldn't make out who or what he looked like but he was there. She could smell him, a fresh manly essence. She could feel him, a gentle being, more than flesh and bones. He felt as gentle as his voice. His presence stirred feelings deep inside her, to her core and she shivered with delight. His voice, like strong, yet tender arms, wrapped around her like a cocoon. The warmth, the smell, the feeling ... let this be real ...

"Lizzy, Wake up! I need to get those flyers to take to work," Dee yelled from the kitchen.

Lizzy startled awake, disappointed that her lover was only a dream. She stumbled out of the bed and headed for the coffee pot.

Dee stood in the kitchen, her eyes bright and alert. Lizzy was tempted to swat at her. *How can anyone be so awake at this time of the morning?* She poured her coffee, wrapped her hands around the warm mug and took a sip with her eyes closed. *Hmmm. Better.* Dee was forgiven her alertness.

"The flyers are on the coffee table. Go look. Tell me what you think. I didn't have a name to work with, though," Lizzy added.

Dee walked in the living room, picked up the flyers and studied them with a critical eye.

"I am captivated. Joe. His name is Joe," Dee announced.

"Joe? Whose name is Joe?" Lizzy asked still mostly asleep. *Had Dee had a guest stay the night? She was captivated?*

"The Music Man, silly. The guy this flyer is about. His name is Joe, you just said... never mind. The flyers are awesome. I think it's better not to reveal his name, an air of mystery. I like it—keep 'em guessing."

Dee picked up the stack of flyers and walked towards the front door then stopped and turned. "See you at six?"

"No, I'm calling in sick," Lizzy whined. "Just kidding. Six o'clock. I'll be there."

Dee waved and walked out the door. Lizzy strolled back to her room and flopped on her bed with plans to return to her dream.

***

Dee opened Buckets that morning. She put the flyers out along the bar top and taped one up in each bathroom. She went to the newly opened businesses in the strip mall and left one in each store.

She called the local paper and just made the deadline to have it printed in tomorrow's paper. Everything was working out better than she'd planned. Falling right into place.

The first of the customers came in and noticed the flyers. Dee had Lizzy's famous goulash simmering on the stove to get the aroma in the air. The chatter of customers floated in and out of her ears. Everyone mentioned Friday's entertainment. It sounded more exciting

163

than the circus coming to town. The unnamed performer was surely the kicker.

Even the patrons that weren't Friday night people wanted to come in, just to see the mysterious musician. Dee was excited about her instinct. She was glad she hadn't second-guessed herself. When Lizzy came in tonight for her shift, Dee was going to let her hear the buzz for herself. She didn't want to influence Lizzy's opinion. In two more days, Joe would be showing his magical music.

As the day went on, the talk about Friday Night lingered all around. Dee had a giddy feeling just bursting to get out. She imagined the magic of music floating in and out of every bar stool, hypnotizing the customers.

Dee was so lost in her daydream that she never noticed Lizzy walk in to go to work. She knew something significant was about to happen, but she couldn't put her finger on it.

***

"Hey, how did it go today?" Lizzy asked, tucking her purse in the kitchen cabinet near the back door.

"Good! The flyers were a hit," Dee said evenly. "Ready to work?"

"Let me eat something first. I am starving. We had nothing to eat at the house." She smiled at Dee. "The goulash smells yummy," Lizzy mentioned as she headed to the stove.

Lizzy knew Dee pretty well. She could tell Dee was dying inside to talk about Friday with her. Lizzy dished up some goulash into a bowl and waited.

"I think Friday is going to go over very well," Dee remarked as she leaned against the stainless-steel sink.

"Really? I think so too. I'm hooked on that flyer. I even kept one for my journal. I can't wait to make another. I was thinking about it all day," Lizzy replied.

Just as Lizzy walked out of the kitchen to take her place behind the bar, the front door opened. In walked Joe the Magical Music Man.

Their eyes met. Joe smiled. His teeth were white, though not perfectly straight. One front tooth slightly over lapped the other. Lizzy almost inhaled her goulash. *Oh, my Lord ...*

She coughed a few times to clear her throat as he walked closer to her. She heard Dee from somewhere behind her.

"Hi, Joe! Check out the flyers we had made up."

Lizzy turned, her mouth all but hanging open; this was the Magical Music Man.

She set her bowl on the bar, wiped her mouth, and stuck out her right hand. "I'm Lizzy," she squeaked. "I made the flyers, I'm working Friday Night." Somehow, she'd gotten that run-on sentence out of her mouth without any hesitation or breath. *Man, do I sound like a dumb blonde or what?* She stifled a groan.

He turned to her and smiled his brilliant smile. "Very, nice to meet you. Lizzy, is it?" He shook her hand. He turned back toward Dee who had moved out from Lizzy's shadow.

"So, it's still a go?" Joe inquired to Dee.

"Yup! Buckets is very excited to have your magic. I mean music, here."

Lizzy sat down and finished her goulash, feeling detached from their conversation. She sensed something in Dee that wasn't familiar … was she interested in the new eye candy, maybe? *Oh, boy ... that could be a problem.* Lizzy gobbled a couple more bites when Joe turned to her again.

"I'll see you Friday. Very, very, nice to meet you." He smiled that smile that seemed to make her heart stop mid-beat.

Lizzy perked up again, coughed after forcing a swallow of food, and tried not to show her excitement.

She lowered her voice an octave. "Yes, Friday." She dared not take another bite and fought the urge to stare at him like a love-sick thirteen-year-old.

"Nice to meet you too, Joe. Right?" Lizzy replied not letting on that she would never forget that name. His *name* was music to her ears.

After he walked out the door, Dee turned to Lizzy. "Friday is going to go over *very* well, don't you think?"

Lizzy battled her feelings, fought not to show how affected by Joe she'd been. Especially if Dee was interested. She took another bite of her goulash so her full mouth would filter her excitement. "Yeah, *eye candy* is right! Hope his music is as good as he looks."

Lizzy stared into her bowl, so Dee couldn't see how attracted she'd been to Joe. The thought of going another day without seeing him upset her already. The phone rang and Dee answered.

"Buckets, may I help you?" She listened, and then her face went white. "Oh my god, where is she? We will be there as soon as possible," she blurted. She hung up, then dialed another number.

"Gracey can you work tonight? Lizzy and I need to get to the hospital. I'll explain later."

Oh God, no, Lizzy thought. *Not another accident. Who could it be this time?*

Dee got off the phone and turned to Lizzy. "Ripley's in labor and wants us there, now. We have to wait tell Gracey comes in, though. She said she'd be here in fifteen minutes."

Lizzy's fear transformed into a beautiful feeling of bliss. "We're going to be aunts, you know," Lizzy said with a grin that must have gone from one ear to the other.

"Yes, we are," said Dee. "We're going to be the best aunts, ever!"

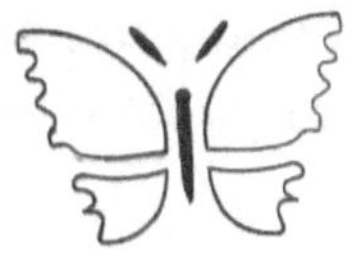

CHAPTER TWENTY-FOUR

Lovely Lindsey

The secret of happiness is to count your blessings while others are adding up their troubles. - William Penn

As Dee and Lizzy arrived at the hospital, Walter came out the door, looking as though he'd stuck his finger in a light socket.

"They just got her to the room," he said in a rush, his voice breathless. "The doctor is on his way. I forgot to bring her overnight bag. I'll be back. Please, go stay with her," he said as he dashed out the door.

As they walked through the doors, a nurse met them.

"Are you here for Ripley Smith?" the nurse asked.

"Yes," Dee replied. "Where is she?"

"In room 106, on the left. She's been asking for the two of you," the nurse added.

"Thanks!" Dee said, grabbing Lizzy by the arm.

They all but ran down the hall towards Ripley's room.

Lizzy wasn't feeling very well. Her goulash was churning in her stomach like she'd been out on a drinking binge. She'd never seen a baby born and wasn't all that excited to see this one, even though she loved Ripley like a sister. She clutched Dee's arm and stopped her in her tracks. "I don't think I can handle watching this. I'm only here, to be here—for her."

Dee shrugged. "Look, I'm sure she doesn't want you to watch. She just wants our support. So, toughen up will ya?"

Lizzy took a deep breath and exhaled. She wasn't going to let Ripley see her fear. Dee gave her a thumbs-up and they entered the room.

In what seemed like only a few minutes to Lizzy, Ripley started to scream like a banshee. She panted and puffed and almost broke the fingers of her best friends. Lizzy and Dee each had one of Ripley's hands in theirs and they did their best to reassure her that everything was fine. The nurse came in and out, completely at ease with Ripley's distress.

"Is everything, okay?" Lizzy asked the third or fourth time the nurse came in. She and Dee were helping Ripley to time her breathing and pushing just as instructed by the nurses a half an hour earlier.

"It is," the nurse replied. "We're going to check and see what's going on since she seems to be ready to have this baby. The doctor is scrubbing right now." With a reassuring smile, the nurse vanished.

By the time poor Walter returned to Ripley's room, a baby girl had already made her entrance and Lizzy thought she'd never seen anything so wonderful in her whole life. The butterfly hatching from the cocoon … the Phoenix rising from the ashes … her new niece making a perfectly normal entrance into the world from her warm, wet cocoon inside Ripley's body. She had only gasped when the nurse had cut the umbilical cord, though it hadn't seemed to hurt the baby at all! She'd laid on her momma's breast and hadn't uttered a peep.

"Wow, that was amazing," Lizzy said from the chair where she'd collapsed. She couldn't take her eyes off the beautiful pink girl wrapped tightly in a blue and pink blanket.

Ripley rested, her smile wide, but tired. "She really is beautiful, isn't she?"

"What are you going to name her?" Dee asked Walter as he stared into the baby's unfocused eyes.

"I like Lindsey. What do you think Ripley?" Walter turned to Ripley for an answer.

"Let me see her face again?" Ripley said in a tired, raspy voice.

He carried is new daughter to Ripley and put her in Ripley's arms. Ripley stared for a minute, a smile slowly appeared. "She has your eyes," she whispered. A tear trickled down her cheek. Then she cleared her throat. "Yeah, she looks like a Lindsey. Lindsey it is."

Ripley held Lindsey close and only gave her up when the nurse needed to check her vital signs and complete her measurements to make sure Lindsey was healthy.

Lizzy and Dee watched as Walter stood by the table, mesmerized by every move Lindsey made. They could see him falling more and more in love with the perfect baby girl that Ripley and he had created.

Lizzy was thankful for Ripley's going into labor when she did. It had kept her mind off of the Magical Music Man. For a few moments any way. He still tortured her mind. What an unbelievable attraction she had to the man. .

Later in the evening, the nurse came in. "Sorry to ruin the celebration, but mother and baby need rest," she said, busying herself with fixing Ripley's pillow.

"Yes, how right you are. We're going and you get some sleep," Dee said. Lizzy stood behind Dee, nodding her head in agreement. She was exhausted herself. They walked out smiling, bathed in the feeling of unconditional love.

Once Dee and Lizzy got to the house they slipped on their...well, Dee wore a cotton pajama and Lizzy loved her silky nighties.

As soon as their heads hit their pillows they were fast asleep, awaiting a new day.

***

She is so close she can smell the musky-sweet scent of his chest hair. He trembles and she wonders if he's as nervous—as excited—as she. She can hear his heartbeat—or is it hers? So close yet not touching. Static energy crackles between their bodies. Contact would be unbearable; the arousal is so pure, so intense she can almost feel what he's thinking to do to her. She knows this is right. The snap and crackle of light around them is all she can see. She knows her fate is with this man.

Lizzy woke up in a sweat from another hormone-driven dream that made absolutely no sense to her. Although she woke, her heart still pounded, her body soaked with perspiration. She secretly enjoyed the excitement her dream had made her feel and she smiled lazily as she stretched.

"Lizzy! Get up! We need another stew for the kitchen today. Gracey called, said she sold the last goulash last night," Dee yelled from the kitchen.

"Okay, how about a chicken and dumplings for today's special?" Lizzy yelled back as she slid her legs off the bed.

She put her robe on. She stumbled out of her room and into the kitchen. The coffee was already brewing.

Dee laughed. "Don't look so surprised. I'm still trying to perfect the coffee for Mr. Price-is-Right. I just can't seem to make it like you do, for him. What do you do different?" Dee asked.

"I showed you exactly what I do. You make great coffee, especially for someone who doesn't even drink it. It's probably as you always say, it's *my* magic," Lizzy said with a sleepy giggle.

"I know what I say," Dee said with a frown. "Can I borrow that magic for his coffee? That's it—just *his*. He's so grumpy without your coffee," she mumbled as she brushed her teeth.

"I thought, I worked today?" Lizzy called to Dee who had returned to the bathroom.

"You do. I'm going to see Ripley and Lindsey this morning," Dee bragged as she walked back into the kitchen.

"Wow, your hair looks great," Lizzy admired. "What did you do to it?"

"Thanks. I colored it this morning. It's called "Magician"—you really like it?"

"Yes, it looks really nice. Whatever you did," Lizzy complimented as she sat at the kitchen table.

"See you later. Ah–how's the coffee?" Dee asked as she opened the front door.

"Perfect. I don't know why he complains about it," Lizzy answered. "Nothing is wrong with your coffee, at all."

"It's just not yours," Dee explained. She yelled as the door shut. "Bye!"

Lizzy got herself another cup of coffee and wandered into the garden for a few minutes. What was up with Dee's new hair color? And why did she worry so about Mr.-Price-is-Right's coffee?

Was Dee going through some sort of change?

***

Lizzy entered Buckets and turned all the lights on, added the small bills she'd gotten from the bank to the register. Then she went back out to the Jeep for the groceries. She slowly strolled into the kitchen. Her dream haunted her.

Lizzy prepared the chicken by cooking it real slow until the meat fell off the bone. As that cooked, she cut up vegetables and pulled out the frozen dumplings. Who was the man in her dreams? Would she know him when she met him?

She pulled the cooled chicken apart and put it with the broth into a large stock pot, tossed in the vegetables and her special seasonings. Last she added the dumplings.

Within an hour the chicken and dumplings simmered on the stove. Buckets smelled heavenly. Lizzy flipped the on the open sign and awaited the business.

Her first customer was Mr.-Price-is-Right. She got him his coffee, remembering what Dee had said that morning.

He thanked her with a reserved smile. "You know, that Dee makes pretty good coffee, too," he mentioned.

"Really? I'm sure she would love to hear that since she's not much of a coffee drinker." Lizzy giggled on the inside. *If Dee only knew.*

171

The flyers, lying along the bar, flapped in the breeze each time the door opened, reminding Lizzy of Joe the Magical Music Man. Almost as though the flyers were taunting her, begging to be held once more.

As the day went on, the talk of Friday night lingered about Buckets. Lizzy tried everything to get Joe off of her mind, but the excitement floated all around the bar, charging the air with an almost-electric charge. Lizzy was at the mercy of the conversations about the "mysterious musician" which bothered her.

The sun slowly faded and Lizzy prepared to go home and get Friday night off of her mind. All she wanted to do was to deal with it when it became time.

Truthfully, Lizzy hated the anticipation of anything. As a child she opened the presents under the tree, then rewrapped them before anyone knew. It helped her get through the holiday without going crazy.

She shook her head to dispel the memories of her childhood and last night's dream. *Well, this is one of those presents I can't open.* She hated how anxious she felt. Almost as if Friday could be something that could change her life, or Buckets' for that matter.

She finished restocking the beer coolers and took a look around to be sure that Dee would be ready to go. All was in order and she was more than ready to go home. She realized how little real rest she'd had in days.

Dee burst through the front door. "Hey, Liz. Lindsey is *so* beautiful. Are you going to go up to see them tonight?" she asked as she walked behind the bar.

"I was thinking about it, but I think I'll go tomorrow. I've got to get some sleep tonight. I haven't gotten much lately. I've been having crazy dreams–not bad–just crazy," Lizzy said. "Oh yeah. Mr.-Price-Is-Right told me today that you make pretty good coffee, too," Lizzy said fanning a coaster in front of her face.

"Really?" She thought on that a moment. "Maybe he does it to me ... so I don't stop trying to compete with your coffee. Smart man, he is," Dee said, wrinkling her nose.

"I'm glad he does it to you. You made me a great pot of coffee this morning, it tasted wonderful."

Lizzy kissed Dee on the cheek, dashed into the kitchen and returned with her purse and keys in hand. "I don't mean to run out so fast. I need to rest; tomorrow is going to be ridiculously busy from what I'm hearing."

Dee stood a little straighter and lifted her chin. "I knew it was the right move."

Lizzy answered with a tired smile. "Sure was. Another great instinct, partner!"

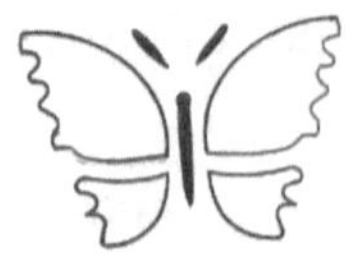

CHAPTER TWENTY-FIVE

Man Crazed

Stop asking for others opinion trust yourself! - Unknown

He is here... It's dark, so dark it feels forbidding. His smell, his voice, but she cannot see him. She feels the excitement of this unexplainable attraction, but still can't see. The tingling sensation, again, surrounds her body as though she's an exposed wire. Yet even unable to see him ... he is there. Pleasure washed over her body, all the way to the tips of her toes and fingers. The adrenaline pumps in her veins...he is here. The darkness hides the motion that drifts around her, the warmth of him radiates, brushing her bare breast. She perspires beads of salty sweat from the heat that he reflects above her body. She still cannot see him, but he is here.

Lizzy awakened to the sound of her annoying alarm clock. She slammed her hand down on the snooze button, hoping to return to the dream. Why can't she see what this being looks like? Growling, she pulled her pillow over her head.

"I can't take these crazy dreams anymore!" she screamed into the empty room.

"Lizzy, are you alright?" Dee asked from the kitchen.

She moaned and tossed off the covers. "Yes, another weird dream is all. I feel like I'm losing my mind. They feel so real." She shuffled into the kitchen. "You leaving already?"

"Yeah, I'm going to get going. I want to clean Buckets real good for tonight's big debut," Dee said as she walked out the front door.

"All right. I'll see you at six," Lizzy mumbled to herself knowing Dee couldn't hear her.

She was bothered by Dee's excitement about tonight. She worried because she strongly suspected that Dee might have an interest in the Magical Music Man, Joe. *Not good.* Lizzy had a powerful and unexplainable attraction to him, and since that was such a rare thing, she wondered fearfully that Joe might be meant to be her mate.

Well, she thought, *maybe he will be a total jerk and I won't like him. He might be like Jessie was, nice looking, but not too bright, which would make me less attracted. Only tonight will tell.*

She dragged herself back to the coffee pot. Dee had made her a pot.

"Got to love her, no matter what. Even if Dee and Joe get together," she announced to the cup of coffee.

As she sipped on her coffee at the kitchen table she thumbed through the sale papers. Lizzy decided to go get a new outfit, something sexy, for tonight's big debut.

"I'll just make him *wish* he had me, right?" Lizzy asked herself.

So, after visiting Ripley and Lindsey, and after her big shopping spree, she walked into the front door of the house.

She laid several sexy tops and two pair of Levi's on her bed. One pair for Dee and the other, for her. Lizzy's wore her jeans tight and always had, but not Dee. The silky tops flaunted spaghetti straps in a pretty flowered print. Lizzy lifted one of the tops, held it against the front of her and smiled.

"Sexy, but not smutty. It's me," Lizzy said smiling to the young woman in the mirror.

Shopping always made her feel refreshed about life. Lately she was comfortable with the way her life was going—happy even. But the anxious feeling she had been having was making her insane. Her peace was gone. Lizzy blamed the feelings on her hormones and the fact that she hadn't been in a man-woman relationship for over two years, now.

Nothing to worry about, right? Everything in its right time.

***

Lizzy strolled through the front door with her new outfit on. Her jeans were a little tighter than any of her others, but she thought they made her butt look great.

Joe was busy setting up his PA. Dee waited on some customers who were seated at tables. Lizzy sat at the bar. Dee skipped over to where Lizzy had sat.

"Do you mind if I have a beer before I start work? To calm my nerves a little," Lizzy asked Dee.

"Why would I mind?" Dee asked. She looked at Lizzy closely.

Lizzy let a short laugh escape. "I don't know, just making sure you didn't," she replied. *I just may not survive tonight ...*

"Is that a new outfit?" Dee asked, brushing the silky fabric with her index fingertip.

Lizzy grinned. "Yep, got you one too. In honor of your latest, greatest idea!"

"You did? I hope my jeans aren't that tight, though," Dee said.

"Oh, do you think they're *too* tight?" Lizzy asked nervously.

"No. Not for you, but me? Yeah. Those would kill me." Dee laughed.

"And what is that supposed to mean?" Lizzy asked.

Dee didn't hear her because Joe had come to the bar and she quickly made her way over to him. Lizzy couldn't tell what they were saying but could tell Dee was enjoying herself. *I can't believe I'm jealous of my best friend. This is too absurd.* She took a sip of her beer to swallow the painful thought.

Joe walked over to Lizzy and leaned on the bar next to her. His smile almost blinded her. "Lizzy, right? Are you ready for tonight?"

Lizzy swallowed down the beer that she'd sipped right before he walked over, and slightly choked on it. *Not again!*

After a cough or two, she put her hand over her heart and answered him. "Yes. Yes I am—ready." *I'd be better off not to talk to him if I'm going to be tongue-tied every time he asks me something.*

"Do you think it will get busy tonight?" he asked, leaning in closer to her as if they were discussing something secret only to them.

"Yes," Lizzy said and looked straight ahead. *Now I look like a snob.*

Joe straightened and backed away from her. "Well, I'd better finish getting set up so I'll be ready to start at six." He turned to walk away.

Quickly Lizzy turned in her stool. "I'm sorry. I wasn't trying to run you off. I was just afraid I might cough again. You seem to always catch me when I have something in my mouth," she babbled. *So much for keeping it short.*

He turned back to her and smiled. "You are too cute."

Lizzy smiled back and felt her insides turn to mush. *He thinks I'm cute! Wahoo!*

She finished up the last of her beer then asked Dee for another.

"You better go easy Lizz, it's going to be a long night," Dee cautioned.

"I'm fine. You look terrific, by the way. Why did you wear that dress today?" Lizzy asked Dee.

Dee had on a cute sun dress with tiny strawberries on it, which wasn't her usual style.

"I don't know. I felt like being girly today. It's funny, the regulars are all saying I look like strawberry short cake." Dee laughed as she looked down at her dress.

"That's funny, but not true. You look great!" Lizzy finished her beer and then got behind the bar to work.

Dee whispered to Lizzy. "Joe thinks we just work here. He doesn't know we're the owners."

"He doesn't?" Lizzy asked. *Wonder why? And I wonder why Dee didn't set him straight.*

"No. He keeps asking if the owner would be willing to have him back."

Once again they were interrupted when Joe walked back over to the bar. Dee worked her way past Lizzy to see what he wanted. She smiled and shook her head at him.

Lizzy rolled her eyes. *Why would he want strawberry short cake when he could have me....? Barbie. Good lord, am I buzzed?*

Lizzy realized the source of some of her stress. She had to tell Dee that she was attracted to Joe.

"Dee, I'm so nervous because ... Joe ... I ... I'm very attracted to him," she confessed. She could feel heat rushing into her face.

Dee looked horrified. "Oh, Lizzy. He has a girlfriend. I should have told you. I'm sorry,"

Lizzy didn't know whether to laugh or cry, but at least she knew that she wouldn't be hurting her best friend.

"Oh, he does? Well hell. That sucks. He's the first, the first I've been attracted to since Lee." She smiled, then took a deep breath. "Now, I guess, I'm not so nervous any more. Maybe now, I can talk to him without choking," Lizzy said.

Dee wrapped Lizzy in a hug and they had a good laugh. And that was the last break they got all evening. Customers old and new flowed through the door in a steady stream all night.

Lizzy's buzz wore off. Joe's voice was incredible, just as Dee had said. Lizzy noticed him glancing at her every so often, but she ignored it because he had a girlfriend. Sure, she was still unbelievably attracted, but she respected relationships.

He sang love songs he had written, and stared at her as he sang through the lyrics of love. She knew she'd never be able to pursue a man who wasn't free to love her completely and she reminded herself every few minutes that he was involved with someone. She was too busy with customers to dwell on Joe's longing gaze.

Nine o'clock came and went and Joe kept singing and customers kept coming in. As the night drew to an end, Buckets stayed packed. Dee and Lizzy shooed them out.

"Have a safe drive home," they said, gently pushing customers toward the door.

As Lizzy wiped down the bar and Dee restocked the coolers, Joe packed up his equipment. Dee went to the register to take out the money to pay him. Joe walked up to the bar where Lizzy was working.

"How did I do?" Joe asked, leaning in toward Lizzy.

"You did absolutely great ... great!" she answered. "Gee, I didn't choke that time," she said with a laugh.

He smiled his mega-watt smile and Lizzy smiled back.

"You have a very nice smile, Lizzy," he said.

"Thanks. I was just thinking the same thing about you," she replied.

"Well, it must be true. You know what they say about great minds thinking alike." Joe quoted. He turned to Dee. "Did you find out if your boss will have me back?"

Dee glanced at Lizzy. "Of course! Every Friday night if you can? We did our record tonight, in sales," Dee said.

He looked delighted. "Wow! That's great. Lizzy are you going to be working?"

"Yes, unless I get deathly ill or choke to death on something," she joked, a lot more relaxed than earlier.

"Thank you ladies, I will be back next week. Have to get home, so the girlfriend doesn't get angry with me." The Magical Music Man, Joe bowed. He picked up his guitar case and exited the building.

"I think that girl is a lucky girl. You know some woman, a very *good-looking* woman, went to give him her phone number. He told her he had a girlfriend. Now that's impressive," Lizzy added as she wiped down the tables.

"All I know is that, that man made us a small fortune, tonight. He's gold, Lizzy."

Lizzy looked at Dee and noticed the dark circles under her eyes. "You know Dee, you could have gone home and gotten some rest. You've worked eighteen hours today!"

"Gracey is going to work my shift tomorrow. I'll rest then. Besides I had to make sure you didn't choke and leave us without a bartender! I knew you were going to like him. I just knew it," Dee bragged.

Lizzy turned off all the lights, then joined Dee to go out the front door. They looked to the sky, at the moon. It was the biggest, fullest, shiniest moon Lizzy had ever seen.

"Wow, Lizzy," Dee said as they walked to the Jeep. "I knew tonight was going to mean something significant." She spun in a circle, wearing her strawberry dress in the silvery moonlight.

"Our record sales!" Lizzy cried and took one last peek at the moon before getting into the Jeep. Maybe she'd have her peace back.

CHAPTER TWENTY-SIX

Truckers and Buckets

"*The biggest adventure you can take is to live the life of your dreams.*"- Oprah Winfrey

She sees the male figure and knows it is Joe. There's a distance between them and a female figure in the back ground. Lizzy can't make out her face. Joe keeps looking back at the female figure but doesn't take his eyes off of Lizzy. She can smell him and feels the anticipation she's felt in the other dreams. Her heart races like mad, she feels remorseful; scared of causing pain to the unknown female. Sorrow fills her throat and she almost cries.

Lizzy woke Sunday morning and decided to forget about Joe and her hormonal reactions. When Lizzy made a decision she stuck to it.

She knew it wasn't going to be easy. Now, instead of looking forward to Friday nights, she dreaded them. It was going to be a battle with her hormones and her righteousness.

She slid on her house robe, made her way to the kitchen, and followed her normal routine, straight to the coffee pot. It wasn't made today. *Dee must have forgot or decided to give up on the "Lizzy coffee challenge."* Starting a pot, Lizzy made her way to Dee's room.

There Dee was, in bed fast asleep. That was unusual for Dee. She always woke up at dawn. Lizzy looked closer and saw another body in her bed.

"Oh, I am sorry. I didn't know you had company," Lizzy said as she backed her way out of the room.

She returned to the kitchen and thought about her dream again. Could that female figure have been Dee? Is that Joe in there? *Dee wouldn't do that to me. She knows I really like him...*

Dee stumbled into the kitchen rubbing her eyes. "Is there any coffee left? Leroy wants a cup," Dee said.

"Sure, there's plenty of coffee," Lizzy announced relieved to find that Leroy was the body in Dee's bed.

Leroy and Dee had been getting close during the past couple months. Leroy was a trucker and showed up at crazy hours of the night. He stopped in when he came to town and needed a place to stay.

Leroy started out sleeping on the couch, like Johnny. Then he slowly upgraded to Dee's bed. Dee said that they enjoyed each other's company. Leroy wasn't a keeper. Leroy only came around every so often.

Lizzy sat at the table. She sipped on her steamy coffee trying to rationalize why she felt all of these crazy feelings. Not only about Joe, but about not trusting Dee, too.

Lizzy loved Dee and knew she'd never hurt her. Why was she feeling such distrust with her friend? The only conclusion she could reach was that her hormones were out of control. She got out the magical herb book to see what might help. She found a tea recipe. It read:

Tea Preparation: Red clover makes an excellent tea, especially sweetened with clover honey. You can also take red clover as an extract. Red clover is often combined with black cohosh in herbal formulas for hormone imbalance.

Then she found another in the book: Fairytale Tea:
A delicious drink for children and adults. A delightful and inspiring infusion, a blend of flowers & magic; perfect for bedtime stories; hormone balance.

Red clover flowers, lavender flowers, Chamomile flowers, Lemon Balm, black cohosh, spearmint, thyme, lemon peel, and a dab of clover honey.

Lizzy studied the different tea recipes and decided the Fairy Tale tea was the one for her. She added just a few extra Lizzy herbs such as sage and some orange zest to give it more citrus flavor. She prepared the tea on the stove. Luckily they had every herb in the garden except the black cohosh. Lizzy just eliminated that. The smell filled the air.

Dee and Leroy were talking in the living room. She appeared in the kitchen.

"Wow, what's that smell? It's dreamy," Dee said.

"Homemade herbal tea," Lizzy said. "It's called Lizzy's Fairy Tale tea."

Dee hated coffee and loved herbal tea. She was always trying the store-bought varieties. Lizzy was pleased. Now Dee could have it fresh from the garden. She poured Dee a cup and then one for herself. They sipped it together and smiled at the delicate flavor.

"Very nice Lizzy. This is much better than the ones I get from the store," Dee said, savoring the flavor.

"This one is good to balance the hormones, too," Lizzy whispered to Dee so Leroy couldn't hear her secret.

"Maybe we should serve this at Buckets—in buckets," Dee replied softly.

"Well, I've got to get to work. Buckets has to open in an hour." She was enjoying her time at home in the kitchen. "Are you and Leroy gonna come up later?" Lizzy asked as she threw her purse over her shoulder.

"Yeah, probably after a while. He wants to go east to take a walk on the beach, since it's so nice out," Dee said.

"I'm jealous," Lizzy disclosed.

"Call Gracey and come with us," Dee offered.

"No. You two spend time together while he's here. Now, *next* weekend, I want to go," Lizzy demanded as she fumbled in her purse looking for the Jeep keys.

"Found them. See you in a while," Lizzy said shaking the keys like a white surrender flag. She walked out into the sunshine to open Buckets.

***

For the next few days Lizzy felt calmer and more at peace. She sipped her special tea daily, deciding it definitely was magical tea. *Well, that or the fact the full moon is almost over.* She took on most the day shifts for the week so Dee could spend time with Leroy while he was in town.

One particular day, a finish-carpenter that was working in the unit next door, came for lunch. Lizzy had made a pot of chili with fresh chili peppers from the garden and homemade beer crackers.

"I'll have your special with a beer bucket, please," he ordered.

"Sure. Are you ok?" Lizzy asked, noticing he looked quite grim.

"I'm fine," he said. He looked her in the eye and she could sense pain. "Just, well, I went to work to keep my mind off of today's date. It's the anniversary of my dad's death," he explained.

"I'm sorry. I'm sure your father knows you miss him," Lizzy replied, not knowing what to say.

"That's just it. There are so many things I would love to have told him before he died. I never got to," the fellow confessed.

Lizzy still not knowing what to say, nodded and excused herself to go to the kitchen for his food. She returned with a steaming bowl of chili and the homemade crackers. She set it in front of him.

"Maybe you could write him a letter and take it to his grave. I know he'll get it and you'll feel better," Lizzy suggested. "It would give you something positive to focus on, on the anniversary of his death."

As he took a bite of the chili he replied, "That's a great idea. When I finish up here, that's what I'll do," he announced as he gobbled down the chili. "Wow, this chili is great. My dad's chili tasted very similar. Strange."

"Put that in your letter, too. Dear Dad, I miss your chili," Lizzy said with a small laugh.

"Thanks, really, I feel much better. Almost refreshed," he said.

Something occurred to Lizzy as she talked with the carpenter and she decided she would do the same. She loved to write and never wanted to feel there was something she regretted not telling her parents. She wrote them both individual letters of her deepest feelings and would give it to them to take to their grave.

She'd often reminded Dee, "If anything ever happens to me, look through my Bible. There are letters to all the people that I cherish."

Manny and Milly walked in about that time. St Patty's Day was only a month away.

"Here honey, this is the recipe I had told you about," Milly said, handing a recipe card to Lizzy.

"Thanks," Lizzy said, looking at the card.

"I'm not going to be able to make it for Manny this year and it is his favorite," Milly said and gave Manny a wink. He squeezed her slender shoulder and kissed her hair.

"Would you care for a cold beer, Manny? And a white zinfandel for you, Milly? "

"Absolutely," Manny answered with a smile. He helped Milly get settled on the stool.

"As for the corned beef and cabbage, I will be honored to cook your recipe."

Lizzy served them, still smiling at the recipe card. Lizzy swore she could hear the recipe card calling out, *make me please.*

A homeless guy walked in and asked for a glass of ice water. Lizzy had seen him in the area for weeks. "Here," Lizzy said, handing him the glass of water. "Are you hungry?" Before he could answer her, Lizzy pointed her finger at him. "I'll be back."

She returned with a steaming hot bowl of chili and gave it to the man. She grabbed a five dollar bill from her tip jar, wrote her name on it with a little note of encouragement and handed it to him.

"Hope that brightens your day," Lizzy said. She turned away at the tears in his eyes, and left him to eat his meal.

It made her feel good when she helped someone. When Lizzy returned from a trip to the kitchen she found him gone.

Dee and Leroy came through the doors just before three o'clock. They were both still wearing bathing suits from their trip to the beach.

"Perfect timing. I'll be able to have a beer with you two, as soon a Gracey comes in," Lizzy said as she fixed a bucket of beer with a scoop of ice.

Milly and Manny were getting ready to leave. They finished the last sip of their drinks. "See you ladies tomorrow," Manny said as he pulled his wife's chair out for her to stand.

"Bye, Milly. Bye, Manny," Lizzy said.

"Bye, guys," Dee added.

Manny held his wife's hand and walked out the door. Lizzy watched admiringly.

"How has she been doing? Did they say?" Dee asked in an almost whisper.

"Good, I guess. Why?" Lizzy questioned.

Dee looked at the closed door. "Manny told me one day, when Milly had gone to the bathroom, that she was having some health problems. He didn't go into detail. It didn't sound good. His eyes got all teared-up. He tried to dry them before Milly would notice."

"They never said a word to me. She was determined to give me the corned beef and cabbage recipe. She said it was Manny's favorite. Also said she wouldn't get a chance to make it this year, which makes a little more sense if she's been sick," Lizzy concluded.

Gracey entered the door and bounced her way around to the bar.

"Guess what?" She asked the trio.

Dee and Lizzy both asked, "What?" at the same time. Lizzy felt her heart drop. *Please don't let us lose Gracey!*

"I met someone. A nice someone and he asked me out. At the grocery store—he manages it," Gracey said proudly.

"Harry?" Dee and Lizzy said in unison.

"Yeah, you know him?" Gracey asked.

"We know everyone, or at least all the locals. He's as local as they come," Dee continued.

"Is he a nice guy?" Gracey asked.

"Too nice. You're going to break his heart," Dee snickered.

"I really like him. I can't see me breaking his heart. Maybe his back," Gracey bellowed. "Just kidding."

Lizzy and Dee laughed until they cried while Leroy sat and watched their enjoyment with a slight smile on his face.

Gracey took over Buckets and bounced the whole night. Lizzy had a couple of beers with Dee and Leroy. She enjoyed their many conversations that chain-reacted one to the next.

Lizzy decided to go home to get some sleep. She hadn't had any weird dreams lately and she gave the tea credit for that. But Friday night was coming and she'd better be well rested.

Come to think of it, she'd better make a pitcher of tea to bring to Buckets, too!

CHAPTER TWENTY-SEVEN

Together at Last

"Dream your dream; and realize that you are more than just a dreamer, you are the point of origin for its reality."- Steve

Maraboloi

Weeks passed and Lizzy became more comfortable with her over-active hormones. The tea helped and she was mindful of it. And, plans for their St. Patrick's Day celebration had begun.

Friday nights and spending time with Joe, stabilized for Lizzy. They became close friends. Joe having a girlfriend made things easier. The friendship helped make matters a lot easier, too.

Mentally, she and Joe had a connection. Joe even mentioned that he felt like he'd known her his whole life. Lizzy relied on that feeling of familiarity to confirm she was where she needed to be, so Lizzy believed Joe had appeared in her life for a reason. If friendship was the reason, so be it.

March 15th found Lizzy cooking Milly's corned beef and cabbage recipe at Buckets for their St. Patty's Day bash. That made Lizzy wonder about Manny and Milly. She hadn't seen them in about a week, which wasn't like them. The fragrance of the corned beef and cabbage hovered through the air. She'd just put the soda bread in bowls to proof when Dee burst through the kitchen door.

"Milly passed away," she blurted out with tears running down her cheeks.

"What? When? How?" Lizzy asked. She fought back her tears. "That's why they haven't been in," Lizzy whispered.

"Cancer. She had cancer." Dee took a moment to blow her nose "Manny said she hadn't been feeling well. He took her to the hospital. The cancer was so bad there was nothing they could do. She died in her sleep," Dee finished. Her red-rimmed eyes still held tears.

"She gave me this recipe. It was hers. You know, I always add something different to make it my own, but I didn't this time. She had told me she wouldn't be able to make it this year. Do you think she knew?" Lizzy whimpered in a tear-filled voice.

"It's possible." Dee sniffled, blowing her nose again.

"When is the service?"

"Tomorrow morning. Manny wants to bring the family back here after the service," Dee said. "Is that going to be okay?"

"Well, I now know why I was supposed to make her recipe," Lizzy said as she grabbed a paper towel to dry her tears.

***

Dee and Lizzy awoke the next morning to prepare Buckets for Manny's family and still had enough time to make it to the service which was beautiful. Dee caught a glimpse of a hummingbird hovering above Milly's family as the pastor said a prayer on Milly's behalf. Dee pointed it out to Lizzy.

"We're going to have a hummingbird visiting the garden soon," Lizzy whispered. She thought back to one of their many discussions after the visit to Madam Lafage.

A hummingbird symbolizes many things. Because it is so fast, the hummingbird is known as a messenger bird and is capable of stopping time. It symbolizes love, joy, and beauty. The hummingbird can fly backwards, symbolizing to us that we can look back on our past. This bird also advises us that we must not dwell on our past; we need to move forward. The hummingbird hovers over flowers while drinking nectar, teaches us that we should savor each moment, and appreciate the things we love.

A hummingbird's spiritual significance has a lot of importance. The hummingbird is a symbol of resurrection because on cold nights it almost appears dead, but comes back to life again at sunrise when the sun warms the earth.

Hummingbirds enlighten the heart of all. When we get hurt, that causes us to close our heart, until it gets a chance to heal, then our hearts are free to love again. When the Hummingbird appears in our lives, our life becomes a wonderland of delights in flowers, aromas and tastes. We have learned to laugh and enjoy creation, and can appreciate the magic of the present moment, and the magic of being alive.

***

Lizzy and Dee returned to Buckets to prepare for Manny's family to arrive. Gracey had gotten there early to help. Lizzy went straight to the kitchen to check on Milly's corned beef and cabbage which sat warming in the oven. Dee set up the tables with beautiful lace table cloths. Everything looked perfect.

The family started to arrive. Gracey took over getting beverages out to everyone. Then Manny arrived with his children and their children. He walked over to Dee and Lizzy.

"Thank you for doing all of this. Milly loved this place and she loved you girls. Thank you, so much," he said.

"You are very welcome," Lizzy said. "We loved her, too."

"Manny we are always here for you," Dee added after swallowing back her tears.

"Sit, we'll get you your drink and some food," Lizzy said. Dee pulled a chair from the table for him.

Lizzy and Dee served up the plates of Milly's corn beef and cabbage, and then made sure everyone's drinks were full. Lizzy watched the faces of everyone as they spent time saying goodbye to Milly. Manny took a bite and smiled as he enjoyed his wife's recipe. In that moment Dee and Lizzy knew Manny appreciated spending time with Milly.

The people gradually left Buckets. Each and every person stopped by to rave to Dee and Lizzy about the corned beef and cabbage.

190

"I can't take the credit. Milly gave me her recipe and I just followed it," Lizzy told everyone. "It was my honor to do this for her."

***

There was plenty of corned beef and cabbage for the Buckets St. Patty's Day bash. Joe was coming in to play, too.

Joe told them he'd been listening to some traditional Irish music and had even written a few songs of his own to play for the evening.

He walked through the front door as Dee and Lizzy were cleaning up the tables. Gracey worked behind the bar talking to the few people that were still lingering from the funeral reception.

"Hey guys, I want to show you something," Joe said excitedly as he walked towards them.

"What-cha got?" Dee asked and Lizzy looked up.

"It's outside. Come on," Joe said as he grabbed their arms and pulled them out the front door.

There was his beat-up 1978 Trans Am looking as though it had been transformed into a brand new car on one of those hot rod shows. The candy apple red paint was so glossy, the clouds in the sky were reflected in the hood which now sported shiny chrome hood latches, too.

"This is the same car?" Lizzy asked, her eyes wide with amazement.

Lizzy always loved hot rods. Lee was the one that had turned her on to hot rods. Hot rods always made Lizzy feel sexy—unexplainable sexy that she never revealed to a soul.

"Yeah. I've been working on it since… not long after I started working here," Joe confided.

"Deanna, well, the girlfriend, says it's stupid to spend the money on fixing it up, but this thing is a classic. They will never make another like this." Joe glided his hand up and down the shiny red hood. "All that I have left to fix up is the interior," he added.

Lizzy watched him telling Dee about the work he'd done. In the time they'd known him, he never mentioned his girlfriend by her

191

name, Deanna. It was always "my girlfriend" or "the girlfriend" which seemed odd to Dee and Lizzy. They'd wondered about it more than once, but never felt it was their place to pry.

"Is Deanna going to come in tonight?" Dee asked.

He shook his head. "I doubt it. She's not much of a people person," Joe said still looking at the hard labor he'd put into his car.

Lizzy gave him a big smile. "I think you did an awesome job, Joe. It looks happy and ready to take you to places unimaginable." He stared at her. Almost through her. Straight to her soul. The burning of his golden-brown eyes engraved something into her heart.

Her breath caught in her chest. "I have to go help Gracey," Lizzy babbled nervously and turned to go back inside.

From inside Buckets, Lizzy watched Joe and Dee talking. It seemed to be a serious conversation. Dee returned inside. Joe started removing his equipment from his classic car.

Dee was almost dancing above the floor tiles. "They are having problems," Dee said in a sing-song voice. She nudged Lizzy with her elbow, and wriggled her eyebrows like Groucho Marx.

"We're only friends. I can't imagine losing my friendship with him because of over-active hormones. Besides, problems can be fixed," Lizzy announced. *Oh my lord, I shouldn't be wishing for what I'm wishing for!*

"Deanna doesn't want to fix things, not him. Seems to me Joe has done everything in his power to fix their relationship. Now that he understands he can't, Joe has turned to his car." Dee looked like a madwoman with that grin on her face.

"I know. I love that car. It's *soooo* sexy," Lizzy cooed, batting her dreamy eyes.

"It can also take him to unimaginable places, just like you said, Lizzy," Dee hinted, the manic grin now more of a smirk.

"Leave me be," Lizzy hissed. *Oh my, can I dare even hope?* She took cleansing breath. *No, if he still loves her, it won't work.*

"Denial—that's what you're going through. Denial." Dee blurted.

"Ok, drop it!" Lizzy snarled and stomped away from Dee to get to work.

Lizzy was snippy with the customers, Dee and Gracey that night. Not even Joe escaped her wrath. She couldn't seem to get over the possibilities being so close, yet so far from her grasp.

"You need to go drink some of your tea, Lizzy," Dee said to her.

"Yeah, maybe I do," Lizzy snapped sarcastically.

"She is a firecracker tonight," Dee whispered to Gracey.

When the night came to an end, Lizzy carefully avoided conversation with Joe. Dee paid him and helped him load his stuff. Lizzy once again watched through the window as Dee and Joe talked about his problems. Lizzy hated that she didn't have the courage to be his friend when he really need one. She just couldn't do it.

***

Friday nights came and went and summer came to a close. One Friday night Joe seemed extremely distracted.

Lizzy could tell he wasn't himself. He glanced at her in the midst of a song of lost love, as though trying to tell her something with his eyes. She did her best to ignore the pull.

Buckets stayed extremely busy, which happened when the moon was full. Dee came in the front door after going home a couple hours to get some rest. She got behind the bar after a few minutes of greeting all of the customers.

"Hey, thought I'd come help for an hour or two. I've got a busy day tomorrow so I need to get some rest tonight. A group of golfers are coming in tomorrow after their outing," Dee told Lizzy.

Oh, no. I'll have to be alone with Joe? Dee usually helped close up, but that wasn't going to be the case tonight.

"Did you see the full moon? It is amazing. Like a golden ball in the sky," Dee said as she wiped down an area of the bar where a beer had spilled.

"Really? I want to check it out," Lizzy said.

Lizzy walked from behind the bar to the front door.

Lizzy stood on the sidewalk looking up at the golden moon. She stared, mesmerized by its golden color. Joe's current love song fit the moment. That familiar feeling hit her hard.

At that moment, the moon beamed a force of energy down onto Lizzy. It hit her straight in the chest and took her breath away. She turned to go back into Buckets.

As she walked through the door, the music stopped and all eyes turned to focus on her, Joe's especially. She had no idea what they were all staring at, but she wasn't going to ask, either. The room had sort of golden glow to it, as though the moonlight had followed her inside Buckets. Time stood still for a split second and love hung in the air like mist along the beach in early morning.

All Lizzy could see was Joe staring into her soul. This time she could feel his gaze penetrate her heart. Lizzy shook her head to get back to reality. She returned behind the bar.

Dee stared at her. "Hate to tell you, you're glowing," she said. "Moon was amazing, right?"

"Unbelievably amazing. I'm unable to find words to do it justice. It literally took my breath away," Lizzy answered dreamily.

The night came to an end. Dee had left after the bulk of the people had gone. Joe packed his guitar in the case and rolled up the cords to the PA system. The door opened and in walked the homeless guy again. He came in quite often. Lizzy wouldn't turn him away. About a week or two before, Lizzy had found out his name and made sure to say it to let him know that he was still a person.

"Art, do you want a glass of water?" Lizzy asked.

"Please. I hate bothering you at this hour. Just don't feel real well. I think I may be dehydrated," Arthur said.

"Have you eaten anything today?" Lizzy asked.

"I had a sandwich from the gas station an hour ago," he replied.

"Do you want anything?" Lizzy asked again.

"No, just the water, please." She gave him the water and he went on his way.

Joe walked to the bar, Lizzy assumed, to get paid.

"Lizzy, can I talk to you?" he asked.

"Sure, what's up?" Lizzy asked around the lump in her throat. *Oh, not now, please ....*

"Deanna and I broke up. Well, she packed up and left. Went back home, where we're both from," Joe said.

"I'm so sorry, Joe."

"Don't be. It was the inevitable. She hated it here. I, on the other hand, love it here. I even think I have my parents convinced to move down," Joe said. "That's not what I wanted to talk about, though. It's me and you ...." he started.

Lizzy's heart dropped through the floor straight to the core of the earth. *Oh please, oh please, oh please!*

"Will you take a ride with me to unimaginable places?" Joe asked Lizzy.

"In the candy apple red hot rod?" Lizzy teased, excited but trying to add humor to cover up her nervousness. "I love hot rods," Lizzy taunted. "Of course I will, Joe. Just let me finish up here and ..."

"Take your time." Joe said grinning.

They closed Buckets and left in the candy apple red hot rod.

"This car is going to be a keeper," Lizzy chimed to Joe as he shifted gears.

Joe smiled at her. He pulled down a dirt road to a lake that hid in the woods.

"I know this place. We use to come here as kids in the summer and swim. How did you know it was here?" Lizzy asked Joe, knowing he wasn't from the area.

"I was drawn here by some strange force. The same as I was drawn to Buckets, like I was supposed to find this place," he said as he turned the car engine off.

They looked out the window of the car. There stood an old oak tree with branches that hung down, almost like hands trying to touch the water. The golden magical moon's light cascaded onto the lake. The ripples of water made it look as though the reflection of the tree was dancing with celebration of what was to come.

When they got out of the car, Joe turned to Lizzy, put his hands to her waist, lifted her up, and sat her on the shiny hood of the car.

If he only knew how sexy I'm feeling at this very moment, Lizzy thought.

Joe leaned towards her. "You're still glowing, Lizzy. You look like an angel."

"Dee said something like that, too. What are you talking about?"

He gently moved her blonde ringlets away from her face. "You went out for a few minutes. When you came back, you were glowing. A faint, gentle golden sort of glow."

"I see," she said, but she didn't. She leaned away from him. Joe was everything she didn't want but everything she had to have. Their chemistry was so intense she ached from head to toe with it. He was *her* magic and she knew it.

Joe's gaze darted to Lizzy's lips, then back to her eyes. Almost as if asking, if he might kiss her. Lizzy grabbed his head in her hands and brought his mouth down to her lips, so she could have a taste of him. She felt as though a lightning bolt had run through her.

Joe ravished her mouth as if he'd tasted ecstasy, taunting her lips, so luscious, plump and sweet. Their hands fought uncontrollable motions, all over their bodies. Their hands were everywhere, as if in a desperate search of something they both needed to find or they'd perish.

Lizzy pulled his shirt off and rolled her nose up through his chest hair. She knew his smell well.

Fireworks exploded in every cell of their bodies. Joe tugged desperately to free her from her tight jeans, kissing every inch of exposed flesh along the way. Once freed of the denim, his hands found her breasts and gently explored them with mesmerizing delight.

Lizzy fought to get another taste of his lips, as hungry as a lioness consuming her prey. She paused the kiss a moment, their lips clung to one another, not wanting to let go.

Joe tossed their clothing to the grass and gently laid Lizzy down. They harmonized their bodies to the same rhythm, then melted together as one. Lizzy felt the fluttering of butterflies not only in her belly, but all over. From the tips of her fingers, to the tips of her toes, the tickling flutter was so intense it caused her to quiver uncontrollably. The pleasure of the fluttering so unbearable she couldn't imagine surviving any more ... Suddenly the fluttering broke the seal of her flesh and flew away into the darkness as the moon glowed over top of their bare bodies.

Joe gathered her in his arms and she looked at their bodies entwined, shining almost as brightly as the gloss of the car.

"Lizzy, I want you to know, you aren't a rebound girl. I have never felt anything as powerful as I felt tonight. From the first time I saw you ..." Joe started to explain.

Lizzy giggled. "You mean the day you made me choke on my goulash?"

"Yes, I was so intrigued by you. So powerful, it terrified me," Joe said staring into her eyes.

"I am scared too, Joe," Lizzy confessed as she turned onto her side. "I'm scared to lose you, to love you, to leave you, most of all to be hurt by you. I didn't want to jeopardize our friendship and I still don't," Lizzy vowed.

"We will make a pact tonight. Under this full moon, we'll be terrified together and conquer the world one day at a time, deal?" Joe declared.

"Deal," Lizzy agreed. They sealed the bargain with renewed exploration that disturbed the butterflies once again.

CHAPTER TWENTY-EIGHT

Mysterious Ways

Be still before the Lord and wait patiently for him – Psalm 37:7

The smile of fall approached and with it, the promise of the winter holidays. Every morning when Lizzy opened Buckets, Art would be out front waiting to have his glass of ice water and help her set up for opening.

Dee and Lizzy both offered him the special of the day in exchange for his help. Lizzy would sometimes get money out of her tip jar and give it to him.

Lizzy always asked, "Do you still have the five-dollar bill I gave you? You know the autographed one?"

Art always replied, "Yes, Miss Lizzy, I do. Right here." Then he'd pat his pants pocket.

Lizzy always laughed. "It will be worth some money someday ... the autograph, that is."

Lizzy assumed of course, that he didn't have that five-dollar bill. Her question was the way she reminded him of the note of encouragement she had written on it for him.

Lizzy and Joe spent every second together that they possibly could. Of course, they still had to work.

"Bills still have to get paid," Lizzy preached. Despite her love for Joe and their growing relationship, they both had plenty to keep their feet on the ground. The world around them hadn't stopped and they knew it.

Buckets haunted the town with the excitement of a Halloween party which was the talk of the town. Dee came dressed as a witch. Leroy came into town and he dressed as her broom. She carried him around all night. When she was tired, she leaned him up against the bar. He wasn't always pleased to be left alone.

"At least I put you at the bar and not in the corner," Dee told him.

Lizzy came as a beautiful butterfly. Joe dressed as a pirate.

"I'm surprised this butterfly is here with a pirate like you. You have a goatee, earring and a tattoo?" Ripley asked Joe. She remembered back to Lizzy's list of the kind of man she wanted.

Joe laughed, knowing about Lizzy's list and glad he'd met her criteria.

Johnny came as the Headless Horseman. His girlfriend Beth wore a police woman outfit.

"If he only knew," Lizzy and Dee whispered back and forth to each other in between their laughter.

Ripley and Walter came as Jack and Jill. They carried their bucket of beer around all night. Of course, baby Lindsey got to spend time with grandma and grandpa.

A wonderful night sparkled throughout Buckets, so many costumes. Lizzy had made a punch as red as blood. Joe showed her how to make it look as though it was boiling. He attached a fish tank bubbler to the bottom of the punch bowl. Every one raved about the punch.

Gracey showed up with Harry from the grocery store. They dressed as bride and groom, only the bride was Harry and Gracey was the groom. Gracey had gotten some dry ice from Harry and they put that behind the bar. Harry's idea of course.

Smiles, laughter, and happiness hovered and haunted the whole night.

***

Lizzy invited Dee to accompany her and Joe to her parent's home for the annual Thanksgiving feast. Lizzy finally introduced Joe to her

199

parents. With Joe being Italian and from the north, Lizzy's traditional Thanksgiving was slightly different from what he was accustomed too. Lizzy's family was extremely southern and he was extremely Italian. Joe seemed to fit right in with her family, considering the differences.

About a week before that, Lizzy had met Joe's parents and his sister when they'd come down to visit him. They looked around at property for a possible retirement home.

Lizzy adored Joe's family. Joe's Mom and Dad were the cutest couple Lizzy had ever seen, except maybe for Manny and Milly. Lizzy admired the fact that they were always holding hands and touching, like high school sweethearts. Lizzy's momma always said, *"You can tell how a man will treat you by the way he treats his mother."* Joe treated his mother with nothing but love and respect. Lizzy was consumed by Joe as she learned his world.

Christmas came on the heels of Thanksgiving and Dee was looking forward to the holiday. Excitement filled the air.

Leroy was going to be coming in for Christmas week. Dee really needed his companionship, especially now that all her friends were pared up. Everyone had someone and he was the next best thing.

Dee had to admit that she'd become a little envious of Joe, mainly because she missed having Lizzy all to herself. Dee liked that Joe was willing to share Lizzy, though. And, they still had their time together at Buckets and that was many hours for friendship.

One particular night that Lizzy worked, Dee stayed to hang out with her. Joe was running later than usual.

"He is never this late," Lizzy remarked with a worried look.

"Maybe he had some car trouble," Dee noted to ease Lizzy's worry. "You are such a worry wart."

"I know. I don't want him to feel suffocated by that, either," Lizzy admitted glancing again at the clock.

Dee tried to change the subject. "The Christmas tree looks great."

"Art helped me last night. You know he said it had been years since he decorated for Christmas, much less any other holiday," Lizzy said.

"Sometimes Lizzy, we take things for granted. Life isn't about staying alive, it's about the experience of it," Dee added with a smile, happy for their friendship.

"I'll take care of the outside lights tomorrow," Dee told her.

"Sounds good to me," Lizzy agreed.

Joe finally walked through the front door.

"Where have you been? I was worried about you," Lizzy said.

"Sorry, lost track of time. I was window shopping. It is Christmas, you know," Joe hinted with a grin as big as the Hoover Dam.

He signaled to Dee to follow him outside. She got up nonchalantly and walked outside with Joe. Lizzy could tell from behind the bar they were having a pretty serious conversation. Lizzy assumed he was showing Dee the Christmas gift that he'd gotten for her. They both returned with "*shit eating grins.*" She hated anticipation of what was to come.

Sirens sounded outside and lights flashed.

Lizzy looked out the window. "Something terrible has happened across the street." The ambulance had pulled up and she saw a body lying on the road. The battered shoes of the body looked familiar.

"Oh no. It's Art!" Lizzy ran from behind the bar, out the door, across the parking lot and into the street where the body laid. A paramedic stopped her.

"Is he alright?" Lizzy cried out.

"He's in bad shape but I think he is going to make it. A lot of broken bones," the paramedic replied.

Lizzy patted her pockets in search of a card, finally found one. "My name is Lizzy. Here's my phone number. He has no family. I need to know how he is doing," Lizzy explained as they loaded Art's body into the ambulance.

"Said your name is Lizzy?" The paramedic questioned. "I have something for you." He handed her the five-dollar bill that she'd given Art months back. "He had it in his hand when we got here. He said to get this to Lizzy. We had no clue," the paramedic said.

The five dollar bill read: *May the road you are on take you to places that is only fit for kings! Love, Lizzy*

***

Dee and Lizzy learned that the man that had hit Art was a multi-millionaire with a heart as big as Texas. The millionaire paid for all Art's medical needs, bought him a house, and hired him to manage one of his many businesses. Arthur later married the millionaire's spinster daughter and was to inherit his fortune.

Lizzy kept the five-dollar bill to remind her that anything is possible in life if people are given encouraging words.

***

Christmas Eve arrived and Dee and Lizzy decided to close Buckets early to celebrate with Joe and Leroy.

Joe's family tradition was a huge seafood dinner. Italians enjoyed their seafood and so did Lizzy and Dee, so it worked out perfectly. Joe was a natural in the kitchen when it came to good Italian food.

Joe made some calamari with a marinara dipping sauce to start the meal. He'd assembled thick tomato slices topped with basil and fresh mozzarella to cleanse the palate before the main course.

"I can help with all this, you know," Lizzy told him when he told her to relax with Dee and Leroy.

He'd kissed her senseless and explained that he was king in his kitchen; she was queen in her kitchen at Buckets. Well, if that was the way it was, what could she do?

He prepared lobster bisque that melted in their mouths. The main dish was shrimp scampi over linguine pasta with fresh grated Pecorino Romano cheese. Next up, hot crispy Italian bread with softened garlic butter was put on the table.

202

For dessert Joe cheated and bought a cheesecake from the newly opened Italian bakery. As they ate the dessert, all eyes were on Lizzy. She wondered if she had something on her blouse but she didn't see anything.

She fumbled with her piece of cheesecake. It appeared to have something in it. When she dug it out, she discovered it was a ring—a diamond ring. Looking up, she saw Joe down on one knee beside her chair. Dee and Leroy stood. Joe reached his hand out for hers.

"Lizzy, I have never felt passion like I have with you; passion for life, passion for laughter, passion for love. Tonight, I want to share your passion, each step that we take together. *Will you marry me*?" Joe asked.

Shocked, shaking, and scared, she willed her trembling voice to answer him. "Yes, I will. Every step."

Later Lizzy learned that Joe had gone to her parents' home first, asked for her hand in marriage and promised to take care of her till death do them part.

He had also gone to Dee and asked for her permission. He'd even secretly asked Buckets, too. It was truly the best Christmas ever.

***

The Buckets' New Year's celebration had the town talking. Everybody that was anybody attended to bring in the New Year. Buckets welcomed them with great anticipation of a year of changes.

Dee cut up streamers into tiny confetti pieces. It took her two days. She stuffed balloons with the confetti and then tied them to the ceiling. A hundred balloons lined the ceiling.

Lizzy made twelve different types of hors d'oeuvres. Lizzy wanted a variety to help people find what they were looking for in a New Year of change.

Dee had ordered several cases of tiny bottles of champagne. Gracey made little tags that hung from the bottle necks with the prettiest ribbon money could buy. The tags read:

Buckets wants to bring you into the New Year with a sweet bubbly taste in your mouth! HAPPY NEW YEAR!!!!

Dee came there with Leroy. Lizzy with Joe. Ripley and Walter. Johnny with his girlfriend Beth. Gracey and Harry.

The atmosphere was enchanted with fairytales that had come true. At the stroke of midnight, the magic of friendship and love glimmered through the air of Buckets.

Lizzy watched as everyone turned to their mates. Everyone hugged and kissed while Old Lang Syne played in the background.

Lizzy knew at that moment she was in the right place and time-by the familiarity of it. She'd certainly learned an appreciation of her life.

***

Valentine's Day was a week away. Lizzy arranged to take off for a trip with Joe thanks to help from Gracey and Dee who would cover her shifts.

On Dee's first shift of covering for Lizzy, she found a note in the drawer of the register.

"Dearest Dee, you know how much I love you, so I'm letting you know that Joe and I will be man and wife when we return from our vacation."

"They eloped?" Dee declared not sure if she was happy or mad. "I sure hope she comes back …"

As the week drew to an end, another letter from Lizzy came in the mail. Dee hesitated to open it, fearing that she was losing her friend. Slowly she opened the envelope.

She read the letter as tears welled up in her eyes. Dee slowly folded the letter and slid it into her pocket.

She sat down at the bar, put her face into her hands and cried some more.

***

Dear Dee,

Joe and I are having a wonderful time on our honeymoon. They really are treating us like royalty. I hope everything is good there. We will be returning in a few days. I know this probably could have waited, but while it is in my heart, I needed to write it. You know me with the writing. You are and always will be my best friend, and nothing will ever change that. As for Buckets, I will be there for you, until we decide otherwise. As life continues to rotate around us, I need for you to know, that what we have is real...a bond, which most can't explain. I will never walk away from what we have. It may seem that we are headed down two separate paths, but that is not true. We may be apart at times, but never in the heart. Just like my grandma and her friends. Please remember that. Every step I take, you are with me. Everything I do, it's you that is there with me. I would never have taken chances on living, if it wasn't for you. You helped me, become the person I always was. I was too scared to be me, because of other people's judgments. I guess I'm not so righteous after all. I always admired you, for not being so judgmental, and not caring what others thought. I love you for that. It helped me break free, from the world of negative feelings and hopelessness. You are so right, being normal is only going to keep you normal. Not being normal, will take you to amazing places in life. Our friendship is like a book, it will take us years to write, and that we shall do. You are like gold to me. Joe, he is my diamond and to hold a diamond, I will always need a base of gold. My dearest Dee, you have not lost a friend, you have gained one! As for Ripley, she too is also gold, but a white gold, to the naked eye appears to be silver, but has compounds of gold. I thank her for bringing us together. Hold down the fort. I'll be home soon, so we can start a new chapter. Let's make it, a never ending story! The rest of our story is still unwritten!

Love always,

Lizzy

P.S. Joe tells me he wants to thank you for being such a great friend, and partner. We owe you one! He truly adores you!

Acknowledgements

If I didn't have these people grace my life, this would have never been possible.

Rhonda Bracewell
Janelle Barbour
Gabe Smith
Aresola Family
Dominic Oliva
On-Target Words
Nicholas Oliva
ClearView Press Inc.
Zachary Oliva
Gwen Lowder
Mike Lowder
Bill Cooper
Mike King
Linda DuPont
James DuPont
Lee DuPont
Tressie D Paytas
Trudy D Tedder
Leah Sebag
Laurie Cuccurullo
Christina Crump
Dallas L. Dixon
Dottie Dills Fylor
The Beer House gang
Countrytime Pub gang
Rose Oliva

Tudisco family
Helen King
Lisa Stratford
Luann Laramore
Dawn Werden
Kimmie Riley
Jen Wood
Shelly Way
Go write classmates
City of Bunnell
City of Flagler Beach
Flagler County
Ron Carnes
Nancy Quatrano
Ray Johnston
I am positive I have missed a lot of people, my apologies to you!-JDO

ABOUT THE AUTHOR:

JORJA DUPONT OLIVA was born and raised in Flagler County, Florida. She is a descendent of the first families who settled in the county, where she still resides. She is a small business owner, wife, and a mother of two boys. She also is a lover of animals and all of God's creatures. She has always been intrigued with the ironies of life. After chasing her own Butterflies--the opportunity to write a book--it manifested itself, due to unconditional love of family and friends. The push and inspiration goes to Michael Ray King's "How to write a book in thirty days" program.

Jorja is now working on book two of the Chasing Butterflies series.

Creatures of Air and Earth - GLOSSARY

Dee believes that creatures of air and earth essence walk through life with us, teaching, guiding, and protecting us. Throughout your lifetime; however, major life changes can cause some your creature's essences to change. As your life changes so can your essence. Dee also believes they can appear to us through dreams, pictures or an attachment to them. She believes that everything living is sacred. A lesson can be found in all things, experiences and that everything has a purpose. Dee believes that life is about HONOR, LOVE, and RESPECT to others and to ourselves. Also being in touch with ourselves and every living thing around us. It is about knowing and understanding that we are part of everything, and everything is a part of us. We are all one, no matter what. Whereas Lizzy believes we are all God's creatures and deserve respect- no matter what we were taught.

ARMADILLO-essence is that of protection. If an armadillo enters your life it is for you to learn boundaries and set them to keep you protected. "Little armored one"

BEE- essence is that of happiness of ones work. If a bee enters into your life, the message is through your work you will obtain wisdom, a connection to your surroundings and to also enjoy your work. "Busy as a Bee"

BUTTERFLY-essence is that of consciousness of your instinct. It teaches us to make changes in our lives to make it possible for our dreams to come true. The butterfly also reminds us that we are constantly in a life of change.

BULL-essence is that of your strength and purpose. The bull tells us not to rush into anything without preparing first.

CAT-essence is that of secrets and self-deception. Black cat is of intuition and dreams. Calico is that of honesty.

DOG-essence is that of faith, reliability and mentoring. It teaches us to examine our loyalty to yourself and to others. Compassion and ability to overlook weakness.

DOLPHIN-essence is that of breathing. It teaches you to inhale new air and exhale the air your body does not need, much like life, inhale the good and exhale the bad. They also mate for life. A deep inhale and a slow exhale often brings about a change in emotions.

DRAGONFLY-essence is that of change and also of deceit. It teaches us that nothing is quite as it seems to be, weather it is a situation or your belief system. It also marks a time of change is happening or is needed.

EAGLE-essence is that of the Devine power, Great Spirit, great creator-God. It is the only creature to fly high in the sky and still see life in its entire lightness and darkness that exists here on earth. This means that we should except the light and dark side of life and know it is to serve a higher purpose.

FISH-essence is that of decision and grace. It teaches us open-mindedness and decisiveness and not to allow fear to hold you back.

FROG- essence is that of cleansing and purifying. It also signifies a start of a new life. To start fresh with positive surroundings.

HORSE-essence is that of strength and power. It teaches us that power cannot be obtained if it is forced only by strength of the person.

HUMMING BIRD-essence is that of resurrection and joy. It teaches us to look back on the past, not to dwell on it and to learn from. It is also teaches us to let walls down so love can enter again and find joy.

PIGEON-essence is that of goals, focus, and perseverance. It teaches us to become in tune to nature. To persevere, and focus to obtain goals.

RABBIT- essence is that of gentleness, fear, and faith. It teaches us to look before we leap. You should face fears that are holding you back from growing.

SNAKE-essence is that of desire and passion. It teaches us through passion we find the wisdom to overcome the poisons of life that we tend to desire.

SPIDER-essence is that of responsibility and infinity. It teaches us to take responsibility for our own actions that will only repeat themselves if we don't.

SWAN-essence is that of accepting change as a gift. It teaches us to accept the great creator-Gods plan as the only perfect plan. The ugly duckling turns into the beautiful swan.

WHALE-essence is that of historical secrets. It teaches us to find ourselves through a blend of one's history and all living beings.